WILLING TO
SURRENDER

SHARON KIMBRA WALSH

Willing to Surrender
ISBN # 978-1-83943-868-4
©Copyright Sharon Kimbra Walsh 2019
Cover Art by Erin Dameron-Hill ©Copyright October 2019
Interior text design by Claire Siemaszkiewicz
Totally Bound Publishing

Published in 2020 by Totally Bound Publishing, United Kingdom.

Totally Bound Publishing books by Sharon Kimbra Walsh

Single Books
For the Love of a Marine
A Fallen Hero
Ambush of Love
Let Him Come Home
Willing to Surrender

WILLING TO SURRENDER

Dedication

To my sister, Tracy

"The higher you build
The walls around your heart,
The harder you fall
When someone finally breaks them down"

Unknown

Chapter One

Annie McKendrick had begun her graduation day by joining four hundred and ninety-seven other seniors from Langley High School in McLean, Virginia, in boarding the yellow school buses provided to take them to Constitution Hall, which was located on the outskirts of the expansive grounds.

She could still picture the glowing faces of the students on her coach and the singing and chanting that had erupted from everyone — including herself — during the ten-minute journey. The excitement had continued, even once they'd arrived outside the imposing, pale-gray stone building with its numerous columns supporting a decorative mansard roof where cheering families and friends had met them.

Just being inside the ornate building's time-honored halls, with its pristine white walls and arched, green carved-and-decorated ceilings and paintwork, had made Annie feel as if she were in a dream. At one point, she had wondered when the bubble would burst and she would wake up.

The two-hour ceremony had passed in a kaleidoscope of noise and color. She'd mounted the stage to receive her diploma, posed for official photographs and had thereafter searched for and found her parents to have more pictures taken with them and her friends.

The emotions she'd felt had been beyond what she'd expected, but the argument she'd had afterward with her boyfriend, Cory Anderson, had briefly dampened her mood and, for a time, had soured her enthusiasm for the upcoming evening festivities.

The quarrel had been about her parents, who were going on vacation the next day. Annie wouldn't be seeing them for a considerable period of time, so she'd decided that she would spend the intervening hours between the ceremony that morning and the celebrations in the evening with them.

Cory hadn't been amused when she'd told him she wouldn't be traveling with him and their friends to the elegant high-rise Ritz-Carlton Hotel at Tyson's Corner where the graduation celebration was to take place.

His familiar tactic of using emotional blackmail to get her to do what he wanted hadn't succeeded, and when she'd refused to back down, he'd exploded. The disagreement that had ensued as a result had tested her patience and resolve, and, at that point, she'd almost ended their relationship.

Annie sighed and eyed the littered tabletop. Thirsty, she searched for her glass of iced water and, after a few moments, found it among the other half-consumed and empty ones crowded together on the surface. She took a sip of the cold liquid and sighed when chilled moisture doused her throat and eased its dryness.

She set the glass back on the table and glanced around to see if she could find Cory. He was nowhere to be seen, and his absence made her feel more irritated than hurt that he'd left her alone to entertain herself.

She'd been dating him for six months. He was a typical all-American boy and had been captain of the high school soccer team. He was good-looking and more than aware of it, but of more concern to Annie's peace of mind was that he was a flirt and didn't give a damn that she knew it.

A short time into their relationship, she had noticed that his charming and appealing manner — very evident when he was in front of his peers or people he thought he needed to impress — was nothing but a veneer to cover his true personality.

He could be arrogant and self-centered, and she'd learned the hard way that he was used to getting his own way. He threw spectacular tantrums when he didn't get the attention he believed he deserved, which always left her feeling drained and numb, as though she'd spent time with an out-of-control, recalcitrant child who had no idea how to behave.

They were character traits that didn't sit well with her. In fact, they showed a side of him she didn't like at all. She'd begun to wonder what she saw in him.

Despite her growing unease, she hadn't wanted to give up on their relationship, but in recent weeks, she had grown irritated and frustrated with the way things were going between them. When she'd found herself making excuses for his behavior to other people, she'd stopped indulging his outbursts.

Thinking about him was making Annie feel uncomfortable, so she let her thoughts drift and studied her surroundings.

The graduation celebration was in full swing. The dance floor was crowded with energetic men and women who seemed to be out to impress each other with their antics. Some of the gyrations were extraordinary, and she smiled to herself and wondered if their acrobatic and somewhat ludicrous moves would be remembered with embarrassment the next day.

The room was a classic formal ballroom with a décor in antique gold and cream and wall-to-wall carpet of the same colors. It was opulent and elegant without being vulgar. Crystal chandeliers hung from an oval-domed ceiling that was carved with Victorian tracery, and lit sconces lined the walls, which were papered in silk and accented with crown molding.

Panoramic windows were festooned with sheer cream drapes, and there were soft brocade seats set around gilt-edged tables and antique credenzas positioned at strategic points about the room with tall, carved cream vases in their centers, holding cascades of gold-and-ivory flowers.

It was a luxurious and beautiful venue, but Annie was restless. She glanced at her watch and saw it was almost midnight. The noise from the music, raucous conversation and outbursts of laughter were almost deafening, and while she'd spent most of the night dancing, she now had the beginnings of a headache and her feet hurt.

Much against her will, she wondered again where Cory had disappeared to. He'd been acting out of character all evening, and while she suspected he might still be sulking from their earlier argument, her intuition told her it was a little more serious than him acting like a spoiled child.

After all, they hadn't parted on the best of terms, and even now, Annie was still annoyed with him. On this day of all days, his fit of angst had made her resent his behavior, and she'd had a sinking feeling that things between them weren't going as well as they should.

Annie wondered what would happen between them when she left for her basic training. She'd joined the Medical Corp of the United States Army, and in a few weeks' time, she would travel from her home nine hundred and forty-four miles to Fort Leonard Wood in Missouri, where she would begin her sixteen-week gender-integrated basic combat training.

If she passed that, she would move on to Fort Sam Houston to commence her medical and advanced courses to become a specialist in her trade. That could last anywhere from sixteen to sixty-eight weeks, depending on any additional skills she wanted to learn.

Annie hadn't chosen her career lightly or taken the step to sign up without a good degree of soul-searching. She'd understood that what lay ahead of her might well be filled with pitfalls and setbacks.

She would soon be leaving her family, Cory and her hometown, where she had lived all her life. While her parents supported her career choice wholeheartedly, Cory had neither given her his support nor shown any interest.

He hadn't told her he would miss her, and she had a feeling that once she was gone, he would move on to someone new. If she were honest with herself, she'd admit it dented her pride rather than her heart to think that once she was out of his sight, she would also be gone from his mind.

Why the hell am I thinking about that time-waster?

Annie pushed thoughts of her boyfriend to the back of her mind. She was eighteen years old and the world was her oyster. She was free of school at last and her future stretched ahead of her, an infinite highway of hope and adventure. She was going to grab onto it with both hands and look back only when she needed to.

Then thoughts of *him* intruded into her mind and a trickle of warmth trailed down her spine when she thought of the incident which had occurred outside the hotel after her father had dropped her off to wait on the forecourt for Cory and their friends to arrive.

She'd noticed a gleaming black limousine with tinted windows pull up in front of her and her curiosity had been aroused, even though it had been no more impressive than the other automobiles dropping off their passengers. She wasn't normally a nosey person, but she'd stared at the windows to see if she could see inside and recognize its occupants.

The rear, left-hand passenger door had opened and a man in formal evening dress had gotten out. The sound of female laughter had come from its interior, and she'd watched as he leaned forward and reached out a hand to whomever was inside.

Her interest had been piqued even more when he'd assisted a young woman of about her own age to alight. A second man, followed by another woman, had appeared from the opposite side and she'd wondered who they were.

The man who had exited first appeared older than the rest of his group and she'd continued to stare as they slammed the doors shut and the two couples moved toward the sidewalk.

Annie had realized her interest was bordering on rudeness, and she'd been about to focus her attention elsewhere when the stranger had turned and had caught her studying them. Like an animal trapped in the glare of a car's headlights, she'd stiffened and a wave of embarrassment had surged through her.

Her face had flushed with heat, but instead of ignoring the man like she should have done, she'd chosen instead to return his look. She'd felt a jolt of recognition.

At Langley High School, they'd been at the opposite ends of the age spectrum, so Annie had never had an opportunity to speak to him. Shyness would have prevented her from approaching him, even if she'd been given the chance.

She'd been a shy, fifteen-year-old ninth-grade sophomore when he was an eighteen-year-old twelfth-grade senior. Any interaction that might have been instigated by her would have failed at the first hurdle because of the age difference, and in terms of a senior's reputation, he almost certainly wouldn't have allowed himself to be seen in her company.

Annie had passed him a few times in the corridors on her way to classes and lectures, and each time she had stolen a glance at him from beneath her eyelashes. On one occasion, she'd caught him staring at her, and the brief acknowledgement had sent tingles coursing down her adolescent spine, the feeling unfamiliar and startling to her young body.

She didn't know the color of his eyes because she hadn't gotten close enough to him to see them. She'd noticed his long but neat brown, almost-black hair and the dark stubble that had always outlined his firm jaw and chin. It had made him look older than his years, and she had never been able to rid herself of the thought of how sexy he'd looked.

He'd stood out from the crowd of other students, his regular mode of dress being faded pegged jeans, work boots and a white T-shirt beneath a black leather jacket, very distinct from the diverse fashion prevalent at the high school.

Although a stranger to her, Annie had sensed he was different from the rest of the jocks that haunted the soccer field, baseball diamond and ice-hockey rink. He must have had friends but she'd never seen him with them, and she had never noticed him at the sports practices or any of the proms she had attended.

Gossip flourished in any school and community, the type that always abounded among adults and teenagers concerning someone who was different. There had always been numerous detrimental stories about him making the rounds, although she'd had no idea they were about him until he'd been pointed out to her.

McLean residents – those who put class and wealth above anything else – had taken great delight in making derogatory comments about those less well off than themselves, and there were plenty about him and his family.

She'd overheard people talking – the conversation spoken in conspiratorial whispers, as though the information wasn't to be bandied about at any cost – that he came from the wrong side of the tracks or, for want of a better description, lived in the poor and less prestigious part of McLean. They said he was a troublemaker and, of more importance, was uneducated.

The scuttlebutt vine had told her his father had fought in the first Gulf War and had returned suffering from combat stress. Unemployed and with no means of paying for medical bills, the man had left McLean, leaving the mother to be the breadwinner to two children.

Annie's own friends had repeated the statements in contemptuous and secretive tones – copying those of their parents – elaborating about those without a six-figure monetary value or who had fathers who did not hold important jobs such as stockbroker, attorney or who didn't have one at all.

As far as they were concerned, people who were not two or even three-car families and didn't live in the plantation-like homes located on the wealthier side of McLean were far less privileged than they, of a much lower class and not to be associated with.

The cruel and unjust words had stirred a righteous anger in Annie's warm and tender heart. As young as she was, she had concluded that the people she knew had shallow minds and *would never understand the true meaning of being a caring human being to others, no matter their monetary status.*

She'd never had the opportunity to find out for herself if the stories about him were true – not that she would have cared if they had been – because one day he was gone.

He had graduated with the rest of the seniors, and at his departure, she'd felt a sharp pang of regret that had lingered through the years that she hadn't managed to get to know him.

He'd been standing not more than ten feet from her, and again, Annie had found herself unable to tear her gaze away from him.

He'd been taller than she'd remembered, and she'd guessed his height to be over six feet. She'd admired his well-muscled physique, which had been emphasized by a black jacket stretched taut across his broad shoulders and chest.

When the breeze had blown the two halves of the garment apart, she'd seen that he wore a deep crimson brocade waistcoat over a crisp white shirt without a necktie, and she'd been impressed that he'd continued to adhere to his own unconventional dress code.

There had been an air of command about him, a presence that showed he was no longer an eighteen-year-old boy. He'd matured in his looks and his powerful-looking body had belonged to someone who worked out and was at peak fitness. He had been even more attractive than she'd remembered and Annie had wondered what it would feel like to have his arms around her and his body pressed to hers.

His face had remained in shadow, and even though he'd faced her direction, she hadn't been able to tell if his gaze had been on her, but she'd felt a familiar tingle she'd not experienced in some time race down her spine and sudden warmth had flooded her chilled body.

Convinced her emotions had been displayed on her face, she'd turned away. Moments later, she hadn't been able to resist glancing over her shoulder once more and she'd seen him walking away, the girl he'd helped from the car holding his arm with both hands, as if she hadn't wanted to let go.

The group had made their way along the forecourt toward the hotel, and Annie's breath had caught in her throat. The man had walked in a graceful but masculine way, his movements like those of a wild beast. He was all-male, and when he'd half-turned to look at her once more, her heart rate had increased and she'd become short of breath.

A pang of jealousy had stabbed her. She'd found herself wanting to be close to him so *she* could touch him. She'd wished she could take the place of the young woman and gaze into his face and have him smile at *her instead*.

She'd been only semi-aware of what was going on around her because her mind had been focused on him, and she'd been surprised that the crush she'd had all those years ago clearly remained as strong as ever.

She'd never experienced such a feeling for a member of the opposite sex before—not even Cory—and she'd found herself musing about what it would be like to be kissed by him.

The man had faced forward just as Annie had heard her name called. The sound had jolted her back to the real world. She'd been bewildered as to what had just happened to her and ashamed of her thoughts concerning a man who was, and would always be, a stranger.

She hadn't looked at him again and he'd moved out of her life. She'd dismissed him from her mind. She had to forget about him, because it was finished and she'd never see him again.

She'd had to move on with the most exciting night of her young life, so she'd forced her lips into a smile and half-turned to watch Cory and her friends alight from their white limousine and make their way toward her.

Chapter Two

Annie surged with impatience at her enforced solitude, stood and grabbed her purse, which hung from the back of her chair. She was eager to be out of the crowd and the heat, and she began to make her way around tables and groups of people toward the exit—nodding and smiling at acquaintances as she went.

She was relieved when she reached the double oak doors and could push one open to step out into a long hallway. It swung shut behind her and the sounds became muted. She sighed with enjoyment when a chilled breeze from an air conditioning unit caressed and soothed her flushed cheeks.

More at ease and feeling a little revitalized, Annie glanced to her right in the direction of the lobby. From where she stood, she could see plush cream-leather sofas and armchairs interspersed with tall and vibrant green fronds and ferns in large urns grouped together on a floor covering that was the same color and just as ornate as the one in the ballroom.

There was still no sign of Cory and she frowned. She couldn't hear him either, so he wasn't with a group of his soccer buddies in the immediate vicinity.

Where in the hell are you?

Perhaps he and their friends had gone to the game room to play pool or something else had caught their attention.

Regardless, she had no intention of spending the rest of the night searching for him or watching him play macho man and hit little balls into pockets — even if that was what he wanted her to do.

Annie bit her lip in frustration and hoped he hadn't stormed off in another tantrum. Right then, she didn't have the patience to deal with him, even if she wanted to give him the benefit of the doubt that he'd only wandered away because he'd needed space to cool off.

If he was still annoyed with her and she left him alone, she wouldn't have to make the effort to placate and humor him. She could go back to the ballroom, play dumb and ignore the reason why he'd left her. He might turn up full of remorse.

Annie looked to her left and saw the corridor went on for a short distance before it made a turn into what had to be another hallway.

Oh, hell. Go for it.

She gave in to her curiosity as to where Cory might be and began to walk along the passageway, her footfalls muffled by the thick carpet. She'd almost reached the corner when she heard low male and female voices. Reluctant to go farther, she stopped.

She was uneasy and didn't know why. The man sounded familiar, and although she didn't believe for one moment it was her date, doubt surfaced in her mind and tension stiffened the muscles in her neck and shoulders.

Do I really want to know if it could be Cory? Annie nibbled her lower lip then shrugged. *Yeah, I do. Then I'll have an excuse to kick his arrogant butt.*

It was only a short distance to the bend in the corridor and once there, she found herself in another long passageway. Electric sconces with artificial flames adorned the walls at regular intervals and shifting shadows at the far end made it hard for her to see whether anybody was there.

Annie stopped again, feeling perplexed. She had no idea where the voices had come from but could still hear people talking in hushed tones. They were close by and she heard the woman giggle in a seductive way, followed by silence.

I'm gonna feel all kinds of a fool if it's someone making out.

She was about to turn around and retrace her steps when the man spoke once more, and although she couldn't make out the words, she recognized his voice this time.

Annie clenched her hand on her purse, digging her fingernails into the lace material. Her stomach muscles fluttered with apprehension.

She held her breath and waited for one of them to speak again so she could pinpoint their exact location. Some moments passed before the woman laughed once more—a sensual sound—and the man spoke as if in answer to it.

Annie tensed and noted the voices had come from a small alcove a few feet ahead of her and on her right. She gritted her teeth and started forward.

As she drew near the opening, blood thundered in her ears and she felt sick. Before she revealed herself, she heard muffled moans and her throat tightened from lack of air.

Unable to bear the tension any longer and needing confirmation that it was indeed Cory, Annie moved toward the recess so she could see into it.

She was sure of what she was going to see but she still froze when she saw the couple standing a little way in from the hallway. They were in each other's arms, mouths pressed together in what looked to be a passionate kiss. Cory had lifted the woman's skirt high up on one side and was stroking her thigh.

Annie must have made a small sound — although later she couldn't remember doing so — and the couple jolted apart then turned toward her, Cory's arm still around the woman's shoulders.

"Well, well. Look who's turned up," he said.

Annie noticed he looked neither guilty nor ashamed at being caught, and any shock and disbelief she felt at catching him red-handed with someone else was smothered when a wave of anger coursed through her.

"*Shit*, Cory. What do you think you're doing?" she asked.

Before he could answer, Annie looked from him to the woman.

Girl, she corrected herself.

Annie wanted to convince herself that her competition wasn't pretty, but she knew she would be lying. The girl must have been at least eighteen years old because she wouldn't have been at the dance if she were any younger.

She had shiny dark brown hair cut in a bob and huge chocolate-colored eyes. Her petite figure was clad in a hunter-green sheath dress that just reached mid-thigh and high-heeled sandals with straps that twined about her lower legs.

By comparison, Annie felt as big and clumsy as an elephant. She also was uncomfortable because she understood why Cory might have had trouble keeping his hands off the girl, but her irritation ratcheted up a level when she saw the smile of condescension and noticed her hand massaging *her* boyfriend's waist.

This elephant has got really long tusks and is itching to use 'em.

In a manner she hoped would convey contempt, Annie looked from the top of the girl's head down to her varnished toenails before she turned her attention back to Cory.

"So, when were you going to grow big enough balls to tell me about your…bit on the side?" she asked.

Cory shrugged and there was a self-satisfied expression on his face. "'Round about now, I guess."

Annie glared at him then glanced down at the large, flamboyant corsage that Cory had given to her, fastened to her right wrist. She fumbled with the ribbon that held it in place. She was seething when she said, "Well, in that case, you might as well have these, honey."

She tore the blooms away and lifted them into the air. Her fiery temper got the better of her and she added, "Oh, and I should have brought you a to-go box, since you seem to want my leftovers so much."

Annie hurled the flowers in the girl's direction, but when they hit her in the chest, she felt no satisfaction — only chagrin that she'd acted in such an immature manner.

The young woman flinched and her body jerked, as if she was about to move toward Annie. "You bitch," she said.

Annie forced herself to laugh out loud before she said with contempt, "You've got a goddamn nerve calling *me* that. Have you taken a good look at yourself in the mirror? I'm not the one who's too stupid to realize a relationship is only for two people, not three." She shook her head. "I feel damn sorry for you, as it seems you have no idea how to count."

The woman pressed herself to Cory's side. "I may be a bitch, hon, but I'm the one who has her hands on *your* man."

Annie saw what appeared to be a self-congratulatory smile cross the girl's pretty face and outrage and embarrassment flared white-hot inside her. To keep herself in check so she didn't fly at the woman with her claws unsheathed, she folded her arms.

She'd been made to look a fool by a slip of a girl and a boy whom she'd sensed for some time was not the man she wanted and who she should have dumped weeks before now.

Besides, the expression on Cory's face was one only a male who saw two women fighting over him could have, and it made her want to punch him. She knew her adolescent behavior would leave her feeling ashamed the next day, but she wasn't about to back down. She waded in with a verbal barrage filled with scorn. "Take it from me, *honey*. You might feel smug and self-righteous now, but stealing someone else's guy doesn't make you special. It makes you a lousy runner-up. Second place never gets the prize.

"Anyway, from what I've learned about this jackass" — Annie jerked her head in Cory's direction — "he only wants you so he can add another notch to his bedpost. So good luck with that."

She half-turned to her now-ex. "As for you... You're a two-timing, arrogant asshole and I don't know why I ever bothered with you in the first place."

Cory laughed, her insults appearing not to faze him in the slightest. "Give me a break, Annie. Life's crap, just like you. If you'd put out even a little bit, this situation wouldn't have happened. You've got one hell of a poker up that pretty ass of yours. You're so prim and proper, like some Victorian governess, that I'm kinda surprised you've found the courage to insult me."

Annie unfolded her arms and clenched her hands into fists at her sides. "You know what, Cory. I love listening to your bullshit lies. They're hilarious. I know *who* you are and *what* you are, so don't lay all this on me. Remember… A real man can stay loyal without getting sidetracked by easy girls. Anyway, my life is too short, just like your dick probably is, to waste it on someone like you."

She glared at the girl, and this time her tone was laced with venom. "I hope you haven't fallen for a dog who's always had eyes for every bitch in high school."

The woman's eyes were almost black, and she rolled them as her full mouth twisted in a grimace. "You'd better back off before I plant one on your filthy mouth," she said.

Annie gave a mock sigh. "Just keep rolling your eyes, *babe*. Maybe you'll find your brain back there."

She knew the situation was getting out of hand, and if it disintegrated into a cat fight, it would destroy whatever credibility and dignity she had, so she inhaled, let the air out of her lungs and tried to calm herself.

"We love each other. Don't we, honey?" the girl said and looked up into Cory's face with an adoring expression.

Goaded into responding once more, Annie laughed again and her voice was icy when she said, "Sorry, hon, but L.O.V.E. in your case stands for Legs. Open. Very. Easy." Then she continued, "Listen… I'm sure you don't like me and I'm one hundred percent certain that I don't give a shit. I'm not going to lower myself by calling you a slut because I don't think you are one. But don't take that as a compliment. You're more like an amusement park ride. Everyone gets a turn, then they have to get off you after a few minutes to find a place to vomit."

The girl uttered a squawk of fury. "I'm gonna —"

"What the hell's going on here?"

Annie whirled around, and when she saw who was standing behind her, her heart missed a beat. She recognized the man who stood in the hallway as the one she'd seen outside the hotel. A random thought popped into her mind. *His eyes are green.*

He was watching the young woman, and while his posture appeared relaxed, there was an expression on his face that told Annie he was angry.

"None of your business, Shay. Stay out of this," the girl said.

"No way in hell. I'm making it my business, Megan," the man replied. "You know the rules."

"I'm sick of your damn rules, bro. I'm not a kid, so back off."

The man straightened, his dark eyebrows lowering over his eyes, which he narrowed at her words. "You're barely eighteen, *kid*, so I don't wanna hear any of your crap."

He turned his gaze on Annie. Her legs began to tremble and her stomach fluttered with what felt like a swarm of agitated butterflies.

His voice was quiet when he asked again, "What's going on here?"

Before she could answer, Cory interrupted and said in a belligerent tone, "You deaf? This is personal between me and the ladies."

The man who Annie now knew as Shay stiffened and he glared at Cory. When he spoke, Annie heard an undercurrent of menace in his voice, "Have *you* got a hearing problem, buddy? I *said* I was making it my business, 'specially since you seem to have your hands on my sister. You got an issue with that?"

There was anger in Cory's voice when he said, "Yeah, it appears I do."

Annie knew from experience that Cory didn't know when to back off. She sensed the tension and antagonism in the air and knew she needed to defuse the situation before it ended in a fist fight between the two men, even though she would get a great deal of satisfaction from seeing the stranger beat the crap out of her deceitful date.

Despite how she felt about being duped, and although Cory was bigger and heavier, she had no doubt the girl's brother was tougher and could handle himself well enough that it might be to Cory's detriment.

She didn't care if her two-timing ex-boyfriend was taught a lesson, but she knew she was better than that, and there was more to life than getting revenge, no matter how good it might feel.

When she turned to confront the couple, she saw they were still touching, as if neither were bothered by the escalating situation. She grew even angrier.

Annie gritted her teeth and struggled to keep her temper under control. "I'd really like to stay here and discuss this pathetic situation, but I've got far more important things to do," she said.

There was an edge to her voice when she addressed Megan, "You're welcome to him. I hope you and he have a wonderful life together. Remember, a cheat is always a cheat, so watch yourself, because payback will be a bitch. Now, I'll leave you in your brother's capable hands."

She turned to walk out of the alcove and almost bumped into the stranger, who had moved even closer to her. She stopped and her gaze locked with his. Despite the chaotic emotions churning inside her, she found herself immobilized by the man's stare.

His face was expressionless but his tone sounded sympathetic when he asked, "Are you okay?"

Annie managed to smile. "I'm fine," she answered.

"I'll deal with this then give you a ride home."

Annie shook her head. "I'll call my father. Just don't be too hard on them. They're just kids."

She felt shy, which was a first for her, looked away then walked around him and along the corridor without looking back. As she turned into the main hallway, she heard raised voices and a bitter satisfaction filled her that, for once, Cory appeared not to be getting things his own way.

This ends the last night of my youth. Could've been better, I guess. At least I found out what a bastard Cory Anderson is now and not later.

Annie realized she'd come out of the incident with her heart almost unscathed, although her pride was a little bruised. Her anger had diminished to simmering embers and she didn't even feel the need to cry.

She wouldn't lose any sleep over Cory's infidelity, and she was going to count herself lucky that it hadn't been serious on her part. She would find it a lot easier to move on and put the immediate past behind her.

Chapter Three

2003

Annie was tired as she walked toward an old-fashioned green hospital screen pulled across to separate the advanced trauma life support section — or triage area — from the operating room.

Early that morning, a mounted marine squad had driven over an improvised explosive device. A light armored vehicle had been wrecked. There had been two casualties classified as critical from the incident and a medevac had flown them to the Thirty-first Forward Surgical Team's field hospital at Forward Operating Base Sykes.

The second of the two patients had needed to be operated on again and, a few moments following his surgery, he'd been wheeled through the short interconnecting tunnel to the post-anesthesia care unit to join the first.

The tension had escalated and the team had rushed into action when complications had developed within minutes of his initial operation—compromised breathing, rapid heartbeat, sweating and bloody vomit—and his condition had begun to deteriorate to a dangerous level.

He'd been brought back to the operating room and a quick and thorough assessment of his wounds carried out. His condition was such that an internal exploration of his repaired injuries had been necessary, and he'd been anesthetized and his surgical incision reopened.

A dissected artery—so small it was almost miniscule, but life-threatening nonetheless—had been discovered, and in no time at all, it had been clamped, sutured and two hundred and fifty milliliters of blood suctioned from his chest cavity.

Once a drain had been inserted, the marine had been monitored until his vital signs had stabilized and he'd begun to improve, albeit still in a critical condition. It had been concluded that both casualties were too unstable to be medevacked out and a decision had been made that they would remain under the care of the surgical team for longer than the usual mandatory hold of six hours for post-operative intensive care, until it was certain they could be transferred without risk.

If both patients continued to remain stable, a Blackhawk helicopter on standby would evacuate them to the Level IV Twenty-first Combat Support Hospital in Mosul. They would then be transferred to the Landstuhl Regional Medical Center in Germany, which was the nearest overseas military hospital to Iraq and operated by the United States Army and the Department of Defense.

Even though they had paid the price for being there, their time in the sandbox was over.

Except for the sounds made by two medics as they cleaned up the bloody aftermath of the surgeries with quick efficiency, the operating room was quiet, an uneasy hush mantling the shelter.

Annie half-turned to watch them as they bagged and disposed of bloodstained sheets, towels and drapes into waste receptacles, wiped down two surgical tables and bed pads and placed gore-smeared, contaminated instruments into an autoclave for sterilization.

Although it was still early morning, it was warm and heat was beginning to build up in the restricted confines of the tents. Portable fans—one in each section—had been turned on but they only served to move the stifling air around and enhance the coppery smell of blood, aviation fuel and oil that was an ever-present reek in the atmosphere.

The hospital had received a few casualties in the four weeks it had been up and running, but Annie could already smell the distinctive iron-tinged and fecal stench that was a manifestation of the terrible mutilations, wounds and the involuntary blameless evacuations from the injured, who had no control over their bodily functions under trauma.

Her gaze drifted downward to the faint blood spatter and smudged crimson outlines of boot prints on the bike-track modular flooring. Someone had tried to wash away the marks but the blemishes remained, a stark reminder of the injured and maimed casualties that the team was determined to save.

Annie's attention turned to the tall and lanky figure of Captain Euan Lloyd, who was seated at a small camping table in the corner of the tent. He muttered as he sifted through the endless paperwork—a by-product of every casualty they treated.

At the sight of him, she smiled with weary amusement, distracted from her morbid thoughts. She noticed how his short black hair stuck up in wild spikes, as if he'd run his hands through it, the way in which his glasses kept sliding off his nose and the abstract way in which he pushed them back on. When he drank from a child's Winnie the Pooh sipper cup, her smile widened.

The forward surgical team consisted of three other surgeons, three registered nurses, two certified registered nurse anesthetists, one administrative officer, one detachment sergeant, three licensed practical nurses, three surgical technicians and three medics.

Annie herself was a specialist medic. She possessed advanced combat casualty care skills and qualifications and was able to carry out emergency procedures such as venous cutdowns, the placement of chest tubes and was able to use special hemorrhage control methods on patients who were bleeding out.

To reflect her capabilities, she held a rank that was equivalent to that of a non-commissioned officer or corporal and had more responsibility than the other medics in the hospital, including the technicians.

The other team members had dispersed, some to the care unit where they would be observing their patients and some to eat or get much-needed sleep.

Annie couldn't rest. Although the frantic pace of the last few hours had drained her and left a hollow feeling in her stomach, she felt restless, as though her body was pumped full of adrenaline.

Her heart hammered from a high fed by endorphins that pummeled her central nervous system, and muscles and nerves in her arms and legs twitched as though tiny electric shocks ran through them.

Her thoughts drifted back to the scenes she had witnessed earlier and she knew it was a sign that she needed to desensitize and get her stress levels back to normal.

Since arriving in-country, she'd learned that if she concentrated on mundane tasks following such incidents, it channeled her mind and freed it from harrowing memories. She could then distance herself, and for a short while, there would be no need for her to think. To keep her mind occupied, she'd decided that cleaning the triage area would be as good a distraction as any.

Annie stopped by the screen and fumbled in the pocket of her creased and blood-stained scrub top. She felt a surge of panic when she couldn't find what she sought, then she discovered the photograph buried deep in the corner where things of importance—keys, money and pens—seemed to remain just out of reach.

The small picture was folded in half to protect the image, and the corners were curled from being handled so often. She unfolded it and stared at the big blue eyes that looked out at her, and her eager gaze took in the toothy grin, cherubic cheeks and thatch of brown hair—as dark as her own. Her heart ached with longing for him.

He was Aiden—her three-year-old little boy and the light of her life—the precious result of a passionate love affair and a painful and disastrous short-lived marriage.

Annie traced her fingertip down the glossy portrait of her child and she smiled. Everybody said he was the image of her and she was thankful for that. His father—Josh McKendrick—had been good-looking and charming but a selfish and callous bastard, and she didn't want to be reminded of the man who had taken and crushed her heart each time she looked at her son.

When she and Josh had met, everything about their relationship had been passionate and intense. He'd swept her off her feet with a single-minded purpose and determination and she'd given him the green light to do so.

After six months of dating, they'd been married. Within a month, she'd become pregnant, and after that, their relationship had deteriorated.

Throughout the months of their courtship and the early days of their marriage, Josh had managed to hide a possessive and jealous streak, but when she'd given him the news that he was going to be a father and would have to share her—even though it would be with their own child—he'd given her an ultimatum. It was to be either him or their baby.

For Annie, there had been no decision to make and Josh had acted out his part in their farce of a marriage until two weeks before Aiden's birth. After laying the blame at her door for becoming pregnant in the first place, thereby causing their breakup, he'd packed his things and walked out. They'd been married for less than twelve months and their divorce had become final two years after their first meeting.

She hadn't seen Josh in three years. When Aiden had been born, she'd tried to contact him to inform him he had a son, but he'd been nowhere to be found, and the Marine Corp and the Army had been reluctant to get involved in a domestic problem, so they'd been no help. Since Aiden's birth in 2000, even though she'd been able to get the news to him that he was a father, Josh had made no effort to see their child or get in touch to ask about him.

Annie had no idea where he was now and she couldn't have cared less if she never saw him again, but she felt bad for Aiden. He hadn't been given an opportunity to get to know his father, even if the man in question was a cold-hearted son of a bitch and not fit to kiss her son's feet.

Annie was uncomfortable with thoughts of a past she would rather forget, and the pain she felt at being away from her child was almost physical and tore at her insides. She kissed the photograph, refolded it and pushed it back into the depths of her pocket before she shoved aside a section of the hospital screen, causing the wheels to squeak out loud, and went through into the triage area.

The hospital performed damage control surgery and this was the area where casualties were first held for assessment that involved prioritizing or ranking the order of wounded personnel based on their individual needs for surgery.

Annie saw the mess in the area and groaned. It looked like a bloody tornado had swept through, depositing gore-stained intubation tubes, used pressure dressings, surgical drapes and casualty blankets on every surface.

The ever-present metallic essence of spilled blood lingered in the air, and Annie wrinkled her nose. The odor reminded her where she was and the horrors they had to face. It also reinforced what she was there to do, to save lives.

Her thoughts were becoming maudlin once more and she pushed them to the back of her mind. More casualties could arrive at any moment and personnel, as well as equipment—both crucial components for saving the wounded—needed to be ready at a moment's notice.

Annie moved toward the closest pair of three-wheeled litter carriers, each with a trolley at its head. When an alert sounded, there was never enough time to load endotracheal tubes and multiple tourniquets or open the kits that contained chest tubes and central lines, so everything was opened, pre-loaded and lined in neat regimental rows for easy access, and ready to go.

There was a blood-stained surgical sheet hanging from the litter and she reached out to pick it up. She stopped when she noticed a man in marine-patterned desert battle dress uniform, tactical vest and wearing a helmet about to exit the hospital.

Annie noticed he was limping and she forgot about the sheet and tried to get his attention. "Excuse me."

At the sound of her voice, the man stopped. His back stiffened but he didn't turn around.

Annie walked toward him. When she was a few paces away, she asked, "Are you hurt? Can I help you?"

The man turned to face her and she saw his combat patch beneath the small one of the United States on the upper part of his right arm. It identified him as a marine, although she couldn't tell his rank because his vest and combats were stained with spatters and smudges of blood.

She also noticed that he looked exhausted. His eyes were heavy-lidded and there were dark circles under them. Beneath a tan, the skin around his mouth was tinged gray from fatigue and his lips were twisted in a grimace.

Annie's scrutiny of him had started out strictly professional but shifted to a study of him from a personal perspective. She found herself assessing and evaluating him as a woman and was a little unnerved at her sudden interest.

He was tall — she guessed over six feet — with a broad chest, shoulders and muscular arms covered in elaborate full-sleeve black tattoos revealed by the rolled-up sleeves of his combat shirt.

She couldn't see the color of his eyes because they were shadowed by the brim of his helmet, but she took note of his square jawline and firm chin, which were covered by dust-smeared stubble.

Annie frowned. She had a feeling she'd seen him somewhere before and thought he might have come in with the injured men earlier that morning. She had seen a male with his build lurking in the triage area, but she'd been far too busy to pay much attention to him.

She was jerked back to the present when the man spoke, his voice husky and laced with exasperation. "Thanks, but no thanks."

Annie was tall for a woman but she had to look up into his face. She saw his eyes were a clear green, like the mineral-filled water of a mountain pool, and fringed with long dark lashes which wouldn't have looked out of place on a woman. They were beautiful and oddly feline, but right then they were narrowed and he was staring at her with an intense look.

A tremor ran down her spine and her pulse beat fast. Again, she felt like she should know the man, and when their gazes locked, she felt nervous and her stomach muscles clenched.

I know those eyes — or at least I think I do.

Chapter Four

Annie couldn't remember if she'd met the man before and she cleared her throat and brought her drifting thoughts back to the present. "You're hurt," she repeated. "Do you need treatment?"

The marine's tone held an undercurrent of irritation when he answered, "Nope. I told you I'm okay."

Annie looked at her dusty combat boots then back at him. He still hadn't moved and she felt intimidated and dwarfed by his height, which was rare for her.

Stubbornness was part of her nature and, determined not to allow his obvious impatience to throw her off course, she raised her chin. "I'm sorry" — she stared at the front of his body armor, made out his rank and continued — "Master Sergeant. I can't let you leave if I feel you need medical attention."

She knew she was being pushy and she held her breath. From the expression on his face, she had a feeling there might well be a verbal explosion — a reaction to her insistence that he stay — and the air was suddenly fraught with tension.

He sounded annoyed when he said, "Do I have a choice?"

It wasn't in Annie's nature to be rude to a stranger, in particular to someone who outranked her, but for some reason, she felt exasperated at the man's attitude and a little disconcerted at his response to her offer of help.

Unnerved but determined not to let him have the last word, she said, "Well, since you put it like that, no, you don't." *What's his problem?*

The master sergeant hesitated then, with an expression on his face that showed the hallmarks of one very pissed-off marine, said, "Hell, I guess it's your call, Specialist. Where do you want me?"

Annie wished she'd kept her mouth shut and had let the man leave when she'd first caught sight of him. She felt ill at ease in his presence and didn't know why, so without answering him, she turned and went to stand by one of the litters.

She gestured to it and said, "Please sit on this."

By the time he started to walk toward her, her patience had worn thin, but she watched him as he reached her side and, with graceful agility, hoisted himself onto the carrier.

Annie struggled to remain professional and said, "Okay. Where are you hurt?"

As she waited for an answer, her gaze caught his and a tremor ran through her.

God. Those eyes are hypnotic.

"Right foot," the master sergeant said, his tone curt.

Annie ignored his obvious irritation and went to the end of the stretcher, where rows of shelves reached from the floor to the roof of the tent and were littered with piles of disposable linens, drapes and open boxes of medical supplies.

After searching through various dilapidated containers, she found what she was looking for, tugged a pair of latex gloves from one and, finger by finger, pulled them on before she returned to stand in front of her reticent patient.

She tried to instill a note of humor in her voice to lighten the atmosphere when she said, "You can remove your helmet, Sergeant. We don't stand on ceremony here."

The marine removed his Kevlar and banged it down on the surface beside him. "Yeah, I can see that," he said, his tone full of sarcasm. "You're sure ready for anything that might go down."

Annie bridled at the implied insult and glanced past her grubby, bloodstained top and khaki shorts to her tan lower legs, which ended in bright pink hiking socks bunched over the tops of grubby combat boots.

She said in as civil a tone as she could muster, "Well, gosh, Master Sergeant, I do apologize for my lack of a dress code."

She bit her bottom lip then inhaled and tried to calm herself. She wasn't about to have a confrontation with the man, even if he seemed intent on goading her into one.

The tone of her voice was firm and to the point when she said, "The team was on forty-eight hours' downtime when the call came in this morning that we had incoming casualties. We've always been of the mindset that patients are more important than our appearance. Changing into uniforms and making ourselves presentable are the least of our concerns in that situation because we drop everything and get ready to save lives.

"One more thing… We don't have sick calls to treat minor injuries or ailments, so I'm doing you a favor. I do hope my…'get-up' hasn't offended you in any way."

Annie hated that she'd had to justify herself to the stranger about why she was not in full uniform and felt resentful that he had the nerve to call her out about it when she was trying to help him.

Dammit. This guy is a full-on jackass.

Silence followed her words, so she felt smug satisfaction and congratulated herself on her success in shutting him up. She leaned forward, lifted his right foot, placed the sole of his boot flat against her thigh and began to undo the laces.

Once she had slackened them as much as she could, she eased the footwear off and dropped it to the floor. The man was wearing a thick sock, and she rolled it down with care then pulled it off, letting it fall to join the combat boot.

"Brace yourself," Annie said and raised the limb so she could examine it.

The smell of sweating skin assailed her nostrils but she didn't flinch. She encountered a variety of noxious odors daily and was used to them. This one didn't offend her senses any more than the others, because she'd smelled far worse.

She saw the master sergeant's injury and wondered how he could have gone so long without getting it treated. There was a large raw area on his heel, consistent with protracted friction from his boot, the roof of the blister having come away to leave behind inflamed tissue. The wound looked sore and swollen.

She was relieved to see there was no sign of infection, but it must have been causing him a great deal of discomfort and she winced in sympathy.

Annie raised her head from her inspection and stared at him. "I see you haven't been taking your own advice, Sergeant."

She couldn't help but notice he had dark, almost-black hair cut in a very short crew-cut. Up close, the color of his eyes was flawless and the look in them watchful, which made her wonder why he was so wary of her.

At her words, an expression of annoyance appeared on his face and he grunted. "What's *that* supposed to mean?"

Annie frowned. "Oh, come on, Sergeant. You know the rules about self-hygiene, especially about looking after your feet in this environment. You must have advised your men to watch out for blisters and have them treated either by your medic or by a medical professional…if they became bad enough, like yours has. It's very important to avoid getting an infection, which is pretty common in this heat and such unsanitary conditions."

She knew she was lecturing. She couldn't help doing it and the man's lips tightened, but he stayed silent and she wondered if her admonishment was so insignificant that it was beneath him to respond at all.

She bit her lower lip. She felt self-conscious, as if she were being treated like a second-class citizen because she didn't know what she was talking about. The fact that they were squabbling about her treatment of him and his stubbornness was ludicrous, and she felt indignant and lowered his foot.

"Look… I'm not here to piss you off, Sergeant. You looked like you were hurt. I offered you medical care. You took it. If you've changed your mind then you're free to leave. I'm not about to force you to have your blister seen to."

As soon as she spoke, Annie envisioned the man losing it and creating holy hell because she'd been insubordinate. She was therefore somewhat taken aback when, on a different tack, he said, "How're the men that were brought in this morning?"

His voice was low and Annie heard a note of concern in his tone. She felt contrite at her harsh words and sympathy for him warred with her irritation.

"Both men are critical but stable," she replied. "Their vital signs are within normal parameters and they're on thirty-minute observations, which is a step up from fifteen-minute obs following their surgeries. That's a good sign.

"If they stay that way and there are no complications, they'll both eventually be medevacked out to the combat support hospital in Mosul. They'll remain there until they can be flown to Landstuhl." Annie softened her tone. "They'll pull through. Were they your men?"

The marine shook his head. "Nope. Just another squad we were working with. We made it back when the mission turned into a clusterfuck."

Annie sensed the man would ignore any danger to himself and help anyone in need. While he irritated the hell out of her, she also felt respect and admiration for him, although more than likely he thought nothing of what he'd done.

She went to the shelves again to collect a small aluminum basin, a bottle of Betadine and a handful of cotton wool. She placed the supplies on the trolley beside the stretcher, unscrewed the cap from the bottle of antiseptic solution and poured a small amount into the receptacle.

She put the cap back on the bottle, set it down, picked up the bowl and cotton wool then stepped in front of the master sergeant.

"Okay. Can you lie face down for me, please?" she said.

The marine's expression changed again and he glared at her as though she'd asked him to perform cartwheels while singing the American anthem. "You gotta be kidding me."

Annie sighed. "No, Sergeant, I don't kid around when it comes to dealing with demanding patients. If you do as you're told, it will give me easier access to your wound and that will make both of our lives a lot easier."

"Holy shit," the man muttered before he swung his legs up onto the litter and in a smooth move rolled onto his front. He mumbled something else beneath his breath and she assumed the language was impolite or crude. "Happy now?" he asked.

"Oh, yes, Sergeant. You'll never know how much I'm enjoying your company. Now, this isn't going to hurt at all."

Annie walked to the foot of the litter, soaked the handful of cotton wool in the liquid and began to dab at the raw blister.

She heard his sharp intake of breath then he said, "Like fuck that doesn't hurt. I love your bedside manner. Are all medics like you?"

Annie pressed her lips together to suppress the laughter that threatened to burst free.

At last. A genuine, non-asshole response. This guy might be human after all.

She was successful in suppressing her amusement and continued with her task. "Nope. I'm one of a kind. They threw away the mold when they made me."

"Now why doesn't that surprise me?" came the chill response.

Okay. My bad, he's a robot. Round one goes to the stoic and humorless master sergeant.

Annie finished cleaning the wound, dried it and moved to the shelves again to hunt through the numerous boxes until at last she found a sealed dressing and an elastic adhesive bandage that would keep it in place. She took the pad from its sterile package and placed it over the raw skin before she shook out and wound the sticky wrap around the ankle.

"There you go, Sergeant. All done. Would you like a treat for being so good?"

As soon as she spoke, she wanted to clap a hand over her runaway mouth.

What in the hell am I saying? I don't even know this man. I wouldn't even talk to my friends like this. Why don't you go ahead and dig the hole even deeper, Annie?

There was no response to her statement and she turned her head to look at him. He was staring at her with an unfathomable look in his eyes and a thoughtful expression on his grimy face, but she could have sworn she saw the beginnings of a grin twitch his mouth.

"I'll pass, but thanks for the offer," he said, and Annie winced at the coldness in his voice. "Am I free to go now? That's if there's nothing else you want to kick my ass about."

Annie's cheeks burned with a blush. She watched as the master sergeant roamed her face as if he were studying her every feature, then their gazes collided and a sudden frisson of emotion passed between them.

Chapter Five

Annie felt shy and awkward. She dragged her gaze from the marine's and took the bowl of used antiseptic solution to a sink in the corner of the tent. She rinsed it with water, and once she'd dried it, she placed it back on the shelf. She threw the sodden cotton wool into a waste receptacle and returned to stand a short distance away from her patient.

"Okay, Sergeant. You're free to go."

He rolled onto his back, sat up and swung his legs over the side of the stretcher. "Much appreciated."

Annie was unsure whether he was still being sarcastic but stayed silent, bent and retrieved his boot and sock then handed them to him. She watched as he slid the garment back on then put on his footwear and tied the laces.

At that moment, a voice sounded from behind her. "So, this is where you're lurking, McKendrick."

Annie half-turned and saw the tall and slender, dark-haired lead surgeon, Major Chad Matthews, approaching her and she smiled. "I guess you've found me, sir," she responded. "To what do I owe the honor?"

Major Matthews reached her side, smiled at her and adjusted his glasses. "I see you've found someone else to boss around," he said, and turned his attention to the marine. "Good to see you, Master Sergeant O'Rourke."

The man nodded his head in greeting. "Sir."

Annie frowned. "Is that meant to be a joke, sir?" she said referring to his earlier remark and pretended to be offended. "You've got me all wrong."

Major Matthews glanced sideways at her. "Yeah, right. I stand corrected then."

He turned his gaze back to the master sergeant. "I'd be wary of this young lady, if I were you. She's bossy, opinionated and downright rude sometimes…but one of the best medics we have."

Annie's face flushed once more. This was a day for blushes—a record number for her—and it was only zero nine hundred hours. She glanced beneath her lashes at the man sitting on the stretcher to see he was staring at her once more, but his features were impassive.

For some reason, she wished she could see behind his tough exterior and the expressionless eyes so she could figure out what he was thinking. That was never going to happen, though, because she thought he might have slapped on a layer of rebar and two coats of concrete to create a veneer that nobody could penetrate.

"I'll bear that in mind for future reference, sir," the sergeant said at last. "Now, I'd better get outta here. I need to get back to my men."

Annie watched him pick up his helmet and hop off the bed. "If your foot gets any worse, you'll need to come back, Sergeant," she said.

The master sergeant gazed at her with a steely-eyed expression. "Yeah, I'll do that," he said, his tone suggesting the complete opposite. He nodded at the major, put on his Kevlar and walked out of the hospital.

Annie watched him go and was a little disappointed that she'd made such a bad impression on him. She couldn't understand why she had, but shrugged and began to tidy away the rest of the supplies she'd used, returning them to the shelves.

Once she'd finished, she turned to the major, who was still watching her, and she cocked an eyebrow. "Sir?"

Major Matthews' voice held a teasing note when he said, "I think you've made a hit there, McKendrick."

Annie's heart skipped a beat. "Who with?" she asked, knowing full well to whom he was referring.

"US Marine Master Sergeant Shay O'Rourke," the officer said.

At the mention of the unusual first name, Annie experienced a twinge of recognition.

Shay? I've heard that name before. But where?

The memory was elusive and she bit her lip in frustration.

This is ridiculous. I'd never forget a man like that.

Annie shrugged. "I have no idea what you're talking about, Major," she replied. "But, with all due respect, you're dead wrong. The sergeant and I didn't see eye-to-eye when I detained him here and he wasn't keen on my forcing treatment on him."

"You mean *the* Annie McKendrick couldn't win him over with her angelic qualities? Now, that's something to put out on the scuttlebutt air waves."

Annie pursed her lips in a grimace. "Yeah, okay, sir. Would you mind getting to the point of this conversation?"

"Master Sergeant O'Rourke happens to be a real legend out here in Iraq. He and his men are known as Delta Team, but people call them the Raptors. Don't tell me you've never heard of them?"

Annie shook her head and the major continued, "I have no idea how many bronze stars he's earned, but it's a helluva lot. The guy never thinks twice before wading into a firefight. People—mainly the ladies—say he's an unemotional bastard because he never shows any fear.

"He's been in here a couple of times with casualties—not his own men, I might add. He sticks around until they're stabilized then goes off on another mission—which is why I think you've made a hit with him. I've never heard him say so much as a dozen words to anyone, let alone a female. You must have succeeded in penetrating that tough exterior with your incredible charm and magnetism."

Annie laughed. "You think?" she said. "I made about as much of a hit with him as I do when I play baseball, which is zip in my book."

Major Matthews laughed out loud. "Go on," he ordered. "Get lost. Go get something to eat and have some downtime. Remember... You need your strength for the volleyball game this afternoon. Mattie's Marauders *will* beat Lloydie's Lurkers, McKendrick, and that's an order."

Annie sketched a casual salute. "Oh, yes, of course, sir. Anything you say, sir."

She about-faced and walked away, leaving the major shaking his head and still laughing.

Back in the operating room, she threaded her way around the tables and portable equipment and entered the tunnel leading to the team's rest area.

As she walked by the care unit she heard the faint beep of heart monitors and the muted hiss of a portable ventilator. When one of the patients moaned, goosebumps rose on her arms and she shuddered.

Those specific sounds always brought her up short. The assorted noises from the medical equipment meant that a battle for life and death was being fought in the closed-off area of the hospital.

Annie shivered again and hurried by the obligatory screen that separated the patients from five cots that had been crammed together in a space that they shared with stacks of boxes labeled Meals Ready to Eat — MREs — and pallets of bottled water.

Five members of the team at a time could sleep or eat in the area, depending on how busy they were and whenever an opportunity presented itself. It was rare that any one person was lucky enough to get more than a few hours' rest at a time, because relaxation was a luxury the surgical team couldn't afford.

Everyone took turns on the cots or any flat surface that would accommodate a weary body, such as operating tables, stretchers or, if desperate, the floor. Lack of sleep resulted in lapses of concentration and mistakes made, so standing orders dictated that at some point every person had to have at most four hours of downtime, even if catching some shut-eye was impossible.

Annie knew, to her cost, that for her it never seemed to work out that way.

The rest area was empty of slumbering bodies and she went to the MREs and searched through an open box. She wasn't very hungry and found a packet of crackers and a bag of M&Ms, then collected a bottle of warm water before she sat on one of the cots.

For a moment, she stared through into the administrative operations area, where she could see more stacked unopened containers, and she prayed she might be given the opportunity to relax and have some peace for a few moments for the first time that day.

Her alone time lasted a couple of minutes before it was interrupted.

"Hey, girl."

Annie jumped, glanced over her shoulder and saw Freya Marshall, her friend and one of the forward surgical team's certified registered nurse anesthetists, sauntering into the rest area.

Annie smiled. "Hi," she said and wondered, not for the first time, how the sergeant could get away with wearing what she did.

Freya had tied a fuchsia-pink bandanna around her head, which clashed with her red hair, and she wore garish yellow knee-length cycle shorts with bright green socks bunched over her combat boots.

Annie mused that in all the time she'd known Freya, which was since basic training, she'd never known her to be conventional in the way she behaved or dressed.

Freya had always been up front with Annie about the fact that she was a good-time girl. She was popular with men and flirtatious, without being over-the-top, and she'd confessed she'd joined the Army to find herself a 'hot man in uniform'.

Annie didn't believe her friend's casual description of herself and was sure the sergeant wasn't as disinterested in her affairs of the heart as she proclaimed. Men seemed to flock to her in droves, likes bees around honey, but she had no idea if Freya had ever been serious about the numerous prospective husbands.

As close as they were, her friend never confided in her about that side of her life, and the men never seemed to last long enough to be able to put a ring on one of her long, slender fingers.

Freya was her superior in rank but their relationship was so close that they could rely on each other for support and emotional strength in testing situations without question. The sergeant, despite her nonchalant attitude toward relationships and life in general, was passionate about her job and the patients she cared for.

"How are our patients?" Annie asked.

Freya walked to the supplies and rummaged around until she found what she was looking for.

"They're doing okay," she answered, and with a bag of peanuts in one hand and a bottle of juice in the other, she joined Annie on the cot.

Once she'd opened the drink, she took a long swallow and sighed. "Oh, man, that's good," she said and continued. "There was a slight complication with a breathing tube and some re-bleeding with the first guy who was operated on, but it's under control now. Bit of a panic for a few minutes, but they're both ready to be lifted out."

Annie felt a deep sense of satisfaction at the news. "That's great," she said.

The two women sat in silence for a few moments, then Annie cleared her throat.

Freya turned to her. "What?" she asked. "I know that sound. What's on your mind, hon?"

Against her better judgment, Annie wanted to know more about Master Sergeant Shay O'Rourke and she wondered whether she should ask Freya. Her run-in with him had intrigued her and the conversation with Major Matthews had fueled her curiosity.

During the short amount of time she'd spent with the marine, something about him had piqued her interest. He irritated the hell out of her and he had about as much charm as a dead tuna, but when she thought about the way he'd stared at her and his rugged good looks, she realized there was a sexy attractiveness about him she couldn't deny.

More than that, the thought of him made her nerves tingle and her stomach flutter as if it were filled with a flock of agitated butterflies.

Oh, hell. Go for it.

Annie glanced at her boots and forced a casual tone into her voice when she said, "Have you heard of a marine team called the Raptors?"

A choking sound followed the question, and when she glanced at her friend, Freya was wiping her mouth and staring at her with an expression of astonishment on her lovely face. "The Raptors?" she echoed. "You mean Delta?"

Annie nodded and tossed a chocolate-coated sweet in her mouth so she wouldn't have to elaborate.

"What planet have you been living on, girl?" Freya said. "Who *hasn't* heard of 'em? Those are some badass marines, despite the fact they're all so goddamn young. If anyone gets into shit outside the wire, it's not the *Ghostbusters* they call but the Raptors. When things get screwed up, they're the ones that go in and clean up the clusterfucks. Why do you ask?"

"No reason," Annie replied and tried to sound nonchalant when she next spoke. "I heard about them from Major M."

From the corner of her eye, she saw Freya glance at her with an expression of curiosity. "Their team leader is Master Sergeant Shay O'Rourke. Scuttlebutt has it—from the women, of course, who else — that he's pretty much an enigma, all alpha-male and sexy as hell. What more could a woman ask for? The downside is rumors have it that he has no interest in members of the opposite sex, which is a bit disappointing. I can also tell you plenty have tried to get into his pants. He's a very mysterious guy, which makes him more of a challenge for some of the ladies on the base."

Annie's heart sank and she wondered at her response. "You mean he's gay?" she asked. *What a waste.*

Freya laughed out loud, and her even white teeth gleamed in the dim light. "Hell, no," she replied. "He's a career marine through and through and straight as a railroad tie, not that I've had much of an opportunity to find out for myself, you understand. I flirted with him once, as was expected of me. I couldn't let the side down, after all. But it was like trying to get a response from a camel spider, and you know how dumb they are — not that I'm likening him to one. I think he thought I was an interesting specimen."

Warmth coursed through Annie's body and an uncharacteristic excitement made her heart lurch. "He's not married then?" she asked, then cringed when she realized how gauche and obvious the question had sounded.

Freya turned and stared at her with a look of suspicion on her face. "Yeah, he is…to the Marine Corp. Whoa, honey. What's with all the questions about this guy?"

Annie turned her gaze away from the other woman's scrutiny and inspected her bottle of water. "No reason. I just heard about him. That's all."

"Uh-uh," Freya said, skepticism evident in her voice. "Come on. Make my day. Spill."

Annie hesitated before she said with reluctance, "He came in with those two casualties this morning. He hung around until their surgeries were over and I saw him as he was about to leave and thought he was injured. I told him I needed to check him over and he got pretty bent out of shape about it."

Freya frowned. "Well, well… What's he really like?"

Annie was reticent about divulging what she thought about the good-looking marine and said in a non-committal voice, "He has about as much charm as said spider, and you know how nasty they are. He's also irritating, sarcastic and damn stubborn."

"Really?" Freya said her tone light. "You seem to know an awful lot about him."

"No, I don't," Annie answered. "He has extraordinary green eyes though, and I'm sure I know him from somewhere, but I can't remember where."

"You got close enough to see the color of his eyes?"

Annie glared at her friend, who was staring at her empty bag of nuts with studied interest, a smile on her face.

"I know where you're going with this, Freya," she said irritated. "Was I supposed to keep my eyes shut when I was treating him?"

Before the sergeant could defend herself against the accusation, the voice of Lance Corporal Darren 'Daz' Kazowski, one of the medics, spoke in a low voice behind them.

"Hey, ladies. The major wants to have a briefing about the game this afternoon."

Freya groaned. "Holy cow," she said. "That goddamn event is driving me crazy."

Annie laughed out loud, relieved her friend's attention had been diverted by the summons.

"Come on, Sarge. Let's move it. Otherwise Major M will go loco and have a field day with us if we don't show one-hundred-ten percent interest in his darn volleyball match."

She stood and held out a hand to Freya, who clasped it with hers and allowed herself to be pulled to her feet.

"I need this like I need a hole in the head," the sergeant said.

Annie pushed her friend ahead of her and both women left the rest area and went into the operating room.

Chapter Six

Shay stopped outside the hospital and flexed his ankle. The sharp pain of the wound had diminished to a dull throb and the dressing the specialist had applied was doing its job well in preventing any further friction from his boot.

He thrust his arm through the sling of his M4 carbine and shrugged it over his shoulder before he scanned his surroundings. His senses were still on high alert and his body thrummed with adrenaline and unreleased energy, the after-effects of the patrol and the incident that morning.

It didn't matter whether he was outside the wire or inside waiting for his next mission, his sixth sense — one which unfailingly sent out a psychic alarm to warn him of danger or signaled that something in a specific situation wasn't right — was working overtime.

He didn't believe in spooks or things that went bump in the night and didn't think it was possible to possess a psychic awareness. He did believe that a human being's senses could be tuned enough to pick up warning signs that others might miss. Even if his eyes couldn't see it, his nerves could detect it... Threat.

Physical intelligence was collated and interpreted from unmanned aerial vehicles — Predator drones — that were carrying out reconnaissance missions and forward observation roles in the run up to the Operation Iraqi Freedom invasion due to commence on March twentieth.

Intel was passed down by command and used as a baseline for strategic and tactical planning briefings. Shay accepted the information he received from the Predators — which so far had proved reliable — but he still preferred to trust his physical senses and his uncanny ability to judge when something was wrong far more than he did military equipment and machines. He always felt uneasy if he couldn't use his eyes and gut instinct in combination with state-of-the-art technology.

Years of training had hard-wired his DNA to respond to a perceived threat, and his intuition had served him well more times than he could count.

Shay inhaled, released the breath then rolled his shoulders. He tried to dismiss the tension that knotted the muscles there, but it was exacerbated by the rage which still simmered inside him, the embers fanned by the recent memory of the two casualties from the morning's incident and at not being able to bring those responsible to justice.

He knew he had to find some way to purge it from his system. Since joining the Marine Corp, he had discovered that he possessed the ability to master and lock down his emotions, which enabled him to operate more effectively in a firefight and when the stakes were highest and multiple variables were in a constant state of flux.

In recent months, however, he'd found it hard to control his anger, and he knew it could become a problem if he let it persist. He wasn't a psychiatrist but understood that the emotional state varied in intensity from mild irritation to intense fury. It could cloud judgment, turn a serviceman or woman's perspective and focus them away from the task at hand.

It could also trigger fear, anxiety and result in reckless and impulsive behavior. When it was uncontrolled, a person could become a danger to themselves or others, reducing combat readiness, effectiveness and the morale of the unit.

On the other hand, anger and fear could become someone's friend. They heightened the senses and boosted adrenaline levels to energize a human body so it could go beyond normal endurance.

Shay had always thought of himself as a man for whom fear didn't form part of his psyche. He knew he had a reputation for being cold and ruthless with a 'don't fuck with me' attitude that warned others not to cross him. While this label was only attributed to him in combat, he was keen to foster the veneer and keep it going.

If he ever felt any semblance of fear when faced with the usual clusterfuck on a mission, he channeled the feeling into aggression and directed it at the cowards who wouldn't face him and his men and who killed for the sake of it and called it 'in the name of Allah'.

He had also never allowed himself to become complacent each time he and his team had completed a mission and had walked safely back onto the base. For a person to let their guard down even for one second could lead to carelessness, and so far, he and the Raptors had been lucky—if it could be called luck, being in the shithole known as Iraq—and they had been left unscarred by their many missions.

He never took survival for granted because it could get a person killed and there was no coming back from death.

Shay remained aware of everything going on around him but let his thoughts drift back to the woman specialist at the hospital.

He spoke her name in a low voice, "Annie McKendrick," and heard the way the syllables rolled off his tongue.

She had treated him with skill and a gentleness he'd found not only touching but arousing. She was spirited and stubborn, and despite being insubordinate in some of her responses to him, he'd found it refreshing. During the short time he'd spent with her, he'd found himself becoming more intrigued and interested in her as a person. He'd almost let his guard down.

On his last few missions he'd felt an encroaching numbness, both physical and mental. It had begun to tighten its grip on him and take control of the part of him that made him a living and feeling human being.

He'd seen so much hurt and death—cruel and unrelenting components of war—that he was inured to it. Each time he was involved in a firefight that resulted in the destruction of the enemy or injuries to someone he knew, he'd begun to care less and less about the real purpose and reasons why he was in Iraq in the first place. He justified each horrific outcome with the words 'same shit, different day'.

The urge to take the fight to the enemy and fuck them sideways had grown stronger. Shay was out for blood and his men howled for it, because insurgents didn't stand toe-to-toe and fight like real soldiers. They used explosives and small coordinated attacks to chip away at the resolve of the troops and the Iraqi people, and he and his men balanced murder and intimidation with providing security and swift justice.

His thoughts, hopes and dreams of killing weren't like the John Wayne myth, but an up close and personal event where he could watch someone's head explode, either from his bullets, butt strokes from his rifle or disembowelment with his knife.

The improvised explosive device event had made him aware — on a higher level — of his growing indifference, and he'd been on his way out of the hospital to collect his gear and go out on another mission to continue bloodying his hands and his boots under his new-found sense of justice. Annie McKendrick had prevented him from leaving and a little warmth had entered his life.

She'd made him feel almost human again, and not only because she was gorgeous — a fact he was very aware of. He wasn't surprised at the strong attraction he felt for her, because he knew her and remembered the effect that she'd had on him in the past.

When she'd stopped him from leaving the hospital, he'd been poleaxed when he'd recognized her. She'd haunted his thoughts for so long that the sight of her had disarmed him and his self-imposed barrier of nonchalance had dropped.

Shay let his mind wander — a rare occurrence for him — and delved into his memories of her, which were still as clear as if they had been created only yesterday.

As a fifteen- or sixteen-year-old Langley High School sophomore, she was lovely then. She was tall for her age and gawky, with luscious hair the color of chestnuts, dark blue eyes and a smattering of freckles across a pert nose and high cheekbones. Whenever he passed her in the corridors, his gaze was drawn to her and he had an almost obsessive urge to get to know her.

He wanted to ask her out on a date, but his own life situation and an angry awareness of the rumors that were going around the school about him and his family had held him back.

He didn't give a damn about conforming to student opinion of seniors dating sophomores – however, he did care about his somewhat disreputable reputation and lifestyle rubbing off on a girl who lived a life of luxury and who didn't deserve to pay for his faults and be tarred with the same brush.

During his early years he hadn't been an angel in relation to women. In fact, he was the love 'em and leave 'em type and he wasn't proud of it. When he saw Annie outside the hotel on the evening of his sister's graduation, all decked out in her short black dress with her long, slim legs accentuated by high-heeled shoes, he was struck dumb for the first time in his life.

Shay noticed her staring at him, and when their gazes met and locked, he wondered why she was looking at him with such intent and whether she felt the same connection to him as he did to her.

She was too young for him, though, but, like a match thrown into a trail of gasoline, a slow burn coiled in his gut and spread to his groin. An intense desire to have her left him shocked at his body's reaction to her, both on an emotional and physical level.

He walked away from her then, but her image stayed in his mind. When he came upon her and his sister late that night, he knew what was going on and he was furious at Megan's reprehensible behavior, getting involved with Annie McKendrick's date.

He had his own rules and values regarding affairs of the heart, and poaching on someone's relationship was taboo in his mind. He saw the expression of humiliation on Annie's face and felt angry on her behalf. He also admired her for her restraint in the face of her hurt at the way she had been treated.

While he was and always would be protective of Megan, he admitted to himself that he was amused at Annie's verbal barrage that was directed at his sister and the man she was with. For that, she also gained his respect.

The images of her had stayed in his mind, provocative and teasing and, despite fighting an internal battle with himself to do so, he had never been able to forget her.

Annie hadn't recognized him. If she had, she might have slapped him again or shot him in the balls. Based on self-preservation, he thought it prudent not to tell her.

In a way he was grateful that her memories of their brief times together had been wiped from her mind. However, if he were honest with himself, he felt regret when he thought of what the alternative might be if she did know who he was.

After his meeting with her in the hospital, he couldn't dismiss her from his mind and, uncomfortable with his emotions, he began to walk toward his accommodation.

For the first time since his deployment, his thoughts weren't focused on where he was and the next mission, but instead, they were concentrated on the memory of dark blue eyes and a heart-shaped face.

Chapter Seven

The dark-haired man with the striking green eyes grasped Annie's hips and pulled her in against him. When he nibbled at the lobe of her ear, shivers cascaded throughout her body and she moaned.

'Do you want me?' the man asked.

'Yes,' she answered. 'Yes, I want you,' and her tone sounded almost desperate.

'Tell me how much you want me, Annie.'

"Annie! Annie, wake the hell up."

The insistent voice penetrated her sleep-induced coma. For a few moments she couldn't distinguish whether she *was* awake or still immersed in the dream, and she felt disoriented.

She groaned and tried to burrow beneath the rough blanket that covered her, sure that if she stayed hidden, she would be out of sight and out of mind of the person who was trying to disturb her rest period.

"Holy shit. Move your ass off that cot, will ya?"

Someone shook her shoulder and she felt compelled to open one eye in response. "What the hell?" she muttered. "This had better be good."

"Nothing is ever good in this shithole. Now get up."

When she realized her tormenter wasn't going to go away, Annie raised her head from the pillow and opened her other eye.

Light shone into the rest area from the care unit and the operating tent and outlined Freya standing by her bed with her hands on her hips.

Annie's voice was laced with irritation when she said, "What's the goddamn emergency that you need to wake me up at" — she looked at the illuminated face of her watch — "zero two hundred hours in the damn morning?"

Freya rolled her eyes and sounded very unsympathetic when she said, "Finally. It speaks. Major M wants a briefing. *Now*. Something about a 'fuck me' dust storm heading our way."

Annie struggled into a seated position and pushed a bird's nest of hair back from her face. "I guess that's emergency enough for me," she said. She untangled herself from the blanket, threw it off her and swung her legs over the side of the cot.

Annie stood and tucked her T-shirt into her desert battle dress pants then patted down the length of her legs to check if anything had crawled up them while she had been asleep.

There were two important schools of thought when it came to catching rack time and getting through it with all limbs intact without an inhabitant of the desert making an unwelcome visit.

A person could get undressed and have a nasty something with long, hairy legs crawl into combats and boots where it—or they—would wait for an unsuspecting someone to put the garments on and push their feet into their footwear, only to be bitten.

Or, a person could stay clothed and have a miniature monster creep beneath the blankets and crawl inside a uniform, where it could sleep the night away next to a warm body and bide its time before taking a nip when it became hungry.

Annie thought it didn't matter which choice she made. She'd be screwed either way. She preferred to go to bed in her uniform and sometimes her boots, which would give her a fighting chance, although she drew the line at wearing her tactical gear. She'd tried that once and it had made for a very uncomfortable and sleepless night.

Once Annie was satisfied that nothing was clinging to or feeding off her body, she pulled a rubber band from her wrist and swept her hair back into a ponytail.

She felt a bit more human and said, "Let's go then. What's keeping you?"

Freya sighed then muttered something under her breath and they left the rest area to enter the operating shelter.

"What were you dreaming about?" Freya asked as they walked.

Annie half-turned to stare at her friend. She frowned and said, "I don't know. What *was* I dreaming about?"

"You were moaning about…something very suggestive and it didn't sound like any nightmare I'd heard of."

Annie knew what Freya was talking about, and an image of Master Sergeant O'Rourke popped into her mind. Her face burned with a blush.

"I was?" she asked in as casual a tone as she could muster.

"Yeah, you were. It sounded like you were having a really great time."

Annie saw the expression of amusement on her friend's face and said, "I still don't know what you're talking about, Freya. If I was dreaming about anything…like that, I don't remember."

"Uh-huh, okay, sleep-induced amnesia on tap. We'll leave it there then, hon, but I think you're offloading some bullshit on me."

Annie shrugged and followed Freya to where the forward surgical team was gathered in a semi-circle about Captain Lloyd, Major Matthews and two other surgeons, Captain Brian Elliott and Lieutenant Dan Byers.

When Annie and Freya joined them, Major Matthews glared at them, cocked an eyebrow then frowned. "Glad you two could join us," he said.

"Sorry, sir," Annie said. "I was asleep and Sergeant Marshall couldn't wake me."

"You got that right," Freya said to her in a low voice. "That dream must have been a real doozy."

Annie dug her elbow into Freya's ribs and felt a perverse satisfaction when she heard her friend let out a gush of air as if she had been winded.

"Okay. Okay. We're all here, so let's get on with it," Major Matthews said. "I've been reliably informed that there's a low-pressure cyclonic storm brewing to the north of us. The natives call it a haboob. Us yanks tend to call it a 'fuck me' dust storm. I don't give a damn what it's called. All I know is that it's heading our way and it's going to kick our asses and create a shit load of chaos for twenty-four to thirty-six hours—and that's if we're lucky.

"For those of you who've never had the pleasure of being subjected to a storm of this kind, I'll do my best to enlighten you. Lightning and thunder will precede high winds and lots and lots of dust. This shit is as fine as flour and it will smother everything, no doubt about that. It will work its way into every crevice of your weapons, garments, vehicles and the hospital. It will also penetrate all your orifices — and not in a nice way, so take that grin off your face, Webster."

There was an outburst of laughter, and when it had quieted, the major continued, "You'll end up eating your MREs with sand — "

"That can't make them taste any worse than they already do," someone interrupted. "Might even make 'em more edible."

There were more chuckles and the major smiled. "Okay, you've had your jokes. Now let's get serious. If you go outside, visibility will be so bad that you won't be able to see anyone, even if they're standing next to you. You could even get lost on your way to the restrooms. If you attempt to do your business outside, you'll have to deal with dust blowing up your backsides, so I wouldn't recommend that option.

"I want screens set up next to the laundry section marking out two separate areas for porta potties with a WAG bag kit in each. It won't offer much privacy, ladies and gentlemen, but we'll all just have to make do for the duration. The temperature will also drop as the leading edge of the storm approaches, so you'll need to stay warm.

"When it comes to equipment and machinery, the more sophisticated an electrical system, the more the dust will affect it. It will clog and may jam if it gets inside. The storm can also create electrostatic discharges that, while not fatal, can have negative consequences on fueling operations and computer or electrical systems.

"There'll be no flying and nobody will be driving, so I hope and pray that we won't receive any medevac or casevac calls, because that'll be a clusterfuck of the greatest magnitude. Of course, we'll do what's necessary — but it won't be easy.

"If you do have to go out, you'll need to cover all areas of exposed skin. Goggles to protect your eyes and scarves over your mouths are the norm. The dust consists of minute particles of sand and crushed rock, and it will abrade any exposed parts of your body like sandpaper.

"From a medical viewpoint, the MNC-I Surgeon's office has said that the long-term risk from breathing dust is thought to be low, however, they do caution against performing strenuous activities when a storm like this is on the move.

"This shit will irritate your eyes, so that's why you need protective eyewear, and you can't inhale the dust into your lungs. During exercise, you breathe many times the volume of air and dust as when you're at rest. Your lungs have a natural process for expelling the fine particles that are inhaled, but until you get rid of the dust, their capacity is reduced.

"We need to seal off each area of the hospital. I want everyone to make sure every section is dug in, because I don't want a shelter to take off into the wild blue yonder.

"We'll turn the generators off, and they all need to be covered in tarps. Someone is always to make sure there's a plentiful supply of coffee kept going. We're all gonna need it before this day is over."

Major Matthews studied the people in front of him. "Any questions?" he asked.

Everyone shook their heads and the officer nodded with satisfaction. "Okay. Let's move. These storms have a habit of coming up real fast, so I doubt we have much time. Dismissed."

* * * *

Annie sighed then shivered as goosebumps covered her arms. Major M had been right when he'd said the temperature would drop as the dust storm drew close. She reminded herself that she needed to get her jacket, because if this was how cold it was now, what would it be like in an hour's time?

Her hands were chilled and she rubbed them together then kicked the bottom of the tent where it met the floor. She was satisfied when she saw there was only a very narrow gap for dust and sand to be able to get in beneath the canvas wall, and she left the small area and went out into the tunnel that led through the center of the hospital to the care unit and rest area.

Outside, she reached up and untied the toggles that held up the flap serving as a door. She let it drop down before she zipped it shut and sealed off the laundry area from the rest of the hospital.

Even though the shelter she had just closed didn't live up to its name and wasn't functional as a place to wash clothes and dry them, it did have a single, rickety clothes washer that rocked and rolled every time it was used and a dryer that rumbled like the engine of a vehicle and sounded like it was on its last legs. But both machines were all the field hospital had and the laundry tent had to be included in the isolation procedure.

Annie's gaze moved on to a small dark tunnel that ran parallel to the laundry shelter and what felt like cold fingers trailed up her spine.

She knew what was at the end of the gloomy, narrow tunnel. She had already checked it and sealed its door before making her escape to carry out the rest of her duties.

The mass fatality temporary morgue section or mobile mortuary dome was the one place in the hospital that everyone was reluctant to enter. Annie remembered the feeling of unease and disquiet she'd felt when she'd gone in.

She knew the heavy atmosphere and her sense of foreboding were a figment of her imagination and generated by what the area was to be used for, but that hadn't stopped her from staring at the aluminum racks aligned in regimental rows with an anxiety almost bordering on fear, that those would soon be filled during the coming war.

She'd almost run from the place after completing her checks, closing the door flap with indecent haste and hurrying back to the well-lit main tunnel, where she had tried to restore her equilibrium and infuse herself with an optimistic hope that the morgue might never be used. It was a fatalistic thought and false when she considered what was going to take place in a few days' time.

Annie walked to the care unit and was about to step through to perform the sealing process when she saw Freya coming toward her, so she stopped.

"Hey, Annie. You need to come see this," the sergeant said.

Annie folded her arms. "See what?" she asked.

Freya grasped her arm and tugged her forward. "Just come on, will ya?"

Annie closed off the tunnel behind her and allowed herself to be pulled through into the next shelter. She waited with impatience while Freya unfastened the flap into the rest area, then she followed her through. After it had been resealed, they continued toward the emergency entrance.

Annie unzipped the canvas to the outside, but before she pushed it aside, she turned to the other woman. "Can I ask the all-important question of why we're going out there? What's the big deal?"

Freya pushed her. "Jesus, lady, just go."

Annie stepped outside and saw that most — if not all — of the forward surgical team were standing in a group in silence and staring northward.

She and Freya joined their colleagues and Annie trembled in the chilly air. "You've gotta be kidding me. It's freezing out here."

"Quit griping, Annie. Look to the north and you'll see."

Before she did as she was ordered, Annie heard shouts from her left and looked to see men tying down the Blackhawk and Chinooks' rotor blades then casting tarps over their engines and fastening them to make sure they wouldn't blow away in the coming winds.

Their actions were methodical but hurried and she saw two men glance toward the distant mountains as if they saw something bearing down on the base.

Annie refocused her attention and looked in the direction Freya had indicated. Her heart skipped a beat and she felt a stab of unease at what she saw in the distance. "Holy shit," she said.

"Yeah, that's what he said," Freya replied.

Dawn was supposed to have broken, but there was no sign of the familiar psychedelic red and gold glow which heralded the rising of the sun. The morning was gloomy and almost as dark as dusk.

For as far as Annie could see, the sky was a mass of low, anvil-shaped clouds that churned and seethed like thick, charcoal-colored smoke stirred to fury by the building strength of the air currents in the upper atmosphere.

The wind blew in urgent gusts. There was a faint hissing and sand and dust blew across the ground. When she stared once again toward the Sinjar Mountains, she saw they had taken on a wavering, smudged appearance, as if they were being absorbed into the very fabric of the approaching storm.

As she watched, the distant horizon grew hazy with a dirty brown band, and the already feeble light began to take on an ochre-tan hue and small particles of sand bit into her exposed skin.

The wind on her face was dry, as if all the moisture content had been sucked from it, and there was a burnt-copper odor in the air that stung her nostrils and made her eyes water with its potent essence.

A brief but loud rumble of thunder rolled across the sky and a flicker of lightning lit up her surroundings with strobe-like striations, the storm ferociously announcing its impending arrival.

A primal fear flooded through Annie as she watched the dust storm roll inexorably toward them, eating up the distance between it and them as if it were a voracious living thing.

It stretched from horizon to horizon, a dingy and amorphous wall with little silvery plumes of dust streaming off its crest in the manner of a tsunami rising from the deep.

Forked lightning ripped its way across the sky again — white and almost blinding — and following on the heels of the electrical discharge came the inevitable enormous crash of thunder that sounded like an explosion.

In the few minutes Annie had been outside, the wind had kicked up. It now whined and moaned like a wounded animal around the trailers and through the narrow alleyways between the tents.

Added to the storm noises was the crack of canvas as it rippled and danced in the building gale and the constant sibilate sand as it corkscrewed into miniature tornados and began to pile up against the sides of solid objects in small dunes and undulating mounds.

Annie flinched as another roll of thunder came rumbling in from the storm. It sounded as if the heavens were about to be torn open, and a fork of lighting filled the air with electricity and lit up her surroundings with a flickering, strobe-like whiteness.

Without warning, she was engulfed in a dense cloud and what felt like minute particles of macerated rock lashed and stung every bit of her uncovered flesh.

It was hard to breathe and she felt as if she were suffocating. She covered her mouth and nose with her hands and began to move backward, as if she could outrun the wall of dust that was almost upon her.

Somewhere close by Major Matthews shouted, "Inside. Now. The hospital needs to be locked down. Move it, people."

Annie turned, stumbled and almost fell. She regained her balance, and with her hands still covering her face and eyes half-closed, she followed in the wake of a ghost-like figure in front of her.

She found the entrance by pure chance and hurried inside. Once safe, she sagged against the canvas tunnel wall with relief and took great gulps of the chilled air.

Chapter Eight

Annie looked up from the paperback she had been trying to read for the past hour and glanced around her. The teams had congregated in the operating tent, and despite the noise from the raging storm, she was amused to see that everyone had managed to fall asleep.

Captain Lloyd was at the desk in the corner, slumped in a canvas chair. His long legs were stretched out in front of him and his head was tilted back as if he were staring at the ceiling, mouth agape, as though waiting to catch a fly. Every now and again, his lips would purse and he would release a burbling whistle like that of a boiling kettle.

Major Matthews had found a space on the floor and was leaning against a waste bin, wrapped in a tattered blanket. He was sound asleep with his head listing so far to the left that Annie thought he might topple over. He too was snoring, his more like one or two snorts intermixed with grunts.

Some personnel had been successful in finding themselves chairs and were sprawled on them in uncomfortable positions. Others had wrapped themselves in whatever they could find to keep themselves warm, had lain on the floor and were either snoring like generators about to malfunction or moaning and twitching their way through whatever haunted their dreams.

Annie couldn't sleep. She'd fortified herself with mugs of strong coffee and, on a hunt to find something to occupy herself, had found the book hidden among the MREs in the rest room. She had hoped the horror novel would distract her and keep her awake, but the noise of the wind kept disturbing her concentration, and at last, she gave up trying to make sense of the words.

Annie laid the book on the floor beside her chair and glanced at her watch. It was zero four hundred hours. She stifled a yawn, stood and stretched to ease the kinks that had taken up residence in her spine from sitting too long. She walked with quiet steps toward the triage area, climbing over and going around slumbering bodies.

When she drew the zipper upward just enough to give her a small opening to get through, it made a harsh purring sound and was louder than she'd expected. She half-glanced over her shoulder to see if the noise had disturbed anyone, and upon seeing nobody had moved, she crouched and shuffled through the gap.

Once she was on the other side, she found she'd been holding her breath. She let it out and rolled her head from side to side to break the tension that had seized the muscles in her neck and shoulders.

She went toward one of the litter carriers with the intention of trying to get some sleep and stopped in her tracks when, above the screaming of the wind, she heard a crash from outside.

Her body stiffened in a reflexive action and she strained her ears in case it was repeated and might pose a threat to the men and women inside the hospital. She didn't hear it again, so she relaxed and took a pace forward, then stopped again when she heard the familiar noise of the entrance-door flap being unfastened.

Annie's heart lurched in her chest. Somebody was coming in, and she was afraid whoever it might be was up to no good. Nobody would be out in the dust storm. It was too dangerous. Furthermore, if it had been a casualty, the team would have been notified in advance, so it was someone wandering the base who had no idea what they were doing or where they were going.

She half-looked over her shoulder again to see if anyone had followed her to investigate the crash, and when she saw she was still alone, she looked around to see if she could find something to use as a weapon.

Her personal rifle was in the administrative section and she had no way of getting her hands on it. It was ludicrous to think that with all the guns and heavy ordnance on the base, she didn't have a weapon on hand to protect herself so, as a result, she was defenseless.

Beside the closest litter, Annie saw a tray covered in blue paper with stainless-steel instruments lined up in preparation for use, and she grabbed a scalpel and held it in front of her.

The slim blade was going to be useless against a determined intruder, who might just laugh themselves silly at the sight of it. Despite that problem, she wasn't going to yell for assistance for no reason, so she went to the flap separating the triage tent from the tunnel and raised the zipper.

Without thinking of the consequences, she ducked through and squealed with shock when she cannoned into a big, firm body and the hand in which she carried the knife was caught in a vise-like grip.

"Freaking out a bit aren't we, Specialist McKendrick?" said a familiar voice, and her makeshift weapon was taken from her nerveless fingers.

Her heart racing and mouth dry with fright, Annie straightened and wrenched her arm from the man's grip. She looked into the face of Shay O'Rourke then at another man standing beside him.

The sergeant's companion was a couple of inches shorter but was also broad across the shoulders and chest. He too was staring at her with a sharp look in his dark brown eyes.

Jesus. What is it with these guys? Do they have to look at someone with such goddamn intent?

Annie turned her attention back to the master sergeant. "You scared the shit out of me," she said, shock making her words sound sharper then she'd intended them to be.

Shay glanced down at the scalpel, which looked miniscule in his large, gloved hand. When he looked back at her, he cocked an eyebrow. There was a note of teasing in his voice when he said, "At least you didn't scratch me with this thing. Although, right this minute I wouldn't put it past you. You look as if you could skin me alive."

Annie tried to calm her shredded nerves. The master sergeant was grinning, he his expression in total contrast to his demeanor at their last meeting. It softened the hard planes of his face and his green eyes sparkled. For a moment she was speechless at the sight of him and her pulse fluttered in a way unrelated to her fright.

Annie tried to pull herself together. The way he had the power to stir her emotions into turmoil startled her with its strength. This occasion — setting aside the fact of the circumstances they found themselves in and that he had scared her almost half to death — was no different, and she realized with a start that the initial animosity she'd had toward him had changed and that she was attracted to him, whether she liked it or not.

He was aggravating, stubborn and bad-tempered but he was also sexy as hell and had the most kissable-looking mouth she'd ever seen on a man. A field hospital, however, wasn't the place to fall for someone and this certainly wasn't the time.

She'd already given her heart once and it had been trashed. She had no intention of handing it over again under any circumstances. There were only two males she was prepared to have in her life — one her son, the other her father.

The two men obviously had spent some time out in the storm because their uniforms were coated with dust. Tiny trickles of it spilled from their shoulders and the folds and ridges of their tactical vests.

Master Sergeant O'Rourke's goggles had been pushed to the top of his helmet and he wore a shemagh wrapped around his head beneath his Kevlar, which was bunched beneath his chin. He was dressed in full tactical gear and held his weapon at his side, muzzle pointed at the ground.

Annie moved backward — as far away from him as she could get without falling through the gap behind her. "Can I help you with something?" she asked.

"This is Sergeant Brax Johnson," Shay said and inclined his head in the direction of the second marine.

Sergeant Johnson nodded at Annie. "Ma'am," he said.

"Sergeant Johnson and I were on a defensive patrol around the perimeter when we decided to check in on you all to see if you were okay. I've also received some orders that I need to discuss with Major Matthews."

Annie felt a wave of curiosity go through her but suppressed it. "We're all fine, Sergeant. The major is asleep but I'll go get him for you. I'm sorry, but I can't let you inside. You're both covered in dust and you could contaminate the air and the equipment."

Shay shrugged. "No problem. We'll wait here."

Annie held Shay's gaze for a moment and her stomach muscles jittered in response. She ignored the sensation, about-turned, pushed through the flap and hurried into the operating tent.

She went straight to the major, crouched beside him and shook his arm. He awoke alert and sat upright. On seeing Annie, he brushed his hand through his unruly hair and said, "What's the problem, McKendrick?"

Annie kept her voice low. "Master Sergeant O'Rourke is here to see you, sir. He says he has something he wants to discuss."

Major Matthews frowned then got to his feet. "He's been out in the storm? The guy's a nut job. Okay, lead on."

With the officer following behind her, Annie made her way back to the tunnel, left the officer with the two marines then went back to her chair. She sat and waited to see if she could find out what the meeting was about, her mind full of the master sergeant and his unexpected appearance.

Some minutes later, the major returned to the operating room and, to her surprise, approached Annie. "I need a word," he said when he reached her. "Let's go into triage."

Questions about the content of the conversation raced through Annie's mind. One was whether the master sergeant had reported her. She'd been rude to him on the one occasion they'd met, but he had infuriated her with his attitude toward her. She doubted, however, that he was the type to bring up such a minor infraction. On the other hand, perhaps she'd pushed him too far. But why would he have waited until today?

Major Matthews led the way into the triage area, stopped and turned to face her. Annie stood in front of him, saw that he didn't look happy and her stomach sank.

I think I'm in deep shit here.

"Is there a problem, sir?" she asked and waited for his response.

The major's tone was abrupt when he answered her, "A request has been made from Delta Team's commanding officer for a medic to go out on a patrol with them tomorrow. Their own has been sent stateside. I don't know the reason why, because I didn't ask. I've been ordered to send a member of the team with them — and you're it."

Annie was taken aback. "Sorry, sir? I'm not sure I understand. I'm not a marine and I've never been outside the wire on a patrol."

Ignoring her polite protest, the major continued, "The intel I've been given by Master Sergeant O'Rourke is that forty-eight hours ago a recon team went to check out an insurgency presence at a compound a few clicks from here. They've gone off comms. Now, it could be their network has gone down with the storm or it might be something more sinister.

"Delta has been ordered to find and assist the missing men and also check out what appears to be a manmade trench system in the area, which seems to be connected to the compound."

Annie shook her head in disbelief. "I'm *not* a marine, sir," she repeated. "Surely you should send someone else who'll know what they're doing — or even a flight medic, if the team are going to infiltrate by helicopter and it's an extraction."

She knew there was vehemence in her words and it would sound as if she was refusing to go, thereby disobeying an order. There was no doubt she was nervous at taking part in such a dangerous mission — who wouldn't be? — even though she was trained for combat patrols and could handle her weapon along with the best of them.

It was more that she didn't think she was the most suitable person to be given the role, considering her lack of experience, and there might be a chance she would not only let herself down but also Delta and the forward surgical team as well.

Major Matthew's expression softened. "I advised the master sergeant that we needed every team member here at the hospital in case of a mass casualty event. He understood, but orders are orders, McKendrick. The missing guys could have gone firm and be safe. On the other hand, they could have been caught in a firefight and are lying hurt somewhere.

"We're thin on the ground when it comes to medics qualified to go on this type of mission. You're a specialist by trade with advanced skills, and you're also a damned good one, from what I've seen of you in action and read in your record. Contacts with the bad guys have been increasing, and it could be we'll all end up having to do things we don't want to do or we're not trained for.

"If something has happened to those men, you'll be needed, especially if there are more than basic injuries that have to be treated. You need to go. If it's any consolation, I'm not happy about sending you, but the brass in their infinite wisdom have said otherwise."

Major Matthews was silent and he stared at Annie as if waiting for her answer.

Annie cleared her throat. She knew she had no choice but to obey the order, even if the major had couched it in terms that sounded as if he would accept an answer from her in the negative.

"Okay, sir, but I want it on record that I don't think I'm the right person for this, and everyone will be knee-deep in shit and my ass will be on the line if I screw up."

Major Matthews smiled. "Eloquent as usual, McKendrick. I'll make a note of your concerns. There's a briefing tomorrow morning at zero seven hundred hours in Section D.

"This dust storm will be a major factor in whether the mission will go ahead or be aborted. Once that's confirmed, you'll be briefed. That's all I know. You'll need to collect your weapon and make sure it's in working order. You'll gear up in full battle rattle and take a unit one pack. Use your discretion about what to include in it, but bear in mind you might need some of the more advanced supplies and equipment. Make sure you have everything you need, including water and MREs. Understood?"

Annie nodded. "Yes, sir."

"Good. Go get some sleep if you can with this wind howling like a half-witted banshee. I'll check in with you tomorrow before you leave."

"Yes, sir."

"Okay. Off you go."

Still shocked at what she had been ordered to do, Annie turned and went back to her chair. She sat, closed her eyes and tried to relax. A thought popped into her head that she would be spending time with Shay O'Rourke. At that thought, she wondered if he knew she had been selected to go with him and his team. She had a feeling he wasn't going to be very pleased.

Chapter Nine

Annie was alone and she was exhausted. She'd had no sleep since being woken by Freya in the early hours of that morning, because it had been impossible to ignore the insane wailing of the wind.

Despite the noise, other members of the team had managed to nap during the day while officers and medics had become embroiled in a game of cards set up on an operating table.

As the game had progressed, it had become rowdier, with the men accusing each other — all in good humor — of cheating, and she'd wondered how they could be so full of energy with a limited amount of sleep.

She'd wandered off to the chill unit where the bloods were kept and had occupied her time by taking an inventory of what remained of each product. She'd then moved on to the storage cabinet for the Class A drugs and repeated the task.

The job had almost certainly been done by somebody else, but as there were no casualties, there was nothing for her to do. She couldn't even do her washing because the generator providing power to the laundry section had been powered down as 'surplus to requirements'.

It had been a long and boring day and it was now twenty-two hundred hours.

An hour earlier, Major Matthews had advised them that the wind was letting up and visibility had improved. Now all she could hear was a shrill keening as it swooped around the shelters, so she thought the mission the next day would go ahead. In a couple of hours, the installation should be in the clear and things could return to normal.

Annie had almost laughed out loud at the thought. How could life on a forward operating base ever be called 'normal'?

In about nine hours, she would have to report to Delta Team. While her concerns that she might screw things up for herself had diminished somewhat, a slight anxiety still gnawed in her stomach.

Thoughts kept popping into her head concerning various scenarios that might play out away from the relative safety of Sykes. To keep her fears under control, she decided to clean her weapons.

Annie studied each item of her M16A2 cleaning kit laid out in front of her on an upturned plastic box to make sure she had everything she needed — rifle lubricant, a wire brush, barrel rods, cotton swabs, cleaning solution and some rags.

She had already stripped down her sidearm — a single-action, semi-automatic, magazine-fed, recoil-operated M1911 pistol — and now she picked up her rifle. She pressed the button next to the trigger to check that it was on 'safe' and pulled back the charging handle until it locked. She checked the ejection port cover for any bullets in the chamber then used one of the rags to wipe the weapon to rid it of all the dust, dirt and oil that might have accumulated.

Her methodical actions soothed her, and her mind wandered to the complex issues surrounding those who worked in her role on the front line.

Medics were purportedly non-combatants but they could protect themselves or their patients and, thus, carried weapons for that purpose. If they used their arms offensively, they could sacrifice their protection under the Geneva Convention, which tended to create problems in the field under hostile conditions.

Tradition dictated that most United States medical personnel wore a distinguishing red cross to denote that they weren't engaged in fighting. However, insurgents faced by professional armies in Iraq and other war zones across the globe either didn't recognize the Geneva Convention or didn't care.

Annie removed the rifle-belt pins that held the upper and lower receivers and pulled out the charging handle. She cleaned the outside of the upper receiver with a dry rag and sprayed cleaning solution inside it. She brushed the interior with the wire brush to get the carbon and dirt out and wiped the inside with another rag.

She'd been trained as well as any infantry soldier. She'd achieved marksmanship on a variety of weapons and was convinced she could handle herself as well as any man.

Her medical training had involved scenarios in exercises involving a medical response, be it a basic first aid-type casualty or a complex clinical-type trauma, on top of her soldiering skills. That ensured she was not only able to get somewhere in good order but could be a competent medic at the end of it.

On a mission—when the worst happened—all eyes turned to the 'doc'. She therefore needed to be fit enough to do the patrol and be a part of it, which included using her weapon if necessary before she could turn around and perform her core role, which was to save lives.

Annie spent considerable time cleaning her weapon thoroughly, readying it for whatever was required of her, then she activated the safety and propped the rifle against her chair. She collected the items that belonged in the cleaning kit, put them back into the canvas bag and pulled the strings around its neck to close it.

She hadn't finished her tasks for the night, however. She needed to check that she had all the medical supplies she would need for the short mission and lay out her tactical gear, so she rose from her seat and went to hunt down the backpack-style bag known as a unit one pack.

She found one propped against a box of MREs and picked it up to discover that it was large and heavy—weighing upward of approximately fifty pounds—although she could reduce the load if she took out items she wouldn't need.

She put the pack on the container she'd used as a table, unzipped the main section and spread the two halves flat then opened each pouch and pocket to check the contents and compare them to the inventory in her head.

Everything inside the bag was well organized.

Annie ticked off the individual items on her mental list then checked the catastrophic bleeds kit. There were two combat application tourniquets which would be used to stop massive life-threatening hemorrhages. It also contained Kerlix gauze and agents to stop bleeding, various field dressings of different sizes including two large ones for abdominal wounds and two more tourniquets, as well as emergency trauma bandages.

The other pouches contained lactate ringers — LR — a solution of saline-sodium chloride used to replace fluids and electrolytes and deliver nutrients to keep a casualty hydrated and prevent shock, and Hextend, a sterile medical IV solution used as a plasma volume expander to replace blood volume.

There was also a supply of various IV catheters and a venous cut down kit. A venous cut down was a quick way to administer fluids under battlefield conditions.

Last, but by no means least, Annie went through the remaining smaller pouches on the sides and underneath the front pocket, which held an assortment of other supplies. There were a few pairs of latex gloves, iodine swabs, muslin and gauze bandages, hypodermic needles and syringes, morphine syrettes and combat casualty cards.

Completing the items of what amounted to a first-aid kit were lightweight splints, duct tape, a sharps bin for disposing of medical waste, a water gel burns dressing, trauma shears and, for minor injuries, glues and sterile strips.

A combat medic was also expected to care for the needs of the men and women in his or her squad. This included their everyday ailments so, in a side pocket, there was a small amount of what were referred to as 'snivel' or 'sick-call meds', which were common over-the-counter medications that did not require a prescription, such as Tylenol, aspirin and anti-diarrhea tablets.

It was all stored in the order that Annie would need to use it, if necessary, and she fastened the main pouch and the smaller ones then placed the pack on the floor beside her weapon.

She was dog-tired now, and when she looked at her watch, she understood why. It was almost midnight and she still had to do a gear prep.

She sighed, picked up the unit one pack and slung one of its webbing straps over her shoulder then retrieved her rifle, pistol and the cleaning kit.

She walked into the rest area and stopped to survey the small space. Two of the cots were occupied, but she couldn't put a name to the slumbering figures because one had wrapped his or her head in a towel and the other was wearing a pair of large fluffy camouflage-colored earmuffs.

Annie moved toward the bed she used, which was also the farthest away, so if she happened to make a noise, she wouldn't disturb the occupants. She set the pack on the thin mattress and placed her sidearm beside it.

After she'd propped her rifle against the canvas wall at the head of the cot, she crouched and reached beneath the metal bed frame then pulled out her combat gear, which she placed on the blanket.

Her Interceptor body armor vest with its heavy and bulky ceramic plates, together with the medical backpack, a load-bearing rig that contained pouches for a full combat load for her M16A2 and her M1911 and her helmet meant she was going to be humping almost eighty pounds of solid weight, and that didn't include bottled water and MREs.

Annie made sure her radio was in place on the left side of her vest and that her medical shears, two combat application tourniquets, latex and combat gloves and her night vision goggles, as well as combat casualty cards and a pencil, were all placed in pouches alongside it.

She slid in a pair of sunglasses and placed her pistol in its armored mount on the right side so it would be within easy reach if she needed it. Last of all, she dug deep into the pocket of her smock and pulled out the photograph of her son.

She unfolded it, stared at the image, then refolded it and placed it into one of the pouches — the one over her heart. She rested her hand on it for a moment, sighed again then surveyed her bed, which now resembled a small armory.

She was finished gear prepping and about to place all the equipment on the floor so she could get some sleep when Freya came into the rest area and stopped opposite her.

"Going on vacation, hon?" she asked in a low voice and glanced over her shoulder at the two occupants of the other beds.

Annie wasn't in the least bit amused and glared at the sergeant. "Ha. Ha," she said, her voice also quiet. "Do I look happy? Am I jumping for joy?"

Freya frowned, then an expression of sympathy crossed her face. "No, I guess not — and I wouldn't be either. Major M has already spoken to me about it, but what's the deal with sending *you*?"

Annie folded her arms and shrugged. "I have no idea. I've done my training like everyone else but I don't have any first-hand experience outside the wire. There're people here who would've been far more suitable."

"You're going out with Master Sergeant O'Rourke's team, aren't you? That'll be…nice."

Annie wasn't sure whether her friend was being facetious or not. She experienced a surge of irritation and replied, "Oh, yeah. It's gonna be a bundle of laughs. We already rub each other the wrong way and I think he's gonna be pissed when I turn up for the briefing later…this morning."

"Ignore him," Freya said. "Just do the job you're good at and don't let him bug you. You need to take care of *you*. Stay out of trouble. I don't want you coming back in a body bag or to have to treat you as a casualty. I'll be pissed about that."

Annie laughed. She knew that while Freya had joked about something happening to her, her friend had been serious and the comment had come from the heart.

Freya walked around the end of the cot and stopped beside her. "You hear me, Specialist?"

"I hear you, Sarge," Annie replied. "Now, will you please bug out so I can get some shut-eye? I'm asleep on my feet as it is and I need to get up in five hours."

"Okay," Freya said. "Seriously, though, you take care out there, honey. Those bad guys don't discriminate between non-combatants and combatants."

"I get it. I'll duck the bullets and get out of the way of anything that goes boom that has my name on it. Now, *go*."

Freya put a hand on Annie's shoulder and squeezed. She didn't speak again—everything that needed to be said had been—and she turned and left.

Annie watched her go, sighed again, then, item by item, she put everything on the floor ready for the morning and sat on the edge of the bed. The metal springs emitted a low screech and she winced at the noise and heard some mumbling from the direction of one of her sleeping colleagues.

She looked at her boots and debated whether to take them off. She needed at least a couple of hours of sleep and wearing cumbersome footwear would not be conducive to that.

Decision made, she unlaced them, kicked each one off then turned them upside down in the hope that one of the many creepy crawlies that inhabited the desert world wouldn't get too adventurous and take up residence inside. That would really suck.

She set the alarm on her watch to wake her at zero five hundred hours and made sure she turned the volume down. Her colleagues were attuned — on an almost psychic level — to any form of warning sound, whether it was for incoming casualties or the 'bend over and kiss your ass goodbye' type.

Annie pushed the blanket back and lay down. She turned on her side to face away from the light that was shining into the area from the operating room and, once she was comfortable, wrapped the cover around her.

She shut her eyes, inhaled a deep breath then let it out slowly to get rid of the tension that was making her muscles taut. She wondered what had happened to the missing marines and hoped it was only downed comms that were the problem and nothing more.

She thought about the mission and wondered if she would be able to cope. She'd read an article once where being a combat medic was likened to breathing. Soldiers required one kind of breathing and medics another. Soldier-medics required a combination of both — the ability to use one lung for soldiering and one for doctoring.

It was both natural and unnatural for a human being to know as much about killing as healing — to have to listen for the sound of bullets in one moment, then for the sounds of the wounded in the next, to love each with a rabid dedication and to hate them both.

A medic had to cross back and forth between the two — pull a trigger, treat a wound — first one, then the other. The ability to be able to instantly cross from medic to soldier and soldier to medic without focusing on the difference was a prime necessity of war, because, in the end, all that mattered was one thing—breathing like a soldier in one breath, then breathing like a medic in the next. War…medicine. Inhale…exhale.

No one's gonna die on my watch.

Annie's thoughts moved on to Shay O'Rourke and to his reaction when he found out she was to be part of the patrol. When all was said and done, though, it didn't matter what he thought, because she was more than capable of doing what was needed, even if this was to be her first time integrating with a team on a mission outside the wire.

What the hell. He'll have to suck it up and so will I. There'll be no time for personal issues and we'll just have to work it out.

As the euphoria that came with the onset of sleep flooded through her, Annie began to relax. It had been more than twenty-four hours since she'd last had some downtime and exhaustion claimed her. She slept with no dreams to disturb her.

Chapter Ten

Annie awoke when her watch alarm sounded in her ear, and she groaned and stretched. The fog of deep sleep cleared from her head and she realized she could no longer hear the wind, so she suspected the storm had moved on. The only sounds to break the silence within the rest area were soft breathing coming from the occupied cots around her and distant conversation from somewhere in the hospital.

Outside, the unremitting thud of generators intermingled with the distant rumble of military vehicles traveling up and down the road, the distant *whup-whup* of rotor blades from an Apache gunship and the engines of a much larger aircraft throttling back as it came in on a short final to land.

Air traffic appeared to have increased overnight but it was still the normal sound of a forward military base going about its daily routine.

Annie knew she had to get going. She didn't want to be late for the briefing and give the master sergeant something else to be irritated about, but she stayed where she was and stared at the canvas roof above her.

She was still tired and weariness tugged at her body. She would have done anything to remain where she was instead of humping God knew how many clicks into the back of beyond to find only the Devil knew what at the end of it. It *was* her job, however, and if any member of the marine recon team was hurt, she needed to be there to do her best in treating their injuries.

Reconciled to the fact that sleep was well and truly out of reach, Annie sighed, then thought that if ten years were added to her age for every time she did so, she would be moving around with a walker in the very near future.

She sat up and pushed the blanket off her body. She swung her legs over the side of the cot then stopped, resisting an impulse to put her feet on the floor without her boots on. She ran her fingers through her mane of hair before massaging her scalp and teasing out the tangles that knotted the strands.

Her boots were still upside down where she'd placed them earlier that morning and she eyed them with suspicion. She'd never had a spider in one before, but if she didn't check them out, Murphy's combat law said there would be one inside.

She bit her lip then reached for a boot, grasped it by its thick sole and, with her arm stretched out to keep the footwear as far away from her as possible, picked it up and shook it.

She was relieved when nothing of a biting or stinging nature dropped onto the floor and she turned the boot the right way up, thrust her foot into it, pushed the bottoms of her combat pants into the top and tucked the laces inside.

She did the same with the other then stood, tucked in her T-shirt and, after shaking her combat sweatshirt, she put it on. She searched for her wash kit, shower sandals, clean underwear, socks and top in her holdall beneath the bed and grabbed her towel.

Annie frowned when she saw how threadbare it had become and how it had the unmistakable aroma of dampness, since humidity wouldn't allow it to dry. Two showers a day and using it as a turban to suck up the moisture when she washed her hair would do that to any piece of material after a while, so when she got back from the patrol, she would write home and ask for someone to send her a new one.

She had to make do with it for now, though, so she walked in silence between the other beds and through the connecting tunnel into the operating tent. She saw Major Matthews seated on one of the surgical tables with Captain Lloyd standing beside him, deep in conversation. When they noticed her, they stopped talking and the captain grinned at her. "You're up early, McKendrick," he said.

Annie twisted her lips in a grimace. "Too early for my liking, sir. But I guess going out on a mission will do that to a person."

"Get out of here, Specialist," Major Matthews said and jerked his head toward the exit.

Annie detected a derisive note in his voice and decided it might be beneficial to her not to say anything more. She smiled at them both and left the hospital.

Outside, the cold penetrated her uniform and entwined itself around her sleep-warm limbs. She shivered and, although she was uncomfortable, she stopped and gazed around her.

Dawn was breaking and the sky had lightened to navy blue. The sun was rising in a golden glow, its feeble rays blazing a wispy trail of red, orange and yellow across the heavens, the trillions of stars scattering and fading before its weak onslaught.

She heard the roar of engines and turned toward the sound. A C-130 Super Hercules was coming in to land and sunlight glinted off its bulbous nose, cockpit window and canted-up tail and struck scintillating sparks from its four spinning propellers.

The sight of the huge, gray, bullet-shaped aircraft chilled her. The runway must have been finished and it appeared that troops had started to arrive. It was further proof that the invasion was imminent.

Annie shrugged off the nerves and looked toward the mountains. She could make out the outlines of their peaks, their ruggedness rimmed in lemon-orange and the occasional sparkle from a tumbling waterfall or a patch of snow on their craggy escarpments.

The smell of cold and damp sand with a faint underlying odor of oil stung her nostrils and she wrinkled her nose. It was so much cooler at this time of day – the sun still depleted of its power and the heat that would increase later not yet in evidence.

A cold breeze wafted against her face and she took a deep breath and began to walk parallel to the hospital, wincing with each step as her boots crunched on the gravel.

The storm had deposited a layer of dust over everything and Annie's feet kicked up small clouds that shimmered now and again in the flaring rays of the newborn sun.

The shower and restroom trailers were ahead of her at the northernmost end of the shelters, and when she saw them, she was relieved that she and the forward surgical team were afforded more civilized facilities than most support hospitals.

Annie increased her pace and headed toward the container that housed the restrooms. The twenty-four-foot trailer was separated into men's and women's facilities by a simple partition and there were two doors, one opening into each.

Annie climbed three metal steps leading to the section designated for females and pushed on the steel door. She went in, dumped her kit on the metal floor outside a stall and let herself in.

She held her breath at the pungent chemical smell while she took care of her business, then, aware that time was moving on, she flushed and washed her hands at one of two sinks, after which she picked up her gear, left and went to the shower trailer.

Annie ascended more steps and opened the door. This time, she leaned in to check if any of the stalls were occupied. The doors had a twelve-inch gap at the bottom so she could see if the occupant was male or female.

Annie was relieved to find that none of the showers were occupied, although as time moved on, she knew this wasn't going to remain the case. She hurried toward the nearest one, grabbed a printed notice that lay on the floor, hung it on the nail which had been hammered at eye level on the door and stepped inside.

The interior was as basic as it could get with a simple shower head and a drainage hole in the metal floor. Accustomed to the conditions, Annie dropped her toilet bag in a corner of the stall, threw her towel and clean clothes over the top of the door and scooted up against it so her bare feet would be clear of the unmentionable substance on the floor once she had removed her boots.

Once she had undressed, she removed her footwear, slipped her feet into thong-style flip flops and went to stand beneath the shower head.

It was always a race against time to lather, wash and rinse her body and her hair before the three minutes of water time allotted to everyone ran out. She knew it would be a pain in the ass if she was left covered in soap and hair shampoo because she would have to beg, borrow or steal bottled water to get rid of the suds and she would never hear the end of it.

Annie turned the knob on the wall and let out a squeal when freezing spray drenched her body. Its frigid splash raised goosebumps on her skin and she ducked and dived around the confined space, dodging the icy droplets until at last the water began to heat up and got warm enough for her to be able to bathe.

The lukewarm temperature was as good as it was going to get but as it pounded her face, the muscles in her shoulders and neck begin to relax and she sighed with relief.

Unbidden, an image of Shay O'Rourke's face popped into her mind and Annie's pulse rate increased. She shivered, and this time it wasn't from the coldness of the water.

There was something about the man—something dangerous, some element of his presence or character that she'd never run into before. Perhaps it was his eyes, which were so intense, or his strength that appealed to her as a woman.

Whatever it was, the thought of him was stirring sensations inside her that made her feel very aroused but uncomfortable, because it was so out of character for those types of emotions to affect her.

Annie lurched from a daze and realized she had drifted away and had been standing with her eyes closed.

"Dammit!" she exclaimed, her voice echoing around the trailer.

Any minute now the water would cut out, so she washed herself as fast as she could, and after toweling her body dry and squeezing the moisture from her hair, she sprayed herself with deodorant, clothed herself in clean underwear and a T-shirt, put her uniform back on and thrust her feet into her boots.

While she was brushing her still-damp hair, the water stopped and she smiled to herself.

Ha! Beat you.

After she'd plaited her long tresses, she wound the result into a bun and, afterward, she felt a little better — more alert. The fatigue had relinquished some of its hold on her. She picked up her wash kit, collected her dirty clothing from the door and let herself out of the stall.

It was almost full daylight when Annie descended the steps and the temperature of the air had warmed by a few degrees. But with no time to take in the bright day, she hurried back to the hospital. She headed for the rest area and checked her watch for the time.

It was almost zero six hundred hours. She shoved her dirty laundry into her holdall and put her tactical vest on over her head then bent and laced her boots, blousing her pants over the top of them.

She withdrew a leather thong holding her dog tags from beneath her combat shirt, took it off, removed one tag and pushed it down under the tongue of her right boot. If she happened to be killed and her body was difficult to identify, someone would find the dog tag in her boot with her ID number on it.

Annie then replaced the thong with the remaining tag back about her neck, belted the magazine pouches around her waist, donned her helmet and fastened its chin strap then pulled on her combat gloves.

She thrust her arms through the webbing of the unit one pack and as she did, she felt panicked. She bowed her head and took some deep breaths, trying to stop the faint trembling in her hands and legs.

This is my job. I'm good at it, it's what I'm paid to do and I need to get on with it. It's not the time or the place to freak out. I'll be no good to anybody if I don't get a grip on myself. The major wouldn't be sending me if he had any doubts that I could do it.

Calmer after the pep talk, Annie completed a final mental inventory of the contents of the pouches on the front of her vest. She made sure her pistol was secure in its armored mount and that her radio was fastened to the side of her chest just below her left shoulder.

She then picked up her rifle, thrust her arm through its one-point sling and shrugged it onto her shoulder. She now felt as if she had concrete blocks on her back and she exhaled through pursed lips at the weight.

She was ready to go, so she left the rest area and went into the adjoining shelter.

Major Matthews was alone and he turned and beckoned her over. "Heading out now?" he asked.

"Yes, sir," Annie answered.

"Keep your head down out there, McKendrick."

"Copy that, sir. I have no intention of getting it blown off."

"Excellent. Just do your job and you'll be fine."

She gave him a weak smile. Major Matthews nodded at her and she turned and walked through the hospital and went outside.

Annie turned to her left and walked past rows of empty tents in the general direction of where she thought Section D might be. She didn't know the layout of the base very well and she hoped she wouldn't lose her way and be late for the briefing.

At the end of the accommodation shelters, she hooked another left and continued walking. Ahead of her was the single dusty road that cut through the center of Sykes.

The base was quiet, so when she heard male voices, she thought she must be heading in the right direction. She was correct, because after a few minutes, she passed a wooden hut and reached a large board nailed to posts in front of a graveled area with a long accommodation tent and a smaller one set up alongside it.

Annie stared at the sign and saw that a marine crest dominated its whiteness. Someone had painted *Section D* at the top and beneath it the crimson head of a rather ugly Velociraptor with a pointed snout and a mouth filled with elongated sharp teeth. Beneath the image was the word 'Raptors' in dripping red.

She had the feeling she might indeed be heading into the den of a man-eating monster as she stepped around the sign. In front of her, she noticed an awning covered in camouflaged netting set up beside the shelters and beneath it a dozen men seated on wooden benches.

She also saw Shay standing in front of them with Sergeant Johnson next to him. Her heart leaped into her mouth and she moistened her lips, which had suddenly become very dry.

Chapter Eleven

Annie walked toward him and Shay's heart jerked in his chest and his gut coiled into a knot that was almost painful.

You've gotta be kidding me. What the fuck is she doing here?

He stiffened when he noticed she was wearing full tactical gear, was carrying a weapon and there was a medical pack on her back.

Oh, hell no. She can't be the medic coming with us.

Shay watched her as she approached. When she drew close, there was an expression of wariness on her face. Her obvious hesitancy was not conveyed in her step as she marched toward him and he had to admire her for her determination in entering what she must have thought was an uncomfortable situation.

Brax nudged his arm. "Someone's put a fucking coyote among the cattle," he said in a low voice.

Shay folded his arms and grimaced. "Fuck, yeah. Tell me about it."

"This is going from bad to fucked," Brax continued, and it sounded like he'd developed a bad taste in his mouth.

Shay glanced at his men. They hadn't noticed Annie approaching because they were too busy jawing and grab-assing around, but when they did, he was in no doubt that her presence would make their day but that their reaction would ruin hers.

Annie reached the briefing area and stopped. She studied the seated men then looked at him. She was about to speak when Shay saw Lance Corporal Mel Williams look over his shoulder as if he'd sensed she was there.

The whistle he gave was loud and piercing before he said, "Who've we got here?"

One by one the men's attention turned to Annie, their noise petering out into silence. They were quiet for a few moments, then wolf whistles and catcalls accompanied by several crude comments rent the air and Annie's smooth, tan cheeks turned red with embarrassment.

"Well, fuck me...an angel," Corporal Allan Lowell said. "C'mon in here, you gorgeous piece of ass. You've come to the right place if you're looking for some fun."

"I dick it first," Lance Corporal Dale Hammond said, and joined the tip of his thumb and first finger of his right hand in a circle then thrust the first digit of his left through the center.

The gesture was obscene and Shay bristled at the implied sexual innuendo directed at Annie McKendrick.

"You wouldn't know how to," Corporal Kyle Webber said, and there was an outburst of raucous laughter at his words.

"You want me to fuck-start your face?" Lance Corporal Hammond said, "you goddamn fuckwit."

"Knock it off, you lot," Shay said. "You're not in kindergarten now, so back off."

The men went silent at his words, although their attention stayed on Annie. Shay saw she was glaring at the team and the expression on her face had changed to one of annoyance. He thought that if given the opportunity, she would kick them all in the nutsacks and enjoy doing it.

After what seemed like minutes but, in fact, were mere seconds, he said in a voice that sounded husky to his own ears, "Specialist McKendrick, I guess you're here for the briefing."

She cleared her throat before she said in a tone that conveyed her irritation, "Unfortunately, yes, Master Sergeant."

Shay almost grinned at her blatant insubordination but stopped himself from doing so just in time. He'd expected nothing less than a feisty response from her and said, "Take a seat so we can get this going. We have a date with a Chinook in thirty mikes."

Each of his marines watched her with avid interest when she stepped into the briefing area. She walked to a space at the end of the second bench and, as she moved, she held their stares—not giving them an inch—until they looked away.

She let her pack slide from her shoulders and stood it on the floor then sat on the seat and propped her rifle beside her. She pushed her helmet to the back of her head, took out a small notebook and a pencil from a pocket on the sleeve of her combat shirt then stared forward at him, her face devoid of expression.

Shay noticed the speculative gazes directed at him by the team but ignored them and turned away to pull down a screen with a large topographical map on it. As he faced front, his eyes caught those of his sergeant.

Brax cocked an eyebrow and Shay glared at him. He felt disconcerted—an unfamiliar feeling for him—together with a simmering anger at the position which the powers-that-be had placed him in.

Regardless of who she is, she's a female on my team. Crap. *Now I'll have to play babysitter and be responsible for her and fuck knows what else.*

He knew his thinking was sexist, uncharitable and very unlike him, as well as being conscious that he was wasting time and his men were becoming restless at the delay. He attempted to dismiss the tumbling thoughts in his mind and focused on giving the mission brief.

Shay pointed with his finger at two red circles on the map. "A Chinook—or as you *gentlemen* like to call her, the Happy Hooker—will drop us down range here. Our area of operations is at this location."

"Holy fuck, Sarge! Do we get to fire our weapons, blow up some shit and kill some tangos?" asked Sergeant Mike Miller in a voice full of gleeful enthusiasm.

"It's another butt fuck," Corporal Webber added, his tone solemn.

"Yeah, Miller. If we come across some bad guys and they open fire on us first, you'll get to play with your weapon. Now, do I have your permission to continue with this briefing?" Shay asked.

At his glare, the men quietened down and a couple of them darted surreptitious glances at Annie, but she ignored them. In fact, she appeared uninterested in what they had to say and the attention they were paying her.

He shook himself and continued, "As you all know, a marine recon unit has gone off comms. They've failed to report in for over twenty-four hours. Their objective, before they went quiet, was a compound where hostiles have been sighted. Drones overflying the area have also taken photographs of a network of above-ground channels that spread out from the walls of the buildings and run for approximately two clicks.

"They're too deep and wide to be used for water irrigation, and it's been decided they're manmade. They're considered suspicious and it's been decided the hostiles could be using them either to infiltrate or exfiltrate the compound."

Shay found his gaze drifting to where Annie was seated. Her presence was disturbing him more than he cared to admit, and he wondered what the outcome was going to be for them during their time together outside the wire.

He had to get a grip. He wasn't about to let personal emotions about a woman interfere with his job and he forced thoughts of her from his mind.

"We'll investigate these excavations," he went on, "then move on to the compound and assist the recon team with whatever they require. Be advised that the risk factor for a firefight is high. Once we've checked out the area and find our missing bros, we'll be extracted.

"The location has not been cleared of IEDs, so you can bet your asses we'll have to deal with a rash of 'em. We'll have our nuts hanging out in the wind, guys, so eyes on and focus. *No* excuses. None of your fooling around or ball-splitting antics, otherwise I'll rip you all new assholes. Is that understood and are there any questions?"

There was silence, and satisfied, Shay said, "Outstanding. Okay, get your asses out of here. One final gear prep and form up by the sign. Now's the time to have a final smoke if you want one."

"Oorah," responded the team, chanting the marine mantra, then there was the thud of boots as the men rose to their feet, picked up packs, weapons and helmets and moved out of the briefing area.

Brax spoke to Shay. "You think there'll be some surprises?" he asked.

"You can bet your sweet ass there will be," Shay said. "Wherever those bastards are, there's always a shitstorm to follow and another clusterfuck to add to the list."

Brax nodded. "I hear you," he said. "Now, I think I need to go babysit those dickheads before they screw someone else over."

Shay watched his assistant team leader stride over to the men, who were doing nothing except exercising their mouths. He went over to Annie. Without any preamble he asked, "You up for this?"

She frowned and there was a note of impatience in her voice when she answered, "Why wouldn't I be? It's always been my job to play babysitter to a bunch of jarheads."

Shay's mouth twitched with the beginnings of a grin. He worked to keep his face straight and said, "Keep your head down, and I want your ass to stick to mine like glue. Do everything I tell you when I tell you. Is that clear?"

He saw an expression of stubbornness appear on her face and her eyes blazed at him when she said, "Certainly, Master Sergeant. I wouldn't dream of doing anything different. My ass is all yours."

Don't I wish. The thought popped into Shay's head and he winced. He'd allowed her to get under his skin and she was like an itch he needed to scratch but couldn't quite reach. However, this was not the time or the place to acknowledge that she was getting to him, so he forced any personal thoughts of her into the dark recesses of his mind.

"I guess that's clear," he said and heard the cold tone in his voice. "Go and join the others and we'll get out of here."

Annie nodded, slid her arms through the webbed straps of her pack and picked up her weapon. Without another word, she strode from beneath the netting and walked over to join his men.

He couldn't help but check her out as she left. He noticed the way her fatigue pants clung to her tight little ass and the way her hips swayed sexily in what he guessed was an unaffected manner. His mouth went dry and he had a sinking feeling she was going to change his life and his future in more ways than he cared to think about.

Chapter Twelve

Annie walked across the gravel-strewn ground and her sixth sense told her that Shay O'Rourke was watching. She could feel his eyes like twin laser beams, burning the delicate skin on the back of her neck, and there was a pleasant tickling sensation between her shoulder blades.

A warm tingle spread through her and burgeoned into an aching fullness between her legs. She wanted to squeeze her thighs together to prolong the feeling and rub herself against something so she could achieve some form of release from the exquisite pressure.

She almost laughed out loud at how ridiculous it was for her to be turned on by a stranger. On this day of all days, when she was about to go outside the wire into knee-deep shit, she had to experience a sexual longing for a man she didn't know — and more to the point, one who exasperated and bothered the hell out of her.

After Josh and their disastrous marriage, she had sworn off men — something that every woman may have vowed to do at some point in their lives — and she had no intention of ever getting involved with a member of the opposite sex again. She just wished her traitorous heart would knuckle down and take heed of the instructions her head was struggling to give.

I need to get in the zone and forget about the guy. Period.

Annie reached the team and stood on the outskirts of the group. Nobody spoke to her or paid her any attention. She felt ostracized and, if she were honest with herself, very much alone.

To keep herself occupied, she concentrated on adjusting the webbing straps of her pack so they rested more comfortably on her shoulders, then she tapped the toe of her boot impatiently on the ground.

"Okay," Shay said from behind her. "Get ready to move out."

The men obeyed the order in silence and moved to form up into two ragged lines, jostling and shoving each other like adolescents. Once stationary, they adjusted their packs, fastened the chin straps of their helmets and held their M16A2s at the low ready. For the first time, Annie noticed the apathetic expressions had gone from their faces and they now looked alert and focused.

Shay strode past her and half-turned to look over his shoulder. "You're with me," he said.

Annie bristled at the order but followed him anyway — as if she had a choice in the matter — and they went to the front of the team.

"Let's go, ladies," Shay ordered and he strode off almost at a jog, with Annie trying her best to keep up with him.

The temperature had already risen at least twenty degrees, and by the time Annie and the marines reached their Chinook, she thought she might pass out from heat exhaustion. As far as she was concerned, her show of weakness would have been the cherry on the cake.

The distance from Section D to the bird couldn't have been more than three hundred yards, however, the pace had been a forced march. After completing the distance, the heat had enveloped her in what felt like a stifling blanket.

She hissed her breath through gritted teeth, sweat trickled down her face from beneath her helmet and her lungs felt tight and burned from the hot air. Dust, deposited by the storm and disturbed by the many pairs of marching feet, hung in clouds and clung to her perspiring skin. She felt as if her face was plastered in a mask of dried clay.

The CH-47 Chinook was ready for them, its twin rotor blades turning slowly. Two door gunners, armed with M60D 7.62-millimeter machine guns, were positioned on either side of the open side door and one of them lifted a hand and stuck his thumb in the air at them.

Annie followed the master sergeant and the men to the rear of the giant helicopter, where they strode up the ramp into the interior, passing a rear gunner positioned at his weapon, who nodded at them as they filed in.

She found a seat opposite the open side door, slid the straps of her pack down her arms and let it fall to the floor before she sat and fastened her harness. She put the medical bag between her legs then rested the muzzle of her rifle on top of it and took a deep breath. Anxiety surged through her body and she squirmed in discomfort when her stomach muscles tightened in a painful spasm.

She was scared about the upcoming mission and there was no use trying to convince herself otherwise. She also had an idea of what Delta thought of her and that made her feel awkward and alone.

There hadn't been time to get to know the men and there had been no bonding process. That meant she hadn't earned their respect or their trust, and by their obvious reaction to her, it was quite clear she wasn't welcome in their close-knit band, which didn't surprise her.

They didn't know her and therefore had no idea of what she was capable of. She couldn't blame them for that. They were used to working with each other and had formed a powerful and close-knit group based on their time together in combat. That was of paramount importance if they were to meld into a cohesive team and watch each other's backs in a hostile situation.

She was an unexpected fly in the ointment, a disruption like the ripples in a still pond after a stone has been thrown into it. It would take more than one patrol and her status as a medic to resolve the issues they had with her.

Annie took another deep breath then let it out. She reminded herself she was just as good as any man, regardless of her lack of combat experience, but, despite her prowess in the field, she was under no illusions that she would need to rely on the marines to watch her back.

Chivalry had no place in the heat of battle, but an inherent primal instinct to protect those who they fought shoulder to shoulder with was a part of human nature. She therefore hoped they wouldn't allow anything to happen to her.

She knew the men needed to trust her as well, so they could all survive the mission, but despite the pep talk she was giving herself, she faced the fact she was terrified of what was to come. She was determined she wasn't going to give them the tiniest reason to show her any further animosity and she was damned if she would let them see how frightened she was.

The marines found their seats. She glanced sideways at them then watched Shay as he moved to the cockpit and spoke to the crew chief and the pilots.

To distract herself from her uneasy thoughts, she studied the interior of the helicopter. She had never been in a Chinook before and was impressed by its size — approximately fifty feet in length and just over twelve feet in width — with two rows of center-facing red nylon mesh and aluminum seats lining both sides of the fuselage.

Known as the 'workhorse', the Happy Hooker's cabin was far from pretty and not meant for comfort. It appeared capable of carrying approximately thirty fully equipped men and women or the equivalent weight in cargo, which included vehicles, because there were hooks with straps imbedded in the floor to lock down wheels.

Annie's thoughts changed track and her breath caught in her throat when she heard the crackle of a radio from the cockpit and the engines began to ramp up. A whine splintered the air.

A harsh whickering sound joined the ascending howl as the rotor blades began to turn faster, steadily spooling up to full power, and the Happy Hooker vibrated and shifted as if straining at invisible tethers.

The forward fuselage tilted upward at a slight angle and the helicopter rose into the air. It hovered for a few moments, then the noise of the engines became deafening and the upward pitch of the nose increased so that Annie had to grab hold of the front edge of her seat to prevent herself from falling sideways.

As they ascended even higher, she got a sinking feeling in her stomach, then the Chinook's pitched angle decreased until the nose dipped toward the ground, her stomach reversed and plummeted and she found herself toppling in the opposite direction.

The helo glided forward, banked to the right then leveled out and Annie sighed with relief that they had made it off the ground without anything catastrophic happening.

Despite the high temperature outside, a chill wind howled and whistled in through the open side door and swirled around the interior. Tremors seized her arms and legs.

She wondered if the trembling was from the frigid air or if she had succumbed to her nerves. She hoped it wasn't the latter, because she wasn't going to be of any use to anyone if she was frightened out of her wits.

The marine who had taken a seat next to her elbowed her arm. Startled, she turned to him. When he had her attention he gestured to her rifle. "Know how to use one of those?" he shouted.

Annie heard the derision in his voice and saw the look of scorn in his eyes. She glanced down at the black, oily-looking weapon. She turned the rifle so she held it by the muzzle, pointed the butt stock at the floor then glared at him.

"I think I can figure it out," she yelled back. "I aim it like this, don't I?"

She almost laughed out loud when the man rolled his eyes in disbelief and shook his head before he turned to speak to the man on his right.

Asshole, she thought with resentment.

Her attention was drawn to Shay, who had taken a seat opposite her, and she noticed he was staring at her, his face expressionless. He didn't look happy and Annie guessed it was because of her. She felt self-conscious under his gaze.

From what she knew of marines, they didn't appreciate an unknown quantity in their midst, and although the military was not sexist toward women, she could understand why a bonded team of men would feel threatened and somewhat jinxed with a female thrust into combat with them.

It irked her that a man of his experience could let such a minor matter irritate him, but there was nothing she could do about it. She hadn't had a choice about being here and she wasn't going to apologize for it.

Suck it up, Sarge.

Annie dragged her gaze away from him and a marine seated two seats away from her, yelled, "You gonna be able to step up to the plate when everything goes goat fuck on us, Specialist, or are you gonna screw the pooch?"

Two men laughed at the comment. Angered at the question, Annie leaned forward. It was obvious to her that the statement was a wind-up to see if she would be offended by the foul language and go all girly-girl on them. She focused her gaze on the man who had asked it and glared at him until he looked ill-at-ease.

"Well, Lance Corporal...Harris. If a bullet has your name on it, you'll find out, won't you?" Annie eventually responded. "Let's hope I don't create a goat fuck of my own when it comes to treating you, because you'll be in deep shit."

Her answer caused a few chuckles from some of his colleagues. Lance Corporal Hammond leaned forward so Annie could see him and said, "Don't mind Harris. He's well known for his brain farts and tends to spout crocks of bullshit most of the time."

The man who had questioned Annie and was now on the receiving end of an insult didn't like it and he slammed his fist on Hammond's Kevlar. "Fucking fuck you, pal," he shouted.

Tired of the wisecracks and determined to ignore any further remarks directed her way, Annie withdrew. She looked between the two gunners and out of the open door, squinted in the harsh sunlight, took her sunglasses from the front of her vest and put them on.

The shadow of the Chinook flashed across the parched landscape beneath them and she could see nothing but flat beige and ochre-crackled earth, dotted here and there with sparse and stunted vegetation broken up by shallow rifts and wadis.

Nothing broke the empty monotony of the landscape, not even the mud-and-brick ruins of a compound or a single animal racing to find shelter from the inhospitable conditions. The tableland looked unforgiving and abandoned.

From the corner of her eye, she saw the crew chief appear at the door of the cockpit and make his way along the length of the aircraft toward the master sergeant. Once he reached him, he leaned toward him so his mouth was close to the sergeant's helmet and spoke.

Shay nodded, and when the chief left to make his way back to rejoin the pilots, he held up both hands and splayed all ten fingers so the team and Annie could see them. It was a signal that indicated they were ten minutes from their destination.

Annie swallowed because it felt as if a lump had lodged itself in her throat. She jerked, startled, when she heard the sudden ominous sound of loud repetitive pinging and metallic clanging against the outer fuselage of the Chinook. She knew what the sounds meant.

Oh, shit! We're being shot at!

The words screamed in her brain and panic gnawed at her insides. The enemy was trying to bring them down. She had to get a grip on herself and rein in her fear before it gained control. She gripped the edges of her seat, the fingers of both hands aching with her death grip.

She saw one of the gunners raise a hand to the side of his helmet as if he were listening to something. His back stiffened and, in the next moment, he and his colleague opened up with their weapons

The pinging against the thin aluminum fuselage continued unabated and the Chinook began to vibrate and bounce in turbulent air as it swerved from side to side in a series of evasive maneuvers.

Annie stared out of the door. Her eyes widened when she saw approximately half a dozen shadows moving across the desert below them and her muscles grew rigid with tension at what that might mean.

She saw the figures stop every now and again as if to fire up at the helo, but they were too far away for her to see their actions clearly. She did notice plumes of sand fountaining into the air as the bullets from the machine guns tracked them, and her belief that they would come through the brief attack was confirmed over the next few minutes as the M60Ds did the job they were built for.

One by one the shadows fell and didn't move and the unholy sounds of bullet contact on the skin of the Chinook fell silent.

Annie released her grip on her seat and flexed her tense and rigid fingers. What had just happened felt surreal, like she was trapped in a nightmare. That was reinforced when she heard a whoop of exhilaration from one of the gunners, who punched his fist in the air.

Shay, his expression blank, as if what had just happened hadn't bothered him in the least, undid his harness and got to his feet. He went to the cockpit and spoke to the crew chief then turned and held up five fingers.

"Gear up," he shouted. "Condition one, guys. Let's get some."

The men erupted with their 'Oorah' salute and unlocked their belts. They double-checked their weapons then sat on the edges of their seats to wait — almost eagerly — for the mission to get going.

Annie slammed a hand on top of her helmet to make sure it was seated firmly on her head then looked over her own weapon to ensure it was ready for use.

There was a change in the pitch of the engines and the Chinook began to sink toward the ground, the rear fuselage dipping downward as if its rear wheels were straining for contact with the solid surface.

Annie tried to control the erratic pounding of her heart and inhaled, held the air in her lungs for a few seconds then let it out.

The marines stood and crowded into the aisle, and Annie joined them. She shrugged her shoulders so her pack was more comfortable, made sure the safety of her rifle was on and pushed the heel of the buttstock into her right shoulder with the muzzle resting naturally down to a point approximately one foot in front of her boot at low ready.

Shay came to stand beside her. "You ready?" he asked.

Annie swallowed and, unable to speak because it felt like the lump in her throat had grown to the size of an orange and was threatening to choke her, she nodded.

The master sergeant's gaze roamed her face, settled on her mouth then, as if in confirmation of her words, he said, "On me, then."

He took up position behind the nearest gunner and held up a gloved fist in a signal to wait. Annie moved to stand at his left shoulder and, when she glanced outside, saw the vast sea of sand stretching in a never-ending vista of hell.

The tension in the air was palpable and she half-turned to glance over her shoulder at the marines stacked up behind her. There was a marked absence of their raucous and jocular humor, as though each man had taken on a different persona.

The air seemed to tingle with emotional pressure and an aura of restlessness, as though each team member was aware of what could happen when they left the safe confines of the helicopter but were eager to get moving, despite the danger.

The moments before landing seemed much longer and the sounds of the rotor blades and the whine of the engines blurred into a deep bass tone then faded away, much like what happened in a nightmare. All she could hear was the harsh sound of her breathing and her stomach churned.

A maelstrom of desiccated vegetation and sand exploded into the air from the downwash of the rotors as the Chinook continued its descent. The rear fuselage tilted down even more before there came a thud as the wheels touched down, then a second one as the front ones followed suit.

The master sergeant yelled, "Go. Go. Go," then he was gone.

Annie shuffled to the door and hesitated. She looked down at the ground and had an image of herself jumping into an abyss and vanishing forever. She flinched when her shoulder was gripped and she half-turned to see Sergeant Johnson standing behind her, his face gleaming with sweat and his gaze intense.

His dark eyes narrowed and there was an expression of sharp concentration on his face as he stared at her. "You need to move, Specialist," he said and jerked his head toward the open door. "We're sitting ducks out here and you're holding us up."

Annie nodded and, dismissing all thoughts of the dangers waiting for her once she left the relative haven of the Chinook, she jumped.

It seemed to take forever until she landed heavily but safely on the unstable ground, but once she regained her balance, a mixture of training and survival instinct kicked in, and she pushed the buttstock of her weapon into her shoulder and aligned her gloved finger along the safety of the trigger so she could release it if necessary and bring the weapon up into a firing position.

With one eye on Shay, she studied her surroundings to confirm that she and Delta Team were alone, then she jogged to stand beside him.

Chapter Thirteen

Shay surveyed the surrounding desert and grimaced. He licked his lips, which felt sunbaked and dry, tasted dust and grit and spat out what little saliva he had in his mouth.

The heat had leached away the moisture, leaving him with a feeling that his tongue had swollen to twice its normal size, and he swallowed and tried to imagine he was standing beneath an ice-cold shower and sipping from a frost-covered can of Budweiser.

Fuck me. What a shithole!

Back in the present, he kept his pace slow and easy. Shielding his eyes from the glaring sun, he scanned a one-hundred and eighty-degree arc of fire, from nine o' clock to three o'clock. Always alert, he knew if anything moved in his line of sight, he would see it and be on it. No hostile would *ever* fuck him over.

Once the Happy Hooker had departed, the only noise to disturb the stagnant and molten air was a muted hissing sound as a hot breeze whipped dust into miniature ghost-like tornados that whirled across the desert.

Ochre-colored, arid parched land stretched for miles. Scorched by the searing sun, it was barren of all but the hardiest of vegetation, which clung to rare shaded areas afforded by a rock or sand dune.

Shay turned in a three-hundred-and-sixty-degree circle, his keen gaze taking in his immediate surroundings, and he cursed beneath his breath. He'd had a gut feeling that the mission was going to be fragged from the get-go. As soon as he'd left the helo, his 'oh shit' meter had kicked on, the hairs on the back of his neck had stood up and a psychic alarm had rung throughout his body.

He knew very well that the sort of down-range territory he and his men were in was the place where the 'boogeyman' from nightmares lived.

There was substance to this form of evil spirit in the guise of buried explosives, which were nearly impossible to spot and which maimed and killed without warning, along with unseen enemies who moved like ghosts and who had no remorse for the lives they indiscriminately took.

Every step was fraught with danger and, out in the open like they were in broad daylight, their profiles stood out on the flat surface of the sandbox for anyone who was interested. And the bad guys — if they were in their location — would be very happy to sight them with their weapons and blow them to smithereens.

Shay tried to shrug off the icy trickle of unease that coiled around his spine and focused even harder on the mission at hand. Distraction meant lack of concentration, which led to mistakes, which equaled a 'kiss your ass goodbye' scenario.

Fucking clusterfuck. As usual.

Once Delta had left the Chinook, they'd headed at a crouch for the start of the trenches, which was their first objective. Shay had jumped into the channel and he'd wondered whether he and his men had been transported to another planet inhabited by some form of insectile extraterrestrials.

The walls were approximately five feet high and consisted of a mixture of hardened sand, cracked earth and a mosaic of gravel and crushed rock. The ditch resembled the nests made by the predators from the movie *Aliens* and its construction made him feel uneasy, as if he and his team were about to plunge into the depths of a subterranean hell.

Two fire teams of four men had recced the immediate surroundings, vigilant for any wires or ground anomalies that might be signs that explosives had been planted in the walls or beneath the thick layer of dust that coated the bottom of the channel.

The all-clear had been given and Shay had ordered an objective rally point to be set up where he and his men could make final preparations before moving out. He had known that while the place was out in the open, it was located close to the compound but far enough away that it would be out of range of small-arms fire. The team would not be seen or heard while occupying the channel and it would serve as a point of reference they could return to if necessary, to regroup.

Shay rolled his shoulders beneath his tactical vest and felt the sweat-soaked material of his combat shirt chaff his skin.

Dust—almost six inches deep under his boots and kicked up by the patrol's march—mushroomed into clouds and hung motionless. It clung to uniforms, and when combined with sweat on exposed skin, created a moist, slimy paste that coated weapons and eyewear with an intrusive and abrasive covering.

Must be over one hundred degrees out here.

Sweat trickled down the side of his face and he lifted a hand from his sling-ready carbine and wiped at the liquid residue before he placed it back on the weapon, a single finger lying across the trigger.

He half-turned to glance over his shoulder at Annie, who was behind him, and the three men who followed her, and he checked on the fire teams acting as flank security, who walked on higher ground on either side of the ditch.

Annie and the members of Delta who walked the trenches still maintained column formation distances of approximately six feet, even though the going was tough.

Everyone was flagging from the heat but they were still vigilant and watchful of their own individual arcs of fire — the first man keeping eyes on to his right, the second to his left and so on.

Shay hated a close-order march and really wanted to increase the distance between each member of his team. If an improvised explosive device was triggered, they would be too near each other and the blast could take out one or two members — or even more.

He was, however, stuck with having them perform as they were and his gaze turned to Annie. He tried to convince himself he was just making sure she was doing her job and not slowing the men down, but when he noticed she was struggling to walk through the thick detritus, an uncharacteristic pang of sympathy shot through him.

It seemed as though the searing heat was sapping her strength and her heavy pack appeared to be weighing her down. With her eyes shielded by dark sunshades, the only evidence he could see of her difficulty was in the way she gritted her teeth and the perspiration that glistened on her face.

She hadn't uttered a word of complaint about the inhospitable and difficult terrain, the temperature or the pace he had kept them at since starting out. Shay admired her tenacity and stubbornness.

With a last look at her, he faced front and eyed his point man, who was sauntering along as if he was meandering through a civilian park with all the time in the world. Shay shook his head in amusement.

The guy was so laid back that he was almost horizontal but Shay had no doubt that if danger threatened, the laconic attitude would disappear and leave an aggressive and highly skilled marine in its place.

Shay decided that in ten mikes he would call a halt and they could rehydrate. For now, they needed to keep moving forward, ever deeper into the network of trenches. He wanted to recce the fortifications, find the missing squad of marines and be out of the area well before nightfall.

He knew that no mission was easy and every job was dangerous. They were in lethal territory and walking through a minefield. No matter how many times a planned route was cleared and secured, only so many explosives could be found, thereby leaving a few behind to wreak havoc on the troops on foot patrol or in convoys.

The *hajis* were notorious for watching a regular patrol area, and when it was cleared and designated a safe zone for future missions, they returned and replaced explosives and maybe mines then vanished into the desert once more, leaving the possibility of death and destruction in their wake.

Shay was jolted from his thoughts when he heard a sound behind him and deciphered the softly murmured words of a song. He recognized the hoarse tones of Corporal Jackson 'Jaz' Murdoch and grinned, waiting for someone else to take up the rendition, which had sounded like a dirge from a funeral march.

Sergeant Buddy 'Stork' Harrison, who was leading the patrol, took up the chant, his singing voice pitched high in a falsetto and sounding very much like the bird his build resembled was being strangled.

At the end of the verse, there were some muted laughs and Corporal Brad Taylor said in a low voice, "Fuck me, Stork. Don't give up your day job, will ya?"

"Why are you such a perv, Taylor?" asked Stork. "Everything that comes out of your mouth is either 'fuck me' or has sexual connotations. Remind me never to bend over when you're around."

There was an outburst of laughter and Shay winced. He hated to tone down the humor but he turned and, walking backward, sliced a hand across his throat. "I appreciate your need to vocalize your enjoyment of this patrol, ladies, but cut it out. Let's practice some noise discipline, shall we, guys? Sound carries in this shithole and we don't want to draw attention to ourselves."

"There you go, Stork, ole buddy," came a further remark. "Even the sarge thinks you're a dick."

"Screw you, Hammond," Stork replied. "You ain't nothin' to write home about. So, stick your dick in your ear and fuck what you heard."

"Bite me, Storky, baby. The broads think otherwise," Lance Corporal Hammond said.

As Stork gave Hammond the middle finger, Shay shook his head and turned back to face front again. His body stiffened when he saw that the trench turned to the left at a sharp ninety-degree angle. It was the nature of the bend that anything lying prone on the bottom of the earthwork was out of Stork's line of sight and wouldn't be seen until he walked into the new channel. By then, it would be too late for him to take cover or return fire.

Shay balled his hand into a fist and raised it in the air, a signal to halt. Now would be as good a time as any to take a knee and assess how everyone was doing.

He spoke into his personal role radio. "Take ten."

The team broke formation, and after each man had scrutinized the walls of the trench for anything that might go bang, bite or sting and finding nothing, they leaned or crouched against them and drank water from the tubes attached to their camelbaks or chewed on some of the rock-hard candy bars that came with the MREs.

Shay sipped some of his own lukewarm supply then checked on Annie. She had found a space to rest a short distance away from the men and was drinking from a bottle of water. He noticed that none of the men were engaging with her. He knew why and felt bad for her.

Even though she was not a member of the team, he hoped that before the mission was over, they would accept her or at least have begun to treat her equal to her status as a medic.

Shay dismissed her from his thoughts and, still not able to relax his vigilance, remained standing and scrutinized his surroundings. He was increasingly uneasy. The feeling that things were about to get fucked up beyond all recognition and deteriorate into a major clusterfuck churned in his gut. He had no idea why he felt like he did, because he could see nothing moving except for the wavering distortion of the heat mirage.

However, he preferred to trust his internal warning system and that was what made him feel so uncomfortable. It wouldn't have sounded off if there hadn't been anything wrong.

After glancing at his watch, he spoke into his radio. "Listen up. The trench takes a ninety-degree turn up ahead. You all know the drill, but for McKendrick's benefit, we stay in the center of the defile. *Do not* deviate from your route and stay alert for signs of anything out of the ordinary, even if it's bullshit. Any questions?"

Silence followed his words and he continued, "Move out."

Chapter Fourteen

Annie was unused to marching long distances over such difficult terrain with heavy equipment. The blistered land radiated the scorching heat and even with sunglasses on, the glare was harsh and irritated her eyes.

The straps of her pack dug into and chafed her shoulders, her weapon felt as if it weighed more than the nearly nine pounds it was supposed to and she was uncomfortable and thirsty.

When Shay called a halt, she sighed with relief and found an area away from the men but within hearing distance, where she could rest. Before she could relax, she searched her immediate surroundings, looking for anything suspicious either on the ground or buried in the wall until, satisfied, she rested against it.

She took a long gulp of water and sighed when it soothed her parched throat. She wiped a gloved hand across her forehead and felt the weariness in her body, the heat and the griping aches and pains in her legs, despite her rigorous training. She was ashamed to admit she was finding the patrol tough going.

It was not in her character to give up or let something beat her, so when Shay radioed that their time was up, she straightened her shoulders and moved to take her place behind him once more.

Annie fell back into her slow and careful stride, walking in Shay's tracks as best she could, and focused on the way he moved. She likened him to a predatory animal and found herself eyeing the flexing of the muscles in his upper thighs and his firm sculptured buttocks.

He's so damn sexy. But we're not going down that route, are we, Annie, honey? Now is neither the time nor the place.

Shay half-turned and glanced back at her and Annie thought she saw him grin. Her cheeks burned as hot as a furnace and it wasn't just from the sun.

Holy shit. Did I just say all that out loud?

She was jolted from her thoughts when ahead of her, almost at the bend in the channel, Stork tripped on something buried beneath the dust. He staggered out of formation, almost fell, righted himself and something detonated beneath him.

A massive blast shook the ground, and for Annie, time seemed to slow down and elongate. She was aware of earth, dust and sand fountaining skyward. Stork had disappeared and she saw Shay tumbling back flip over back flip in slow motion toward her.

A force shoved on her chest, her feet left the ground and the shock wave threw her against the right-hand wall. Her helmet hit a protruding root and she bounced off the fortification and landed on her back, her sunglasses flying off her face and her Kevlar sinking through the deep layer of detritus to rebound off the solid earth beneath. The wind was knocked out of her.

She was hit by a wall of sound — rather like a long, drawn-out boom — which faded into a deep croak followed by a moment of complete deafness.

A tinnitus-type noise in her head filled the void left by the blast and Annie could hear her own harsh struggles to breathe. She grunted and tried to fill her lungs with oxygen, and for what seemed like an eternity, she lay prone with her eyes closed.

Dust coated her face and she choked on a mouthful then spat it out. The sound in her ears obliterated all other noise and she opened her eyes and lifted her head.

She could see nothing but a churning curtain of dust and wisps of blackened debris swirling in the turbulent air and she squirmed with fear.

Get it together, Annie girl. You need to move your ass. Now!

She sat up with care and patted her arms, torso and legs to check for injuries and areas of pain. The back of her head ached where it had impacted the ground and her brain felt like it had rattled around in her skull from the concussive force, but aside from those abnormalities, she had survived unscathed.

She thought of Aiden, and when she realized how close she had come to being killed, depriving her son of his mother and never seeing him again, hot tears filled her eyes. For a moment the world spun and she thought she was going to pass out.

She shook her head and thumped a clenched fist into the side of her helmet, as if by doing so she could rid herself of the high-pitched ringing noise in her ears and knock the feeling of disorientation and shock out of her.

Fucking get a grip, bitch. Move!

Annie's hand shook when she reached for a root buried in the wall, grasped hold of one close by and began to pull herself to her feet. She was almost upright when a second blast knocked her onto her back again. She rolled onto her side, pushed her chin into her chest and curled into a fetal position.

Chunks of earth and crushed rock rained down on her body in an avalanche, and while her torso was protected by her tactical vest, pain flared in her arms and legs as they were pummeled by tuberous roots and gravel. She gritted her teeth to stop a scream of panic erupting from her.

A small faraway voice in her head advised her that if she lived through the nightmare, she would have some very nasty bruises to deal with later.

Annie lay still, hardly daring to breathe. She felt that if she took one single intake of air, it would create another more lethal explosion. Even though her mind was screaming at her that she needed to haul ass and see if anyone had been hurt, her body refused to uncoil itself from its instinctual protective position.

She had no idea how long she would have lain there if she hadn't heard a voice, muffled by the tinnitus in her ears but edged with desperation and panic, shout, *"Medic. Medic. Doc. Man down."*

She was on her feet before she was able to process the words and again, she patted down her arms and legs in a hasty body assessment to see if she was still in one piece. She would be no good to anyone if she bled out or if she'd sustained her own injuries.

Annie pushed aside the sense of relief that flooded through her when she discovered that apart from some tender areas where projectiles had struck her, she'd come through the second explosion as unscathed as she had the first.

She looked about and saw that clouds of choking dust hung motionless in the hot air and obscured her view of the scene. She could taste and smell the taint of the blast and coughed to clear her throat. There was so much adrenaline pumping through her body that her nerves shrieked in protest.

"Medic. Holy fuck. Get your goddamn ass up here."

Annie heard the shout — which was almost a scream — and she blanked her mind to all further thought and urged her bruised legs to move forward to where she'd last seen Stork.

She passed Shay, who had regained his feet, and she studied his face for any signs that he might be in pain from an injury. She felt a wave of relief when he nodded at her as though to confirm he wasn't hurt.

She kept to the center of the trench and made her way with careful steps to where it branched off into the next channel. When she saw the scene in front of her, she stopped as if she'd hit a brick wall.

Lance Corporal Hammond was kneeling beside a crumpled pile of bloody rags that looked as though they had been tossed into the center of a large red-and-black stain at the bottom of a shallow, man-sized crater.

A crimson-coated combat boot lay two feet from her and Annie's brain tried to absorb the shocking impression that there was something inside it. Close by was a combat helmet covered in a glistening coat of red. The chin strap was still fastened and the Kevlar rocked back and forth in slow motion, as though it had a life all its own.

The fire team to her right had assumed a defensive perimeter but the three remaining marines on the left were staring down into the channel. The looks of horror on their faces would be something she would remember for as long as she lived...*if* she lived.

She saw blood on the ground and smelled its metallic essence together with the sickening odor of burned flesh, and she felt as if time stood still. She was trapped in a cocoon of fear that was leaching oxygen from her lungs and threatening to choke her. A scream began to build inside her and she knew if she allowed it freedom, she wouldn't be able to stop.

Sounds impinged on her hearing — shouting, someone on a radio calling for a medevac and a deep gargled moan that sent chills down her spine.

Thoughts pounded her mind. The pile of shredded and blackened uniform was Stork. She could see that now, and in less than five minutes he would likely die there in the dust, right at her feet.

She knew she possessed the medical skills to save his life or, at the very least, give him extra precious time so he could be medevacked out for damage control treatment.

She had been trained as a war fighter to help her think and act decisively, but at that moment, she was paralyzed with fear and shock had wiped out everything she had ever learned. She was without direction.

There was a man dying in front of her and Iraqi insurgents could attack their position at any moment.

She had to control her breathing, unlock herself from the terror that had her in a strangling grip and use her medic and soldier minds. Time, however, had come to a standstill and so had she.

Something heavy slammed into her and she almost fell. A firm hand clenched her shoulder and she half-turned to see Shay standing behind her. His face was covered with sweat and dust but his green eyes were piercing and he glared at her with such intensity that her breath caught in her throat.

Annie didn't—couldn't—respond and he shook her then dug his fingers into the soft muscle surrounding her shoulder joint. "You with me, McKendrick?"

The pain caused by his grasp made her wince and she drew in a deep breath, held it then nodded.

"Don't bail on me now, Specialist. Move your ass," Shay said.

Annie pulled her shoulder free and turned away from him. She dropped her rifle, shrugged out of the straps of her pack and, like a disjointed doll, fell to her knees and slammed it on the ground beside her.

Stork's features came into focus, and while she undid the main compartment of the pack then its smaller pockets and pouches, she studied the man who lay so still in front of her.

She bent forward until she was almost leaning over his chest, shook him and shouted, "Stork, can you hear me?"

There was no response and she took off her combat gloves and pushed them into a pouch on her vest, removed a latex pair and, after a brief struggle, managed to pull them on.

She did a quick visual body assessment and saw the man's primary injury. His leg had been amputated just below his left knee and what remained was nothing but a bloody shredded stump with splintered bone glistening in the harsh rays of the sun and red liquid trickling onto the dust.

Annie took a combat application tourniquet from the pouch on her body armor and shook it out. She grasped the marine's thigh and was about to lift it so she could slide the omni-tape band over it and up to his groin when he screamed.

His body began to jerk and writhe in a paroxysm of agony. The shrieks rose until they sounded like the howls of a wounded animal and shattered the deathly hush of the desert.

Stork screamed with such violence that the vessels in his neck distended and pulsed and he tossed his head from side to side. He even tried to lift his head, and to her horror, she saw that one of his eyes was wide open. He was aware of what had happened to him and what she was doing.

How the fuck is he still conscious?

"All right, marine, take it easy," she shouted, steadying her voice. "We'll get you fixed. I've got you."

If she knew for sure he could hear and understand her, she would have lied through her teeth and told him he was going to be all right, because she couldn't tell a man who was in torturous pain and scared that he might only have a few minutes to live — unless she could perform a miracle and prevent that from happening.

She took hold of his jerking limb and felt the violent tremors of shock coursing through his body. All she could think about at that moment was stopping him from bleeding out, and she blanked her mind to the piercing bellows of pain and slid the tourniquet's loop onto the leg and upward until it was approximately four inches above the stump.

She knew what she was about to do next was going to hurt him even more, but she pulled on the band as hard as she could anyway. When she estimated it was tight enough, she secured it onto itself with the Velcro fastening.

Stork thrashed when she attempted to twist the windlass rod and his screams, if possible, grew even louder. The agony he was suffering had given him an uncanny strength, and Annie couldn't keep him still.

"I need some help here," she yelled. "Anyone?"

Moments later, someone moved past her and Shay knelt on the ground at the injured man's head. "What do you need me to do?" he asked.

Annie stared into his eyes, and when she saw a calm expression in them, some of the panic eased out of her.

"Hold his head," she said. "Talk to him."

The master sergeant placed a hand on either side of Stork's face and bent over him. She heard him say something to his man but couldn't hear what it was.

She twisted the windlass three times then inserted it into its clip to lock it in place, after which she threaded the excess band through it and secured it with its strap.

"How's his breathing?" she asked and watched the blood ooze from the wound, hoping and praying that it would stop.

"Fast and a bit labored but he's doing okay," Shay said, and again, his cool and measured tone washed over Annie, soothing her.

She had a limited window to prevent the rapid onset of shock and she took her medical shears from the front of her vest and began to cut away what was left of the material of the marine's combat pant leg.

The fiber was thick and she cursed beneath her breath as she struggled to complete the job, conscious that time was winding down for her casualty. She helped the scissors along by ripping at the garment with her fingers.

Once she'd finished, she pulled out packets of hemostatic dressings and bandages from her bergen and scattered them on the ground beside her.

With hands that trembled, she tore open their protective coverings then pushed aside the two halves of the material to expose the wound so she could see the full extent of the injury.

She knew a thick pad would absorb drainage from the amputation and help protect it from additional contamination and further injury, so she grabbed a handful of gauze and created a pad four-deep before laying them in an overlapping pattern on the stump to cover it.

She then selected a wide bandage and laid its end just below the tourniquet at an angle to wrap it around the limb. She did it a second and a third time, after which she brought the bandage down diagonally across the front of the leg, over the dressing on the stump and to the back.

Annie continued the wrapping procedure, overlapping each layer about one-half the width of the previous one until the dressing and stump end had been covered. She secured the whole with an elastic roller bandage to make sure everything wouldn't unravel during his evacuation and onward transition for further treatment.

Satisfied she'd done the best she could in treating the most severe wound, she waved away the flies which had begun to hover over herself and her patient and surveyed him for further injuries. She noted the left sleeve of Stork's combat shirt was ripped, torn open and soaked in blood. She shuffled around to his side on her knees and again retrieved her shears and began to cut away the material.

She saw an open fracture of the humerus with a large, metallic fragment embedded alongside the exposed bone. Although the bleeding was minimal, with the amount of life-sustaining fluid the marine had already lost from his primary injury, he needed all his remaining blood to survive the trauma. She took her final tourniquet from its pouch and performed the same procedure as she had with the leg.

Annie retrieved more wads of gauze and laid them around the bone and shrapnel to stabilize them, being careful not to move or dislodge them. She then wrapped the arm in a bandage, paying extra special care to wind it in an X around the broken bone and the shard of metal.

When she'd finished, she glanced at Shay, and for a moment noticed the gentle way he held Stork's head.

The injured marine was now silent, his eyes closed. He was very still, and she saw his pallor and didn't like it at all.

Annie cleared her throat. "How's he doing?" she asked.

Shay focused his attention on her and she felt a pang of sympathy when she saw the look of pain in his eyes.

"He's unconscious," Shay said. "His breathing's still not so good but he's holding his own."

Annie nodded. "Any ETA on the medevac?"

She took a marker from a pouch in her vest and leaned forward and wrote 'T x 2' on Stork's left cheek, which would alert the forward surgical team that two tourniquets had been applied.

"The medevac is on its way," Shay said. "ETA is two zero, twenty mikes."

Annie shook her head. "We don't have twenty minutes," she said. "Could someone advise them we have a category A-immediate status here? And, Master Sergeant, someone needs to bag the limb and boot, because it'll have to go with Stork in case it's viable and can be re-attached. Wrap it up in this. *Do not* do it in front of him and keep it out of sight."

Chapter Fifteen

Annie took a casualty blanket in a sterile bag from her pack and tossed it to Shay. He caught it in one hand and glanced at Lance Corporal Hammond. "You heard the lady. Get the…item stowed away and hang on to it out of Stork's sight."

Annie glanced at the lance corporal and saw an expression of horror twist his features. He looked sick to his stomach and she felt angry at him for showing weakness and reluctance in such a situation.

"This is no time to throw up, marine," she said, trying to keep her tone even and not show how she was feeling. "If you can't do it, get someone who can. There's no time to screw around. If you were in Stork's position, wouldn't you want someone to make the effort to secure your limb and send it back with you on the off-chance it could be saved?"

The lance corporal's body jerked as if he had come back from a dark place in his psyche, and he glared at Annie. "No problem at all, doc."

Shay studied his man then threw him the blanket. He caught it and, moving as if he were walking on eggshells, he went behind Annie toward the boot.

Annie turned her attention back to her patient, but from the corner of her eye, she watched the marine crouch and tear open the blanket's protective bag.

He shook it out and laid it flat on the ground alongside the limb, then hesitated for a few moments. He reached out and touched the bloody footwear with a shaking hand.

Tremors palsied his fingers and he clenched them into a fist, then at last, he grasped the sole of the boot and dragged the whole into the center of the cloth before he folded the blanket around it until it was well protected. Once he had finished, he glanced at Annie, who winced at how pale his face was and the expression of sadness there.

Her stomach knotted with emotion and she wanted to apologize for the way she had spoken to him. She suppressed the anguish welling up inside her and nodded her thanks before she reached for the pack to pull it with her to join Shay. She shuffled on her knees between the wall of the trench on her left and Stork's limp body.

Annie carried out a visual check of her patient to see if his condition had deteriorated in any way then said, "Can you turn his head to the left so the fluid in his mouth and trachea can drain away? Otherwise, he might choke. It'll also ease his breathing. And I need to look at those injuries on his face."

Shay kept his attention focused on his man and obeyed without comment. Annie examined the marine's head wounds. His face was peppered with shrapnel and he had macerated facial and scalp wounds impregnated with crushed rock and dirt. His combat shirt was burned black by the blast.

He had sustained extensive facial injuries, which probably involved fractures of his jaw and soft-tissue damage. There was a large gouge below his right ear, from which a continuous trickle of blood leaked—a wound that might have been caused by a high velocity projectile that had torn away the skin and muscle.

Annie studied the amount of escaping fluid and saw there was no spurting. She thought that it was a miracle his carotid artery had not been severed, because he would have bled out in minutes.

Again, she searched inside the pack and found more hemostatic gauze and a roll of duct tape. She tore open the sterile bags, extracted two dressings and scrunched both into a ball then packed the open wound.

It was rough at best but it would help stop the bleeding and prevent an infection. She tore a couple of strips of tape off the reel with her teeth and laid them across the pad to keep it in place before she found more gauze pads and a bandage and began to layer the dressings across the man's face and his swollen right eye.

She had no idea if his sight was damaged, but thought that with the severity of his injuries, the odds were that if he survived his ordeal, he would be partially sighted. She also suspected he might have sustained a traumatic brain injury, and if he had, it didn't bode well for his future.

"You're doing good, McKendrick."

Annie held the dressings in place with her left hand while, with her right, she wound a bandage around the marine's head and secured the whole with another piece of tape.

Once she'd finished, she glanced at Shay. He was staring at her, the look in his eyes steady and reassuring, and again some of the tension that knotted her muscles eased and the numbness that had encased her heart relaxed its hold to allow some feelings to return.

"I'm just doing my job," she said in a low voice and checked to see if Stork was still unconscious and unable to hear her. "We'll see if I've done any good when he pulls through."

Annie took out a plastic packet containing an unused single eighteen-gauge large bore catheter. She tore it open, extracted it then tapped the back of the man's hand and managed to raise a vein so she could insert the sharp, hollow needle into it.

Happy to see bright red blood back up into the needle, she screwed on a length of narrow tubing then attached a five-hundred-millimeter bag of Hextend.

She tore off another piece of tape and used it to stick the cannula to the man's skin to prevent it from tearing out of its entry point, and turned the drip to 'fast' to push the fluid into his body to replace the blood loss and reduce the chance of shock. In less hostile conditions, she would have added lactate ringers to the infusion, but there was no time.

She put the bag of fluid on Stork's chest then found a morphine syrette, pulled off the long cap protecting the point and, without hesitation, plunged it into Stork's thigh and squeezed the contents from the slim tube.

Annie used her marker once more to write an 'M+1', denoting the single dose of morphine given, beneath her original writing on the man's cheek, and knowing she had done all she could for him, she sat back on her heels and pushed her helmet to the back of her head. "That's all I can do for him. We need that medevac now, otherwise it'll all go to waste."

At that moment, Sergeant Johnson spoke behind her. "They need intel on the injuries."

Annie glanced over her shoulder at him. "There's a complete amputation below the left knee," she answered. "We have the limb but it might not be viable. He has an open fracture of the left radius with an unstable foreign body embedded alongside. There are multiple lacerations of the right side of the face and scalp with foreign bodies and possible fractures of the maxilla and mandible with query damage to the right eye."

Sergeant Johnson nodded and disappeared from her view. Annie turned back to her patient, checked to make sure the plasma was flowing freely then took a casualty card from her vest and began to fill it in, detailing the injuries she'd dealt with and the treatment she had given.

Once she'd completed and signed it, she found a safety pin in one of the smaller pouches in the pack and pinned the card to the right sleeve of Stork's combat shirt.

After watching the rise and fall of his chest, Annie couldn't detect any signs of rapid breathing, which would have indicated hypovolemic shock. She touched his hand to check the temperature of his skin and found it to be neither cold nor clammy, which would have been another sign of the condition, and she sighed with relief.

The sun beat down mercilessly on her head and sweat trickled from beneath her helmet and slide down her face. She wiped the liquid away with her hand, then realized her glove had been covered in blood, so she scrubbed her face with her right forearm.

She glanced at Shay. "Do we have a litter? We need to get him ready for extraction."

Shay nodded and moved his left hand from where it supported Stork's head to his radio. He spoke into it, and a moment later, Corporal Taylor appeared behind Annie, carrying a folded stretcher.

"Watch your footing," Shay said. "Don't move beyond me. Put it down and we'll sort it out."

The corporal laid the litter on the ground and backed away, scanning his immediate surroundings.

Annie picked up the piece of equipment, unfolded it then laid it flat so it rested parallel to the marine.

"Can you take his shoulders and I'll get his legs?" she said. "Just make sure the needle doesn't come out."

Still without comment, Shay took Stork's shoulders and Annie grasped the thigh of the marine's good leg and the upper part of the injured limb. They slid his body across the ground onto the narrow litter.

Once he was in place, Annie straightened his limbs as best she could and fastened the straps across his chest and abdomen to secure him. Again, she checked the drip to make sure the tubing had not kinked during the move, took his pulse — which was rapid but not unduly so — and checked his temperature from the feel of his skin and found that he was cold.

She took a second packaged casualty blanket from the pack and, after tearing open the sterile bag, shook it out, laid it over him and tucked it around his body.

While the ambient temperature of the air was hot, with the severity of Stork's injuries and the drastic and sudden depletion of his body fluids, his could plummet and add to the seriousness of his condition.

She was grateful that he seemed to be stable but wondered about her own state of mind when weariness flooded through her. She rubbed the back of her neck and rolled her shoulders to ease the stiffness.

Shay rose to his feet and she glanced up at him and saw he was looking down at her.

"I need to go," he said. "Will you be okay until the medevac gets here?"

Annie nodded. "I'll be fine. Can you get me an update on its ETA? I also need Stork's limb."

Shay nodded. "Sure. If his condition deteriorates, shout out. Understood?"

He spoke to someone behind Annie, stretched out a hand then handed her the packaged boot and amputated limb.

Annie inclined her head, took the folded casualty blanket and set it on the ground beside her then watched as Shay moved around her and started to shout orders to the rest of the team.

She felt lost once he'd gone and she had a sudden urge to cry. The momentary weakness irritated her. There was no time for emotions now. If the need arose, she could collapse later — when it was over.

Annie placed her hand on top of Stork's. If he regained consciousness, he would feel her touch and she hoped it would give him some comfort to know someone was with him.

She felt as if she were trapped in a nightmare with no prospect of waking.

To distract herself, she glanced at her watch. The hands told her it was zero eight thirty hours and she thought she would remember that time for the rest of her life.

She grew aware of the rapid beat of her heart and the nausea that coiled in her stomach. She glanced around her and realized that shock was beginning to set in. She couldn't allow it to.

What they needed now was for the medevac to arrive, but the minutes dragged by with what seemed like an eternity of tension. Her ears strained for the whine of distant engines and she felt a growing sense of isolation for herself and Delta.

They were sitting ducks with limited firepower and a critically injured man. If hostiles had a plan to ambush them, now would be the time for them to do it, because they had no cover and no place to retreat to.

Annie could see Shay talking to his men. A perimeter had been set up encircling the area where she and Stork were and the two fire teams were prone on the ground with their weapons facing outward.

Even so, she felt as if she were in her own private prison, and when she saw the expressions on the faces of the men, she sympathized with them. They were seasoned warriors, veterans of past firefights and, in some cases, were used to dealing with death and destruction.

But right then, they were helpless spectators in the life-and-death drama being played out in the Iraqi desert and Annie knew it must have been hell for them to have witnessed a team member and buddy getting hurt and them unable to have prevented it from happening.

As for herself, she welcomed the partial feeling of numbness that had enveloped her once she'd started treating Stork. Suppressing her emotions was vital if she was to do her job. On the battlefield, she couldn't give in to anger and aggression or fear, pity and guilt.

The urge to scream out her sorrow and anger at the futility of it was all-consuming—but she couldn't and didn't.

Her intuition told her that Stork at least had a chance of survival. It also said that if he ever made it home, he would live in pain for the rest of his life. No matter that he was still alive because of her treatment, she couldn't make him whole again, and worst still, she couldn't take away his suffering, except with mind-numbing drugs.

She was also alive because she could still hear, even if the sounds were those of Stork's labored breathing, the clink of the equipment of war and the harsh static from radios.

Fear also made its own kind of sound and she had to learn to live with it. It told her that her medical skills might never be enough, and because of that, someone might die in the future, even though she'd tried. She had to shake off her fear and keep moving forward.

She might end up in a firefight, and men and women would depend on her to make the right decisions. She needed to think and act without hesitation amid the chaos and screaming of combat.

What she was in right now was real. The fear, the blood and the shit were real, and worst of all, death was real.

She was aware that the feelings she suppressed would come back to haunt her later, but for now, Stork was the only person that mattered and keeping him alive was the most important reason for her being there.

Time lost any meaning and Annie looked at her watch once more, thinking an hour must have passed, only to find that two minutes had elapsed since the last time she'd looked.

She examined Stork again and noticed with trepidation that his breathing had grown uneven. Panic clutched her throat when she realized she might have to perform a cricothyrotomy to increase his air intake.

She was relieved when she studied his lips and saw there was no blue tinge — although they were pale from blood loss — so there wasn't a sign of oxygen deprivation and she could hold off performing the cut down.

Annie released Stork's hand and began to put loose dressings and bandages back into the pack. She closed the main pouch and smaller ones then heard a faint but familiar noise coming from the southwest.

For a moment, she wondered if she was imagining things, but when she scanned the horizon, she saw the distant specks of two helicopters coming and relief flooded through her.

At last, she dared to think the injured marine might have a chance, and she checked the stretcher straps to ensure they were secure about him, that the fluid bag had enough plasma in it to last for as long as it took for the medevac to reach them and that Stork was as comfortable as he could be.

Annie was startled when Shay crouched beside her.

"ETA on the medevac is five mikes," he said. "When it lands and while we get Stork outta here, you need to keep your head down. The downdraft from the rotors could activate pressure plates buried in the sand and I don't want to add you to my list of casualties."

Annie shook her head. "Negative, Sergeant. Stork is *my* patient and I need to go with him when we take him to the bird. Any movement could cause his condition to deteriorate, and if it does, I need to be there to prevent it from worsening."

Shay shook his head and Annie saw a look of irritation cross his face. "That's an order, McKendrick."

Annie frowned at the stern tone of his voice and anger simmered inside her. "Screw your order," she said without thinking. "I'm going with him."

Shay didn't respond to her final words, but his eyes narrowed and there was a cold look in them. "I'll deal with you later," he said at last—and he sounded furious.

He stood and walked away. A few moments later, Lance Corporals Williams and Harris and Corporals Lowell and Taylor joined her.

Annie shrugged and watched as the Blackhawks drew closer to their position. She lifted her pack, thrust her arms through the webbing straps and shrugged it onto her back then picked up her rifle and the bulky package.

She watched as Sergeant Johnson climbed out of the trench and walked in a methodical manner toward what was going to be the landing zone. She then realized the reasoning behind Shay's request for her to stay behind.

There was no way of knowing whether there were mines or explosives planted in the immediate area, and as she watched Brax move in a straight line, she understood that he had taken his life in his hands by going to meet the incoming medevac. It was the only way in which the ground could be checked before the helo landed.

The sound of the rotor blades cut the air, and as the first bird came on station, a maelstrom of dust and debris spiraled upward in a choking cloud, threatening to bury them all.

Sergeant Johnson turned his back as the Blackhawk descended and he was obscured by a curtain of thick detritus. Annie's concern increased and she bit her bottom lip.

When the helicopter's wheels touched the ground, Brax shouted something to someone in its open doorway and she and the marines with her were on the move.

They bent forward, each grasped a handle of the litter and lifted the comatose man in the air. Annie took the bag of volume expander from Stork's chest and held it up to keep the tubing as straight as possible to avoid kinking and blockages.

"Be careful of the needle in his hand," she said, "and try and keep him level. Don't jostle him too much."

It was difficult to maneuver in the confined space but Annie and the marines managed to turn and face in the direction of the medevac. The two lance corporals balanced the head of the litter on the edge of the trench while the other two raised their end so it remained as level as possible.

Williams and Harris boosted themselves up and over the wall then took back the head of the stretcher while Annie handed over the plasma bag to Williams and laid her precious package with care on the edge of the trench.

One-handed, she levered herself up until she was resting on the lip, managed to gain a toehold in the crumbling earth and Harris reached down, grasped her upper arm and pulled her upward and onto her feet.

She took back the IV bag, picked up Stork's limb then all three slid the litter away from the edge to allow Lowell and Taylor to join them.

Once they'd picked up the stretcher and Annie had checked to make sure Stork was still strapped in, they set off at a jog toward the helicopter, following the route taken by Sergeant Johnson.

As she ran, blood pounded in her ears and her breath hissed harshly through her clenched teeth. The air was stifling and sweat began to trickle down her face, the salty wetness running into her eyes and stinging them, blinding her so she couldn't see what direction she was going in.

The distance between herself and the Blackhawk seemed endless. A heat haze shimmered all around her, rippling the air and distorting the outline of the aircraft and the gap between her and it. Dust from her own and the marines' thudding boots obscured her vision as it plumed up from the dry ground.

Terror washed over her when she realized that her profile was etched against the flat terrain and she was exposed and vulnerable to an enemy out to make a killing.

She felt as if somebody was staring at a spot between her shoulder blades. The hair rose on the nape of her neck and she swallowed, her mouth devoid of moisture.

I won't make it, she thought. *Someone will put a bullet in my back just as I reach the helo.*

She knew that stress had created the morbid thoughts popping erratically into her mind, but she also knew that fate enjoyed stepping in and destroying hope and complacency in all manner of ways. She picked up speed, her boots thudding on the hard ground, heavy pack pounding her back.

Fuck. Fuck. Fuck!

The words in her mind seemed to pound in rhythm with her boots and she wanted to let out a primordial howl of fear.

She almost went down when she stumbled but regained her footing. Then the aircraft was in front of her. Everyone slowed their pace and duck-walked to avoid the arc of the rotor blades and Annie saw a flight medic waiting for them. She handed him the bag of plasma and the bundle.

She and the litter bearers slid the stretcher inside the helo, where it was surrounded by members of the forward support medevac team and Stork was lost from view.

Annie grasped the flight medic's arm to get his attention. "Take care of him," she shouted.

The sergeant stared at her for a moment then nodded. "You can count on it," he said and climbed aboard the Blackhawk.

Annie and the four marines turned, and as the rotors spooled up, they retraced their steps to the trench and jumped into it.

As she did, Annie felt as if she had been swallowed by a depthless hole and unease settled onto her shoulders like a suffocating mantle. She turned and watched as the medevac took off, pirouetted on its nose and sped off across the desert, the second helicopter taking up position behind at a higher flight level.

They vanished into the hazy undulating horizon and relief that at least Stork was out of the kill zone and on his way to receiving treatment for his wounds swamped her.

His life would be in the capable hands of the surgical team, and hope that he would survive and return home dispersed some of the sadness and anxiety inside her.

Annie half-turned and a swarm of the kamikaze flies that had been a buzzing annoyance since Stork had been hurt, descended on her. They were insane and insidious and they hovered about her face and hands and settled with irritating tenacity on her upper body. She swiped at them before she noticed the reason why they had locked onto her.

Her gloves and the lower sleeves of her combat shirt were covered in blood and, sometime during her treatment of the marine, she had gotten his life fluid on her tactical vest and the tops of her combat trousers.

There was no way she was going to be able to clean herself, and she grimaced at the thought that she would have to wear her uniform in the state it was in until she got back to base.

She tore off the medical gloves, balled them up and clenched them in one hand.

If *we ever get back.*

Chapter Sixteen

Annie winced as heat from the harsh sun hit her like a slap in the face and she squinted against the glare. There wasn't a breath of wind to dissipate the clouds of dust stirred up by their passage and it hung almost motionless in the stagnant air.

The desert was silent, the temperature suffocating, and she tried to ignore her discomfort as she turned in a slow circle, her defenseless eyes trying to pierce the distant haze to see if the team was alone.

She could see nothing beyond a few hundred yards and she focused her gaze to her front on the cluster of partially ruined, sand-colored buildings that formed a ragged oval. It was some fifty yards distant, surrounded by an outer wall of dried mud approximately nine feet high.

There were no insurgent guards posted on top of the walls and no sign of the recon team. The habitat appeared as empty and desolate as the desert, and that could mean one of two things. Either the *hajis* had known they were coming and had taken cover to wait for them to approach close enough to be ambushed or they had bugged out to pastures new.

Her gaze was drawn to a hole in the wall of the trench they were in, which they had discovered when they'd reached the end of the network of channels. It was high and wide enough for an adult to crawl into. Shay had surmised it was the entrance to a tunnel that led to the buildings and was almost surely either an entrance or an escape route.

Annie studied it and a stealthy anxiety trickled down her spine. It was pitch dark inside and the thought entered her head that it looked like a passage to Hades. She shivered despite the heat.

Something didn't feel right. The cavity looked ominous and everything was too quiet—the type of silence that was fraught with menace and manifested itself in a gut-punch feeling of impending doom. She didn't like it at all.

Shay had ordered the team to stay out of sight, so she and the men had hunkered down low enough so their bodies were almost hidden from enemy eyes but they were still able to brace their weapons on top of the wall and keep a visual on the buildings in front of them.

He and Sergeant Jackson were crouched down to minimize their own exposure and were scanning the compound with small field glasses. As Annie was positioned to Shay's right and within earshot, she heard his spoken discussion with his assistant team leader.

"See anything?" Shay asked.

"Nope. Not a goddamn thing," Brax answered. "Not even one of those shit camel spiders."

There was silence while Shay panned his binoculars from left to right and scanned the terrain in front of him.

Then he addressed the sergeant again. "There's a slight berm running in a straight line from our location to the outer wall. See it?"

"Copy that."

Looking down, Shay stepped backward, glanced at the tunnel entrance then crouched and peered inside. Annie watched as he picked up a handful of sand and let it trickle absentmindedly through his fingers.

He had a thoughtful expression on his tan face, and when he rose, he said, "I'm sure this thing runs straight to the walls. I think the dirty bastards use this a lot because they've reinforced the roof to prevent it from collapsing, which is why it's higher than the surrounding desert."

"I hear you," Brax said. "I hope to fuck your plan A doesn't involve us going in there for a recon."

Shay shook his head. "Nope, but it's still a screw up. The terrain between here and the compound is flat and there's no cover whatsoever. This mirage shit is making spotting tangos almost impossible.

"There's one good thing that's come out of this clusterfuck, though. They won't have planted any mines or IEDs inside or on top of it, because they wouldn't want to blow themselves to shit. There's a good chance we'll have a clear romp to the objective and nothing'll go bang. So, that'll be our infil route.

"Okay, kiddies, listen up," he said and turned to wait for Delta to focus on him before continuing. "It looks clear so far, so we're gonna move out in ten mikes. Lock and load, everyone."

Everyone slid back their M16A2's charging handles, chambering rounds. To Annie, in the solitude of the desert, it was the loudest metallic noise in the world, and her heart tried to break free of her ribcage, one pounding thump at a time.

Her hands shook as she followed the procedure with her own weapon then listened as Shay spoke once more. "We'll stick with the original three fire teams, callsigns one, two and three, and go in at five-mike intervals. I'll lead the first one in. The rest of you stand by to give covering fire if the shit hits the fan.

"You can bet your sweet little asses we're gonna be tracked by the bad guys, because I guarantee they'll be holed up somewhere close by.

"My gut tells me there're no IEDs or mines out there because the *hajis* won't want to blow up their only bug-out route, but one or two of the motherfuckers might get trigger happy and want to bag a couple of US marines for their trophy room. They may be crap shots but they've got the balls to try to take us out and give us a fucking hard time in the process.

"You all know the drill and what to look out for. These guys will hide and wait for some poor sons of bitches like us to appear, then ambush or remote detonate their party pieces."

His gaze was intense when he glared at his men, all of whom were listening with fierce expressions of determination. "I don't have to tell you how dangerous this is gonna be. Go slow, stay focused, stay alert. Watch the ground and your sixes, and keep your heads on swivels. Any questions?"

The team remained silent, all shaking their heads.

"Outstanding," Shay said and turned to Annie. His gaze met hers and she saw an emotion there that she didn't understand. Whatever it was, and despite the situation they were in, warmth flooded her that had nothing to do with the temperature.

After a short silence, he said, "You'll go in with the second fire team. Stay low, keep your eyes peeled and watch where you put your feet. Understood?"

Annie could only nod her agreement because nerves had dried up all the moisture in her mouth and she found it difficult to speak.

Shay turned away from her and she raised herself and squinted through the haze at the buildings. She couldn't see any movement, although it was difficult to make anything out through the shifting distortion of the heat mirage. She was about to resume her crouched position when there was the sudden nightmarish sound of a single gunshot.

It whip-cracked from the direction of the buildings, shattering the hush and echoing in ever-decreasing decibels across the desert.

Annie froze when a small fountain of sand shot into the air no more than six inches from her face.

"Get your fucking head down, McKendrick," Shay shouted. "What the hell were you thinking? You're attracting fire."

Annie ducked and pressed herself against the wall, her heart beating a rapid tattoo against her ribcage.

"That was a feat of epic stupidity," Webber said from his position two men down from her. "I guess they know we're here now."

"Taking fire," Sergeant Johnson shouted.

"No shit. You think?" Shay said but didn't take cover himself. Instead, he glared in the direction from where the shot had come from as if he found it a personal affront to him that they had been fired upon.

"That must have been an ass-puckering moment," Hammond said beside Annie and slapped her arm.

Annie felt all kinds of a fool and her voice was breathless when she said, "Yep. Copy that."

"Did anyone have eyes on where that shot came from?" Shay asked.

"Negative, Sarge," Webber replied.

"The bastards must be dug in deep," Harris added.

"Not a motherfucker in sight," Lowell said. "What're we gonna do, Sarge?"

"Try to not get killed, for starters," Shay replied. "Will that do you, Lowell?"

As he finished speaking, sporadic shots rang out and bullets dug miniature whirlwinds of dust and little chunks of soil from the ground.

Everyone ducked and Shay swore. "What the fuck? Someone's grown some balls and is having a good day."

"I got movement," Brax said, "at my eleven o'clock. They're popping up and down like ducks in a shooting gallery."

"All right. Condition one, guys. Let's throw some hurt back and see if the dumb fucks show themselves. Pick your targets if you see 'em and use controlled, three-round bursts."

Without regard for their own safety, Delta Team rose from their crouched positions, braced their rifles on the lip of the trench and let loose all hell as they began to lay down a ferocious provoking fire.

Annie's legs felt like jelly when she tried to straighten up, but she hesitated for only a moment then was on her feet. Without thinking of her actions, she focused on the buildings in front of her, flicked off the safety of her weapon and aimed the rifle in the general direction of the compound.

Her heart in her mouth, she tried to squeeze the trigger but her finger was frozen and wouldn't cooperate. She closed her eyes and inhaled molten air into her lungs, then she tried to remember everything she had been taught by the instructors during her combat basic training.

Annie compartmentalized her anxiety, squared it away and shoved it to the back of her mind. She managed to slow her breathing and narrowed her concentration until she was able to focus solely on what she had to do.

On the periphery of her consciousness, she could hear the repetitive crack of M16A2s, a fusillade of small arms fire that belonged to the enemy and deep pops and sharp cracks and chatter that sounded like two AK-47s.

She took another deep breath and increased pressure on the trigger.

You can do this. You've got *to do this.*

Her mind was blank of all but the need to join the firefight, because just one more weapon might give Delta the advantage. She began to fire calmly and steadily at what she hoped were the warm bodies of the enemy.

The noise around her was deafening and a small voice in her mind questioned whether she would still have her hearing once the firefight was over.

The bolt slide stayed open, showing the magazine of her weapon was empty, and she shouted, "I'm out. Loading."

She spun about and slid down the crumbling wall. She retrieved a full magazine from a pouch at her waist, released the empty one and slammed the new one into the weapon, hearing a faint satisfying click as it locked into place.

She rose to her feet, yelled, "Back in," and continued firing, this time less frenetically, studying the outline of the building — searching for movement.

The small arms fire stopped, as did the unique and distinctive sound of the AK-47s, and Annie saw movement at the southern end of the compound. She stopped firing and squinted her eyes against the fierce glare of the sun.

There it is again. A figure raced from the corner of the building and her breath caught in her throat. She saw a second person followed by a third and she knew who they were.

"Squirters," she yelled. "My three o'clock, about six feet away from the south corner of the building."

She gritted her teeth and lifted her rifle. She sighted in and centered her vision on the first fleeing figure then increased the tension on the trigger.

Doubt overwhelmed her. She was about to shoot a human being, perhaps even kill him. Faced with the choice of the hostiles or herself, Annie made a decision that she knew would change her life. It was kill or be killed, and she opted to defend herself and the men around her.

She felt a massive rush of blood to her head and took in a mouthful of dust when she reminded herself to breathe. She remembered Stork and what he'd suffered. Anger boiled inside her.

With that powerful thought in her mind, she held her breath and, with purpose, engaged the running figure and fired two shots in quick succession. The enemy she had targeted stumbled, lifted an arm as though in surrender then fell to the ground and lay still.

Even though she had just killed someone, Annie watched with indifference and wondered if he or she had known they were going to die.

Get waxed, she thought, then a wave of nausea churned in her stomach and she turned her head to the side and dry heaved.

When she'd calmed herself, she glanced to where her kill lay and saw other bodies lying in various contorted positions about it.

A feeling of elation swept through her, followed almost immediately by guilt that she'd taken a life. That wasn't who she was or what she'd trained for.

You or them, Annie, honey, she thought, trying to appease her remorse and justify her actions.

It would never be right to claim a kill as a medic, but at the end of the day, her target no longer had the ability to engage and hurt anyone again. That was all she was concerned about.

"Fucking ace shot, doc," Hammond said.

"Yeah," Annie said, although the satisfaction she had felt at protecting herself and the Raptors was now nothing more than a faint triumph.

"Cease fire," Shay ordered.

The weapons fell silent and once more the desert became soundless. Oppression closed in on them like a smothering curtain. All Annie could hear now was blood pounding in her ears and the rapid breathing of the men around her.

"Good job, guys and lady," Shay said. "I need to call this in, then we'll get the fuck outta here. Stay focused. There could be more of 'em around."

Annie sank onto her haunches, stared at her boots for a moment, trying to regain her equilibrium, then picked up the empty magazine and checked the one in her weapon to see what ammunition remained.

She'd used up over half of it and she ejected it and slammed in a full one, putting the empty and half-full one into a pouch at her waist.

"Is anyone hurt?" she called out and was relieved when she received a chorus of negative answers.

She sank back against the crumbling wall and closed her eyes. She wished more than anything that she and the men could end the mission, call for extraction and get the hell out of Dodge. She knew, however, that it wasn't over, and she had a feeling there was more horror to come.

Chapter Seventeen

Shay spoke into his radio and Annie wondered how he could remain so calm and cold after what had just happened.

The rumors about him being an emotionless and fearless man appeared to be true, but she suspected some of it might be a front and that he was just as vulnerable as the rest of them.

After all, she'd seen his guard come down when he'd been with Stork, and she wondered if he'd learned the hard way how to hide behind a mask, something she would have to develop one day if she was to keep her sanity out here.

"A bird will come 'n pick up the tangos," he said after he'd ended the transmission. "Okay, let's put this fucked-up place behind us."

His words were followed by a low and heartfelt 'rah' from the men.

"Fire team one, on me," and Shay boosted himself up and over the top of the wall. He rose to his feet, crouched to reduce his profile, moved forward a few paces then gestured with two fingers for Williams, Lowell and Webber to follow.

Annie watched wide-eyed as the four men began to move at a slow and disciplined pace along the edge of the raised bank. They walked heel to toe, rifles held at high ready, each man stepping in the footsteps of the one in front of him, their heads on swivels as they surveyed their surroundings for the enemy and the ground for IEDs and anti-personnel mines.

She locked her gaze onto Shay and her body stiffened with tension. The farther he moved away from the relative safety of the trench, the more the danger increased, and she wanted to call out to him to come back.

By the time the fire team had reached halfway, her nerves were at a breaking point. They screamed in protest and her muscles became as taut as whipcord.

If the men were attacked now, there would be nowhere for them to run or hide. If they had to retrace their route, it would take just as long to come back as to go forward. Whichever direction they chose, they would still be easy targets and could be picked off one by one.

She didn't want that to happen to Shay or anyone else in Delta. If he was injured or—in a worst-case scenario, a situation she couldn't abide thinking about—killed, it would affect her more than she cared to admit.

What had happened on the mission had emphasized the fact that life was too short. Each moment needed to be lived to the fullest.

The dangerous situation they found themselves in had reinforced the pull of attraction she felt for Shay, and while she was aware that *insta-lust-love* existed for some, she was fighting an internal battle against the thought that it had happened to her.

Thinking about him like this is a one-way trip to getting my ass shot off.

"Okay," Sergeant Johnson said, tugging her back from her inappropriate thoughts. "Fire team two, you're up."

Sergeant Miller took his place at the wall and, slinging his rifle, he jumped and heaved himself over the lip. He got to his feet, raised his weapon and gazed around him before he signaled to Corporal Murdoch, who climbed out of the channel next, followed by Annie, with Lance Corporal Hammond as rear end Charlie.

Annie took a step away from the trench, then a second, and as they drew farther away from what she pictured in her mind as a place of protection and safety, she hesitated.

A thought popped into her mind that the *hajis* who they had killed could have been a small part of a much larger force, with the remainder still hidden inside the compound.

With a surge of panic, she studied the walls ahead of her. They reflected the sun and the rays bounced off them with searing brightness. She scanned them for movement but couldn't see anything.

Her eyes stung and watered. She licked her lips, tasted the salty tang of perspiration and smelled her fear, which seemed to ooze from every pore of her skin.

After a brief struggle with her fight-or-flight mode, her training kicked in and she gripped her rifle in hands that shook with faint, involuntary tremors, lifted it and followed Sergeant Miller along the artificial ridge.

Annie tried to focus on the task at hand and place her feet in his footprints. Despite what Shay had said about the possible absence of anything that went bang, she was ever mindful that somewhere on the ground could be the tell-tale disturbed earth and half-buried wires that denoted the presence of explosives. She tried not to raise dust clouds with any sudden or sharp movements that would obscure her vision and hide the dangers.

She kept behind the sergeant, carrying out the same deliberate pacing that she had seen the others do, and as the distance to the false safety of the buildings decreased and they joined fire team one, she heaved a sigh of relief and swore to herself that she would strive to be a good person for the rest of her life.

While they waited for the third team to join them, Shay gestured for everyone to stand back against the wall, and Annie pressed herself to the crumbling masonry behind her and wished she could sink into it and disappear.

Fire team three's trek across to them was uneventful and, at Shay's hand signal, Annie and the squad hunkered down with their weapons pointed outward, all eyes focused on their immediate surroundings.

Shay spoke into his radio, his voice low and clear. "Okay. Lowell, Williams, sweep the entry point. Everyone else, wait till you hear the all clear."

The two named marines moved toward a crumbling church-style arch that was cut into the wall. Lowell stopped at the left side of the opening, Williams on the right.

Tension mounted and time dragged as both scrutinized the curved masonry before — starting at its base and inch by inch — they slowly and carefully ran their fingertips up along its edge until their hands met at the top.

Corporal Lowell turned, inhaled and said, "Clear, Sarge," and Annie breathed an audible sigh of relief.

"Fire teams one and three," Shay said. "Once we're inside, I want a thorough sweep carried out on all the buildings. Do it quick and easy. Remember… Go through the doors, clear your near corners, run your walls, collapse your sector and communicate. McKendrick, you're still with fire team two. Brax, let's do this."

Shay didn't wait for a response from the team or his sergeant. He edged along the wall until he reached the closest edge of the entry point and Sergeant Johnson followed and moved to stand opposite him.

"Fire team one, on me," Shay said in a low voice. "Three, on the sarge."

Both men raised their weapons to high ready and kept their backs pressed to the wall while the two teams formed up, three men behind Shay, the others to the rear of the sergeant until all eight marines were stacked up on either side of the opening.

Shay nodded at Brax and they button-hooked the entry point and, followed by the rest of the teams, disappeared from her view.

The next few moments seemed like the longest of her life and all she could hear was the rapid beat of her heart and the rush of blood in her ears before Shay's voice came over the radios, "Clear," and fire team two, including Annie, moved to join them.

The entry point opened into a narrow no-man's land, a roofless passageway with a sandy floor that led off to the left and right and followed the oval shape of the outer fortification.

The inner barricade appeared to be made up of the rear walls of buildings and had another opening that, when she glanced into it, seemed to Annie to lead into a courtyard.

Shay and Brax were once again standing by the second entry point while Lowell and Williams carried out another sweep for explosives. The rest of the teams had taken up security positions, scanned for threats and were watching the entrance to their rear.

Shay raised a clenched fist before he said, "Once we're inside, we move as slick as shit off a duck's back. Stay firm till I give the all clear."

With his final words, he and Sergeant Johnson followed the same procedure taken at the first entrance and entered the courtyard in a concerted rush.

Annie waited with bated breath to hear Shay's steady voice come over the radios but when they didn't receive confirmation of no threat, she glanced at the other marines.

There was concern on Webber and Harris' faces as the seconds passed, and she was about to voice her anxiety when Shay's said, "Clear. McKendrick? Get in here and on me."

Annie heard an undercurrent of warning in his tone and alarm raced through her. She sensed that something bad had gone down and her heart lurched. She bit her lip and followed Sergeant Miller into the dark aperture, and as soon as she exited into the inner courtyard, she stopped.

The smell hit her like a slap in the face. The essence held something unmentionable and hung like a viscous cloud in the hot air, cloying and full of death. She also heard a strange noise, as though a buzz saw was being operated in the distance.

She froze and the hair on the nape of her neck stood on end. Somewhere deep inside her, she knew what had happened.

"Motherfuckers."

The voice held both fury and a helpless grief.

Chapter Eighteen

Annie glanced around her and her gaze came to rest on the center of the courtyard. Hot tears filled her eyes and she pressed her lips together to stop herself from moaning out loud.

We're too late. We were always too late.

Through blurred vision, she saw six contorted shapes lying on the ground. She studied them for signs of movement that would show someone was still alive, and when she saw nothing that gave her hope, she blinked back the burning liquid and stepped forward.

Someone grabbed her arm and brought her to an abrupt halt. Shay's voice, icy and controlled, said behind her, "Okay, Marines. Save it for later. Fire teams, do your sweeps. Three, go with Sergeant Johnson and get up on the perimeter wall.

"Keep an eye out for the bird coming in to remove the kill, then two men go and assist them. The rest? If anything moves, don't ask questions. Just shoot the fuckers. *Move.*"

Sergeant Johnson left at a run with his fire team while teams two and three moved off toward the first of several doorways that resembled black screaming mouths ringing the courtyard.

Annie turned to face Shay. "Let me go," she said, her voice steady and cold. "I need to go to those men."

Shay released her. "Are you up for this?" he asked and studied her face.

Annie was relieved to feel anger beginning to simmer inside her and she let it feed on the mixed emotions of sadness and guilt that were already there. "Do you have *any* faith in me at all? I wouldn't be here if I wasn't *up* for it," she said. "Don't worry about me, Master Sergeant. I won't screw the pooch."

She spun around and began to jog toward the supine bodies, hoping and praying that she would find injuries she could treat and give somebody a chance of survival.

She was about ten yards from the first one but it seemed like she was farther away and that for every stride she took, the distance lengthened. The need to reach them and render treatment became all-encompassing.

On the periphery of her hearing, she noted the angry and frustrated voices of Delta Team echoing from inside the buildings and the harsh static from radios.

Worst of all, in the few strides she had taken from Shay's side, her emotions had shut down and she had grown numb—both mentally and physically. She could sense a deep, dark void inside her. It frightened her.

As she approached the first body, a black cloud rose into the air, spinning and dancing like a malevolent tornado, and she realized that flies had found the men. She swiped at them and cursed beneath her breath.

When she came to a stop, dust spiraled into the air. She coughed hard and rubbed her eyes to try to clear the grittiness then dropped to her knees beside a man and let her pack slide from her back.

He was lying face down, and before she could carry out a quick visual assessment to check for injuries, she saw, with a stab of horror, that his hands had been zip-tied behind his back.

"Can you hear me?" she asked and her words shattered the stillness that hung like a menacing thundercloud over her head and around her.

She took her medical shears from the front of her tactical vest — Stork's blood now dried to a dull sheen on the blades — and snipped the plastic cuffs in two. The man's hands fell to his sides, raising their own miniature dust clouds, but there was no response at his release.

Annie pulled on a pair of medical gloves and carried out her now all-too-familiar visual assessment, and she noticed the reason why the man had died. He had received a gunshot wound to the back of his head and the damage to his skull and brain was extreme.

When she touched his hand through the thin latex material of her gloves, she found he was cold to the touch. She leaned over him and rolled him onto his back. Deep down she had known, but when she received confirmation that he was dead, a suppressed sob strangled her throat.

His eyes were wide open, the pupils cloudy, and he stared sightlessly up at a sky he would never see again. His face was a little bloated where he had spent time in the sun and livor mortis or hypostasis had discolored his skin, due to the pooling of blood because his heart could no longer circulate it.

While she knew the undeniable truth, Annie still reached out her hand and placed her fingertips on his neck where there should have been the strong beat of a carotid pulse. She felt nothing, and when she stared at his chest, there was no rise and fall to show he was breathing.

The numbness disappeared as quickly as it had come and anguish knotted Annie's stomach. She looked skyward, stared at the limitless blue expanse and wanted to scream her anger and helplessness at the heavens.

The howl of pain built inside her and the urge to release her torment at the intolerable injustice of what had happened to the six marines was almost unbearable, but she quashed her emotions, pressed her lips together and shuffled on her knees to the next man, dragging her medical bag along with her.

He lay on his side with his hands also tied behind his back, and again, he had been killed by a single shot to the back of the head.

Annie followed the same procedure as before. She snipped the cuff and pulled the man toward her so he was on his back. She checked for a pulse and breathing, and when there was none, she moved on to the next.

By the time she'd reached the fourth, she understood that this was the marine recon team who had not checked in, and she knew without a doubt that they had all been executed — killed while kneeling, their hands confined and with no way out.

Annie dealt with the fifth and sixth victims then rose to her feet and stood looking along the row of bodies. A white-hot fury consumed her and she wanted to kill someone — anyone. What had happened to the team was unjust and unfair, and she wanted payback for their deaths.

Hold it together, girl. Don't lose it now. That won't help anyone and it won't bring them back.

She was so deep in thought that when Shay spoke behind her, she jumped and almost squealed in shock.

"Well?" he asked.

Annie spun around — almost losing her balance — and the expression on her face must have said volumes, because he narrowed his eyes.

He was silent, as if waiting for her to speak, but clenched his hands into fists at his sides.

Her tone was flat and emotionless when she said, "Six angels, killed by shots to the back of the head."

She saw a distant look in his eyes as if his thoughts were far away, then he looked at the dead marines. "*Fuck me,*" he said, and although his tone was quiet, it was full of menace and chilled her with its controlled fury.

Over his shoulder, Annie could see Delta Team approaching, and she wanted to run. The expressions on their faces were ones she never wanted to see again and their emotions, so blatantly displayed by such hard-boiled young men, wrenched at her heart.

They formed a semi-circle in front of Shay and herself and stood staring at the bodies in silence.

"Those fuckers took all these guys' kits and weapons, even their fucking Kevlars," Sergeant Miller said. "We found nothin'."

There was a short silence then he continued, "We going for payback, Sarge?"

Shay half-turned to stare at him then studied his men. "You want revenge, Raptors?"

"Hell, yeah."

"Fucking A, Sarge."

"For our bros."

Annie heard the hate and bloodlust in their voices and a chill like ice flowed through her veins.

"I can go with that," Shay said, his voice calm and casual. "We *could* tag us some bad guys and kick seven shades of shit outta them. There'd be nothin' better then red misting some *haji* ass. But that would mean leaving our bros out here to rot some more, enough so their poor families wouldn't recognize 'em. You think they deserve that?

"So, holy shit, yeah. I'd sleep a lot better knowing I'd killed those motherfuckers, but we ain't gonna do that. We're goin' to call in a dust off and have ourselves extracted the hell outta here. We'll get these men sent home to their families and we'll take the fight to those dirty bastards another day.

"That might not sit well with you, Raptors, but I *can* guarantee those dumb fucks won't like what'll be coming their way when we *do* come back out here. And we *will*."

Annie saw disgruntled expressions on the marines' faces but nobody argued with Shay's logic. They remained silent while he radioed command, gave them brief details of what had gone down and called in three dust offs.

Once he'd signed off on the transmission, he turned back to his men. "ETA on the medevac and extraction is thirty mikes," he said. "Hammond and Webber, I want you to help McKendrick with whatever she needs.

"Sergeant Miller? Take the rest of the men outside the walls and set up a landing zone. Sweep the area and form a security perimeter ready for when the birds land. Pop some smoke and watch your sixes. We've no idea if there're any more hostiles around. Let's get it done and get the fuck outta here."

One or two members of the team and Sergeant Miller hesitated, indecision on their faces, and Annie thought for a moment they were going to rebel at Shay's words. But they seemed to come to a collective decision, and the sergeant nodded and yelled out at parade ground volume level, "Okay, let's go. We're not here for our health. Move it, Marines, double time."

With an inscrutable look at Shay, the sergeant set off at a jog toward the arch and five marines followed him, their boots thudding on the hard ground. Hammond and Webber stayed behind and moved to stand by Annie.

"Ma'am?" Hammond said.

Annie felt detached from what was going on around her and she looked at the man distractedly and wondered why he was being so polite to her.

"What do you need us to do?" he asked.

For a moment, Annie's mind remained blank until she gave herself a reality check and said, "We have to…get these men into…body bags and ready to go. Also, we need to check for any personal possessions and collect them. You'll both need some gloves."

She took off her own bloodied ones, balled them up and thrust them deep into the pocket of her fatigues then knelt beside the pack, opened it, found the items she required and handed them up to the two marines. "You'll need these as well," she said, her voice sounding small to her own ears.

After she'd unzipped a pocket on the back of the main pouch, she brought out six plastic-covered packages. She stared at the body bags in her hand then handed two to Hammond and the same to Webber. Then she rose to her feet.

"If we each do two…men, we'll be done quicker," she said.

The two marines nodded at her and turned away. Hammond slapped Webber on the back and they both slung their weapons and returned along the line of bodies.

Her insides quaked at the task ahead of her. She thrust her unsettled thoughts into the back of her mind and tore open a sterile bag, took out its contents and shook it out.

She made her way to the first dead man, laid the bag flat on the ground at his feet, unzipped it and drew apart the two halves. She stood astride it, lifted the marine's legs and slid the top of the bag under them, then rested them back down.

She then grasped both legs and pulled until — inch by inch — the man slid onto and partway into the vinyl pouch. Now and again she had to stop to straighten out the material where it had bunched up beneath the body but, at last, he was inside.

Annie gently closed the man's eyes with her fingertips then checked the area where he had been lying for anything that might have fallen out of his uniform or from his body. She couldn't see anything and she rested her hand on his forehead, bowed her head for a second then rezipped the bag, sealing him inside.

Annie moved on to the second victim and carried out the same procedure. Once she had finished, she was sweating profusely and her legs felt weak. All she wanted to do was find some shade to sit in, rehydrate, close her eyes for a while and try to erase what had become a day from hell from her mind.

A faint but familiar sound in the distance distracted her for a moment, and after listening, she heard helicopters approaching and knew the choice of whether to take time out or not had been taken out of her hands.

She closed the pockets and pouches of the pack, picked it up and thrust her arms through its webbing.

Hammond and Webber joined her and she saw their faces were pale and they looked sick to their stomachs.

Hardened marines though they were, they were only human, and she empathized with them because she knew how they felt.

"Thanks, guys," she said.

The two men nodded but made no comment, and Annie suspected they didn't want to talk because they couldn't find anything to say that would alleviate the horrors of what had happened.

The sound of three sets of rotor blades was louder, and she turned in the direction from which the noise was coming and waited for the helos to appear.

Hammond and Webber left her to join Shay, and Annie, alone for the moment and not sure what to do with herself, saw a Chinook approach. It veered toward the south end of the building and disappeared in a cloud of dust and sand.

A medevac Blackhawk flew in to a point almost overhead and she glanced up to see its cockpit and the door gunner before it veered to the right.

A pillar of green smoke drifted into the air as the marines laid down the markers for the landing zone and the aircraft descended out of sight beyond the low buildings, its huge propellers creating a billowing cloud of detritus that obliterated its outline.

Annie watched it fade from sight and wondered whether they were all going to get back to the base alive or end up in the same condition as the marine recon team.

* * * *

Apart from the marines forming a security perimeter around the Blackhawk, which would take the dead marines away, Annie and the rest of the team filed up the ramp of a second Chinook that had arrived for their extraction.

The men shrugged out of their equipment, chose their seats and, after sitting, placed their packs between their legs and locked their harnesses. Once settled, many of them leaned their helmeted heads back against the metal skin of the fuselage and closed their eyes.

Annie found her own seat opposite the open side door and fastened the safety straps across her shoulders and waist. She could hear Shay yelling orders outside, then he and Sergeant Johnson jogged up the ramp with the remaining members of the team bringing up the rear.

Brax Johnson took the seat on her left and Shay the one on her right. He barely acknowledged her, but once he had buckled himself in, his leg came to rest against hers and she could feel its warmth through her combat pants. Even as tired and emotional as she was, faint tingles coursed up the traitorous limb.

Annie rested her head back against the cold metal skin of the helicopter, even though her helmet made it uncomfortable, and she shut her eyes. She heard, as per normal procedure, the engines start to rise in pitch, the rotor blades speed up, then, with a jolt, they were in the air.

Images began to pile up inside her head, agitation set in and her eyes flew open. She brushed strands of hair from her face then rubbed her forehead as if the action would wipe away the nightmarish pictures.

She glanced about her at the men and saw that some still looked as though they were asleep while others stared into space, and she wondered what hellish thoughts they were thinking. They were unusually silent and haggard weariness showed on their faces.

Her thoughts drifted back to the sight of the bodies of the marines being carried away one by one. The scene had left her feeling cold and the muscles in her stomach had knotted like wires. She had felt sick.

She now felt trapped by her morbid thoughts and she needed a respite from them. Despite what she had been through that day, her thoughts turned to the man beside her.

She didn't know whether it was a reaction to the tension and stress or whether she was going crazy, but the feel of Shay's leg against hers and the flexing of his muscles through his combat shirt as his arm touched her, turned her churning angst into shivers of warm arousal, which thawed some of the chill that surged through her veins.

She found her reaction to him distasteful under the circumstances, but she couldn't quell the surge of emotion that flooded through her at his closeness.

She needed an outlet for her suppressed feelings and it was either throw the biggest hissy fit in history and scream herself hoarse or let the building tension turn into another, more primitive emotion.

At the idea that she could be turned on despite the horrific events of the day, Annie cringed and dismissed the inappropriate thoughts from her mind.

She was determined to relax, because she was physically and emotionally exhausted. When at last she was able to shut her mind to everything going on around her, she managed to doze.

* * * *

Annie jerked awake a short time later and, for a moment, she was disoriented. The Chinook was descending and there was a slight thud of the landing gear when it touched down. She realized where she was and unbuckled her harness.

The helo taxied to its position on the flight line and the marines stood, put on their packs, collected their weapons and Annie joined them as they filed down the ramp.

Outside, she glanced about her. Even though it was only late morning, it was very hot. The sky was a pale, hazy blue and the sun a searing white orb beating down on bare and helmeted heads alike.

The ground and tents shimmered and the smell of aviation fuel was thick in the air. Enhanced by the heat, the odor mingled with the smell of scorched sand, oil and plastic that was heating up in the rising temperature.

Her mouth was dry and her throat and lungs were irritated by the dust. The noises of the base were loud and continuous with the roar and scream of aircraft engines and the chopping sound of rotor blades from the distant runway.

Everything appeared so normal—or as close as it could be on a frontline military installation—but Annie knew that after today, nothing would ever feel the same again.

In a world of her own, she walked away from the Chinook. She thought she heard her name called but wasn't interested in finding out who might be hailing her, and she continued to make her way toward the field hospital.

She was desperate for a shower and to get some sleep, in that order, and she didn't want a debrief or to have an in-depth discussion with anyone. If she were honest with herself, all she wanted to do was find a place to hide so she could lick her wounds, get a grip on herself and try to make peace with the events of the day.

Chapter Nineteen

Annie sighed and stared at the cleaning kit spread out in front of her. She rested limp hands on her weapon and mental exhaustion tugged at her. Apathy had her in its grasp and she felt wrung out—her thoughts dull, her body lethargic and unresponsive to her brain's instructions to at least try to motivate herself to do something active.

She mentally kicked herself and began to strip down her rifle. The corrosive components of dust and sand might have infiltrated its fine mechanism and could pose a problem when she next had to use it, so whether she liked it or not, she had to stop procrastinating and get to it.

Her hand movements were slow and methodical, like those of a robot, as she did what she had to do, but her mind drifted as it had been doing since she had arrived back from the disastrous mission, to earlier in the day.

After leaving the Chinook, she entered the field hospital and met Major Matthews, who was lurking about, as if waiting for her.

Annie stopped when she saw him, knowing he would want to speak to her. He did, but only very briefly.

'That bad, McKendrick?' he asked.

Annie nodded. 'Yes, sir,' she replied, her tone emotionless.

Major Matthews stared at her and her expression must have told him enough, because he said, 'Okay. Go get cleaned up and get some sleep.'

'Yes, sir.'

Annie bowed her head and walked past him. She hadn't gone far when medic Corporal Malcolm McAllister, who was checking some equipment, asked, 'How'd it go, Annie?'

How do you think it went? *she thought.*

Annie tried to give a polite response. After all, he'd only asked the question out of curiosity, but it had still irritated her. 'Sorry, Mal. I don't want to talk about it,' she said and tried to keep her tone even. 'It's been a shit day. I've got blood all over me, I've been eaten alive by kamikaze flies and I just want to wash up. We'll talk later.'

She didn't wait for the medic to comment but hurried into the rest area, where she dropped her gear on the floor by her cot, stripped off her tactical equipment and crouched to retrieve her wash kit and a clean uniform from her kit bag.

She straightened up just as Freya walked into the rest area and came toward her. 'Hey, girl.'

Annie was thankful the sergeant hadn't asked how it had gone, because she would have screamed out loud.

She picked up her towel and moved to the end of the bed. "Hey," she said. 'I'm just going for a shower. Talk later?'

She avoided Freya's gaze and tried to sidle by, but her friend was having none of it. 'You okay?' she asked.

Annie sighed and tried to keep the impatience out of her voice when she answered, 'I'm fine. Just the same shit, different day. Sorry. But I need to get cleaned up. I stink.'

She hurried outside and was relieved that no one else tried to waylay her.

She made her way to the shower trailer, found it to be unoccupied, hung a notice on a stall door and locked herself inside.

The water was cold but she didn't care. She spent what little water time she had scrubbing her skin over and over until it tingled and grew red. Perhaps if she washed herself hard enough, she could obliterate the events of the day.

She'd just finished rinsing her hair and body when the water cut out and she stared at the shower head as if by doing so, she could make the water start again, but at last she realized that magic was never going to be a part of her life.

She reached for her towel and random spasms attacked her hands. She stared at them, fascinated, then frowned when tremors began to ripple her thighs as if something was crawling beneath the surface of her skin. Her stomach began to churn, her heart raced and scalding tears filled her eyes.

Oh, no!

She'd known it would come, and that when it did, that she wouldn't be able to stop it. She clenched her fists and put them over her eyes. She tried to blot out the images of Stork and the dead marines, but the pictures refused to go away. A tear trickled from the corner of her eye and a small sob escaped her.

Her emotions broke through the mental shield she'd erected and Annie cried – quietly at first, then, as the emptiness inside began to disperse, she sobbed as though her heart would break.

She bent double in the shower, covering her face with her hands, her body shaking as though she was freezing cold, but the icy feeling was deep in her heart.

She wept for the loss of life and for Stork, who might never be whole again, and she felt alone and guilty at the fact that she hadn't been able to save the recon team and hadn't done better by the injured marine.

She cried so hard that she became dizzy and had to prop herself against the cold sides of the stall to prevent herself from falling. She gagged and choked on emotion that was like a physical lump in her throat. If she didn't calm herself, she would lose it completely.

She bit her bottom lip hard so the resultant pain would force her thoughts away from her grief and she took several deep breaths, dismissed the bitter emotions deep inside her mind and locked them away.

When she felt steadier on her feet, she dried herself and dressed in a fresh T-shirt and combat pants, pulled on clean socks and laced herself into her boots.

There was nothing she could do about the splatters of blood on her footwear. With constant use, the marks would fade in time. Until then, she would have to tolerate the constant reminders of how they'd gotten there.

She left the shower trailer and went back to the hospital and the rest area. With disjointed and clumsy movements, she collected her dirty uniform and made her way to the laundry shelter, hoping the washer wasn't in use. It was empty and she dumped her clothes inside, added powder, turned it on then went back to her cot.

She laid down, dragging the blanket over her body and ignoring the urge to cover her head. She closed her eyes and tried to sleep, but her mind darted back in time, intent on refusing her even a few moments of respite.

Annie concentrated on each part of her body, trying to relax. She wanted to freeze her feelings and quench every single emotion, even if it was only for a few hours, but tears threatened to disarm her again.

I will not cry. Ever. Again, she thought.

It was some time before sleep crept up on her, but at last, she dozed, and even though it was only for a short time, her slumber was free of nightmares.

Annie didn't notice that Freya had joined her until the sergeant sat down on the floor in front of her and held out a bottle of water.

"Here," she said. "You haven't eaten, so drink this before you keel over."

Annie glanced up from what she was doing and reached out her hand to take the drink. "Thanks," she said. "Have you been spying on me?"

Freya took a mouthful of her own water and shook her head. "Nope," she said. "Just keeping an eye on you like any good friend would."

Annie put the bottle on the floor beside her chair and went back to cleaning her weapon. "There's no need. I'm okay."

Silence fell between them then Freya spoke again. "Did you get some shut-eye?"

"Some," Annie answered then looked at her friend. "What do you want me to say, Freya?"

Freya shrugged. "Whatever you need or want to."

Annie shook her head in exasperation. "There's nothing *to* say — unless it's about the guy who lost half his leg today and probably an eye or the six marines who were executed. Oh, and let's not forget the fact that we were too fucking late to help them. There. Are you happy?"

Freya stared at her in silence and Annie glared back before she sighed. Her warring emotions made her feel jumpy and restless and she knew she had to get what was worrying her out in the open.

"I couldn't handle it," she said at last. "I think I fucked up in a big way."

"That's not what I heard," Freya said.

"Yeah? What *did* you hear?"

"The boss got a briefing from the master sergeant, who was pretty impressed with you. He said you handled things like a pro."

Annie snorted. "Well, he must have the wrong person, because when Stork was injured by the IED, I froze, and the sergeant had to shake me out of it."

"It happens."

Annie forced herself to speak again, "No, it doesn't, Freya—not in a situation where you need to keep your cool and there are people relying on you. I couldn't get a handle on my emotions. One minute I was numb, the next angry, then back again like a pendulum. And when I went to get cleaned up, I bawled like Aiden. I thought I was going to throw up."

Freya leaned forward. "Look, honey. We've all been there and done it. There've been times when I've been so goddamn angry, I've wanted to kill someone. I hate to spill personal shit here but there've also been occasions when I've found a quiet corner of the hospital and howled like a crazy person. When it comes down to it, we do our job, but afterward, we need to get the crap out of our systems. Otherwise, we'd all lose it. Don't beat yourself up."

Annie shook her head again. "I've said my piece. Can we please change the subject? How's Stork?"

Freya took another mouthful of water. "You did a good job on him. He was stable when he was medevacked in. We patched him up, set his arm, treated his facial and head injuries, kept an eye on him, then he was sent to the combat support hospital."

A surge of relief sweep through her. "That's great."

"It's all down to you, honey," Freya said. "So, I don't wanna hear no more bullshit about how you can't handle things. That's an order. Do I make myself clear?"

"About as clear as mud, Sarge," Annie said, because she wasn't convinced that she accepted her friend's words of wisdom or her morale-boosting statement.

Freya got to her feet. "Okay. I'm for some delightful MRE chow, otherwise I'll die of hunger. You want anything?"

"Nope. I'll get something later. I need to get this done then clean my gear."

"Okay. Catch you later."

Freya left and Annie watched her go. The tension had eased its grip on her but she was still restless. She continued with the cleaning of her weapon, being more meticulous than usual and taking far longer than was necessary, purely to keep her mind occupied and free of nightmarish thoughts.

Chapter Twenty

Annie leaned against the side of the hospital tent and shivered in the chill air. She gazed out toward the perimeter fence and heard a faint sound of gravel crunching beneath boots as an unseen person patrolled the area or made their way toward one of the guard towers. With that exception, silence hung heavy about her.

There was no moon that night, the sky and stars obscured by cloud cover. Feeble red lights shone from each of the towers, but outside the wire there was nothing but impenetrable inky blackness. Any patrols out in the harsh and lonely desert could count themselves lucky, because their movements would be hidden, blanketed by darkness.

Annie still shied from thinking about the events of the day. Her thoughts remained foggy, her movements apathetic. Her muscles were tense and achy and her nerves jangled from the waves of adrenaline that still coursed through her body.

Annie needed to be by herself now and she straightened up and began to walk parallel to the medical shelters, trying to tread as softly as she could on the gravel.

She wasn't surprised when she thought of Shay. She wondered where he was and what he was doing. When she reached the end of the hospital tents, she continued onward, head bowed and deep in thought. She was unaware of the shadow that stepped out in front of her until she heard the crunch of stones other than her own. She stopped and gasped. "What—?"

"McKendrick?"

Annie's heart stuttered with fright and blood pounded in her ears. She almost turned and ran, then the moon appeared from behind a cloud and outlined a familiar face and body. She sighed with relief.

"I'm sorry I scared you," Shay said in a low voice.

Annie inhaled a deep breath then let it out. "You seem to make a habit of doing it, Master Sergeant. What're you doing here? Is there a problem?"

"Nope, no problem. I came to see if you were okay."

Annie was irritated at his words. "I'm fine. What *is* it with everyone asking me if I'm all right?"

Shay was silent for a moment then said, "Have you thought it might be because they care about you?"

A lump formed in her throat. She didn't want to discuss something as sensitive as emotions or caring or loss or what had happened that day. She shrugged and shook her head. "I appreciate yours and everyone else's concern, but as I said, I'm okay. I won't break."

"Well then, I guess I need to apologize for being here," Shay said and she heard the curtness in his voice. "Tell me about Stork and I'll leave you in peace."

"He was stable when he got here. They did damage control surgery. He remained under observation until he was able to fly, then he was medevacked to Mosul."

Shay nodded and Annie realized her words had been too harsh, but before she could say anything more, he about-turned and strode away from her.

Oh, hell. I screwed that up.

She shook her head, annoyed with herself, and half-turned to make her way back to the hospital when the sound of his footsteps stopped. She glanced back over her shoulder and watched as he stood immobile for a few moments, then he turned around to face her and before she could utter a sound, he had moved toward her, grasped her upper arms and turned her to face him.

He dug his fingers into the muscle beneath her combat shirt and she uttered a small squeak as he pulled her toward him and held her against his body.

She couldn't move, and when she looked at his shadowy face, her breath caught in her throat because their mouths were only inches apart.

No!

She knew what was going to happen next, and before she could verbalize any protest, Shay bent his head and slammed his mouth into hers. Sparks exploded and all thoughts of stopping him fled from her mind.

His lips were hot and moist, the kiss raw and intense, and desire clenched inside her and heat began to coil in the lower region of her stomach.

Annie's response to him was instant and without reservation, and when he parted her lips and their tongues entwined, she moaned and sexual arousal hit her so hard that her knees almost gave way.

His lips bruised hers with urgent need, and without conscious thought, she kissed him harder and thrust her tongue into his mouth. At her eager response, Shay took back control of the kiss and became even more forceful.

He groaned, a deep and meaningful sound, and she struggled in his grip. She wanted to get close to him and feel his powerful body pressed against hers. In the space of a few moments, she'd discovered she wanted this man more than she had ever wanted anyone.

Shay released her and she staggered backward, shocked and bereft that he had taken his warmth from her. For a moment, they stared at each other, the passion that had been ignited between them almost a tangible thing. He said in a husky voice, "Goddamn you," before he turned and strode away, vanishing into the dark.

What?

Annie stared after him, her heart racing, and she raised a hand to her mouth and traced her lips with trembling fingers.

Her thoughts were chaotic, her emotions in turmoil, and the past few minutes seemed like a dream. The intensity of their kiss then his abrupt leaving posed more questions than answers, and the mist of passion that had fogged her senses began to dissipate and she felt cold and confused.

Her lips felt tender and kiss-sensitive, and her stomach quivered when she remembered how she had responded to him and the sensations he had awakened in her.

Oh, hell. What have I done?

Annie wanted to follow him, but she denied herself and turned to start walking back to the hospital. The brief but passionate kiss with Shay O'Rourke had started a whole new problem for her, primarily how she could have allowed herself to lose control with a man she didn't know and what the hell she was going to do about it, if anything.

Of secondary importance was what Shay's own game plan was and whether he was just playing with her or had other things on his mind.

She knew what she wanted and it was something a lady would never voice, not even to her friends. All the promises she'd made to herself after her break-up with Josh had been blown out of the water and she had no chance of rebuilding the barrier she'd erected to protect herself from being hurt by another man.

Chapter Twenty-One

Annie counted the units of blood left in the chill unit and nibbled her lower lip with concern.

They were almost out of the life-giving plasma and she made a note on the form and wrote 'urgent' in large capital letters at the top.

Her jaw cracked when she yawned and she shook her head to try and rid it of the sleep-deprived fogginess that had taken over. It felt like her skull was stuffed with cotton balls and her eyelids drooped with fatigue.

After she'd shut the chill unit's door, she turned and was about to leave and report to Major Matthews to advise him of the critical depletion of the blood and other products, when Freya appeared.

Before she could greet her, Annie yawned again and Freya laughed out loud. "Hell," she said, "that looked like the black hole of Calcutta."

Annie was not amused because she was, in fact, exhausted, having had all of two hours' worth of sleep in twenty-four. "Very funny," she said, "which it's not. What do you want?"

"Touchy, aren't we?" Freya teased. "I'll get to the point. I've got a message for you. It would appear there's some guy outside who wants to see you. And no, before you ask. I don't know who it is. I don't have the time to check out your admirers."

Annie frowned then felt a pleasurable tingle of anticipation.

Shay. It's got to be him. Who else could it be?

A surge of energy revitalized her and she thrust the paperwork at Freya. "Here," she said. "Can you give this to Major M and tell him we're black on all fluids and we need an urgent resupply? I gotta go."

Freya snatched the form from her. "What did your last servant die of?"

Annie hurried through into the connecting tunnel. "Not helping a friend out when she asked."

She made her way through the rest area and the operating room and was almost running when she went outside.

It was early morning and the sun was coming up, its weak rays blazing a wispy trail across the cobalt blue sky. Citrus yellow, fiery red and burnt orange flared together in a translucent mist on the horizon and bathed the mountain peaks in luminous light which outlined their ruggedness.

A cool breeze wafted against her face, and she breathed in the air and thought that even though she was in a country which was drowning in grief and hardship, the rising of the sun was the one permanent and unchangeable feature that would continue regardless.

Annie stared about her for Shay but there was no sign of him, and she frowned.

So, who – ? Oh, hell, no!

Josh, her ex, had stepped out from behind an accommodation tent and was walking toward her. Her heart plummeted and her spirits sank.

Her limbs refused to move and she remained where she was, her gazed fixed on him. As he drew close, she saw he was more muscular than she remembered and also better looking, with a new air of maturity about him. He looked every inch a marine, but her scrutiny was detached and impersonal and she was glad she felt nothing more.

Her ex-husband stopped in front of her, almost close enough so their bodies touched, and there was a shit-eating grin on his face.

"Annie," he said, and there was such delight in his voice she thought she was hearing things. She almost looked behind her to see if he was speaking to someone else. "It's great to see you."

"What're you doing here, Josh?" she asked, trying to keep her voice steady, unsure whether to be angry or shocked at his sudden appearance.

"I've been in the sandbox a coupla days," Josh replied. "I was deployed to replace some guy who got himself blown up."

Stork.

Annie bridled at the casual way he spoke about the injured marine, but she quashed the simmering anger she felt and stayed quiet. She tried to give her ex-husband the benefit of the doubt since he had no idea of the circumstances behind how Stork had come to be hurt.

Josh went on, seemingly unaware of Annie's reaction to him, "My new team were talking about some woman medic who'd gone out on a mission with them and who'd treated their guy. My team leader mentioned your name and I knew it was you, so I decided to pay you a visit."

At the mention of Shay's name, Annie felt even worse than she had on first seeing Josh. Shay had provided information about her to her ex-husband and now a whole new clusterfuck had reared its ugly head.

"What do you want, Josh?"

Josh stared at her and the smile disappeared from his face. She saw a fleeting image of the petulant and arrogant man she'd known, married and divorced.

"That's hardly the sort of greeting I was expecting from my wife," he said, his tone sounding disgruntled.

Annie snorted. "If you got the divorce papers, you know I'm not your wife, Josh. I haven't been since about a year ago."

"Well, that's why I'm here. I've been thinking about you for a while and I want us to get back together."

Annie gasped at the bombshell he'd dropped but kept herself together. He hadn't bothered to ask about their son. She could barely keep her anger in check when she said, "Dream on. There's no way in hell that's going to happen, not as long as I live and breathe."

The mask dropped from Josh's face. He looked angry and sounded it when he said, "Why the fuck not?"

Annie almost punched him in the chest. "What?" she said, unable to get her head around what he was saying. "You have the balls to ask me why? I'd hit you but that would be animal abuse." She took a deep breath and tried to calm herself before she did something she would regret. "Josh. You walked out on me two weeks before Aiden was born then you disappeared."

Her ready temper was firing on all cylinders and she knew that if she continued to talk to him, she would end up losing it.

Josh seemed to change tack. "How's the kid?"

Annie tilted her chin at him in defiance. "He's not a baby goat and he's fine, no thanks to you."

"I wanna see him," Josh said.

Wow. Two bombshells in the space of a few minutes. Why don't you go for a grand slam, you dick?

"How do you propose to do that, Josh? We're at war in Iraq and you haven't been in his life for almost three years. I tried to find you when he was born but nobody knew where you were. Now, you turn up expecting to pick up where you left off?"

Josh frowned and he looked as if he was about to throw one of his infamous temper tantrums.

"He's my kid as well, Annie," he said. "You can't stop me from seeing him. I'll even go for the custody thing if I have to."

Annie stiffened and clenched her hands into fists at her sides. "Don't threaten me. That's the worst thing you can ever do."

"You've changed," Josh said, "and not for the better. You've turned into a first-class bitch."

Annie laughed out loud and it wasn't with amusement. "Having a husband walk out on you when you're pregnant and disappearing will do that to any woman. Being in a war zone can also do it. You'll learn that the hard way. It's not all fancy uniforms, playing with your weapon and being a badass marine."

Josh shrugged. "So, I guess that's it. You're gonna fight me about Aiden, are you?"

Annie sighed. She was tired and didn't need the added complication of Josh threatening her with a lawsuit to get access to their son or, knowing him as she did, to try for full custody.

This is not the time or the place to slug it out with him. Back off, Annie, and let him think he's got you where he wants you.

"Look… Let's talk about this like rational adults," she said, hating herself for what she perceived as backing down. "Here is not the time or the place to discuss something as personal or as important as this. I'm not saying you can't see Aiden, but he doesn't know you and things need to be taken slow and easy.

"My deployment ends in six months. When I get Stateside, I'll get some legal advice from a lawyer and we can go from there. We can't do anything now, so you need to wait it out."

Josh stared at her, the expression of annoyance still on his face. At last he said, "I guess I don't have a choice. But don't try and get one over on me, Annie. It won't work. The kid's mine as well and I deserve to see him."

Fucking dickhead. And this is the father of my child. No word of missing him, needing or wanting to see him. As usual, it's all about Josh McKendrick and what he thinks the world owes him.

Annie kept her expression neutral, even though she wanted to snarl like an animal protecting its young. "Okay, I get the picture," she said.

"Hey, maybe we can spend some time together," Josh said, changing the subject again.

Well, shit. That was bombshell number three. Not until hell freezes over, buddy, and that's never going to happen.

"I'll take a raincheck on that," Annie said. "I'm on duty almost twenty-four hours a day and with what might be going down soon, I doubt I'll have any downtime."

Not for you, anyway.

"I get it," Josh said.

Annie wanted to get rid of him as fast as she could. "Look. I need to go, otherwise they'll send someone to look for me and it won't go down well with the Major. I'll be shit-canned," she said.

Josh stepped backward and nodded. "Okay, but this isn't over, Annie. I'll catch you later."

Not if I catch you first.

Annie watched him walk away, then, feeling out of her depth and irritated beyond measure that her ex-husband had put her in a position where she now had a personal threat involving her child to consider on top of everything else, she turned her back on him and made her way toward the hospital.

Once inside the entrance tunnel, Annie stopped and leaned against the wall.

Her temper was blazing and she wanted to scream her frustration at the top of her lungs. She felt an urge to find a place where she could be alone to sort out the turmoil in her head and get her thoughts together, but there was duty to consider, and she couldn't just disappear without getting a roasting and a court martial if she left her post.

She was reveling in the quiet when she heard footsteps and Freya appeared on the threshold of the triage shelter.

"So?" she said.

Annie sighed. "You wouldn't believe me if I told you."

The sergeant walked toward her. "Try me. Shit. You look like you've seen a ghost."

"Something worse than that. It was Josh."

Freya looked shocked. "Holy shit. Don't tell me he's deployed here?"

"Yep. He's replacing Stork on Delta Team."

"That's so screwed. What did he want?"

Annie rubbed her fingertips across her forehead as if the action would wipe away the recent memories of her talk with her ex-husband.

"He wants me back," she said. "And he wants to see Aiden."

Freya sounded incredulous. "Now? Here? After all this time?"

"Yep. He's even threatened me with a custody lawsuit if I don't allow him access."

"What an asshole."

Annie shrugged. "I can think of worse names to call him, but it wouldn't help."

Freya folded her arms. "What're you gonna do?"

"There's nothing I *can* do until I return Stateside," Annie replied. "I told him that and said we'd deal with it when we both get home."

"And what was his answer to that?"

"He said he wanted us to spend time together out here and I made some excuse that with everything kicking off, I doubt it would happen."

"Hon, that's so fucked up," Freya said and sounded as exasperated as Annie felt. "You really don't need his shit right now."

"No, I don't. But there's not much I can do about it except stay out of his way. If I know Josh, though, he won't keep his distance and he's going to end up being a pain in my butt."

"I know the best thing for you, honey," Freya said and squeezed her arm. "Get yourself a new man or let's go for a coffee while we can."

For a moment, Annie forgot her woes and laughed out loud. "I don't want another man," she said, and thought of Shay.

Liar.

"I'll go for the coffee though," she continued.

"I'm buying," Freya said as they went into the adjoining shelter.

Chapter Twenty-Two

Annie shivered. It wasn't as cold as it had been on previous nights, but the temperature still had the power to raise goosebumps along her arms beneath her T-shirt, and she wished she'd thought to put on her jacket before leaving the shelters.

As she walked parallel to the hospital, the blackness surrounding the base was almost soothing in its cocooning silence. After the intense and emotional roller coaster she'd been on over the past few days, both with casualties and on a personal level, she was thankful for the quiet that was only disturbed by the sound of the generators she'd become used to and now hardly noticed.

Ahead of her she saw the faint glow coming from the shower and restroom trailers and, wanting to prolong her solitude, she headed toward them, rubbing her arms to instill some warmth into her body.

When she was almost at the facilities, she decided to continue her trek along the perimeter fence. The guards had become used to her nocturnal wanderings, although they still challenged her — which was procedure — but they'd stopped targeting her with their weapons after the third occasion.

The mutual cease fire had done wonders for her nerves, now that there was no risk of her being shot at, and her chances of being prostrated from shock every time she heard the harsh voices shouting out to her in the night had decreased.

Annie was about to turn in the direction that would bring her alongside the barbed-wire fence when a figure stepped out of the shadows and blocked her path.

"Hey," Shay said in a low voice.

Annie managed to take a gulp of air before she said, "You!" To her chagrin, it came out as a husky whisper and not the annoyed tone she'd hoped for.

Despite her irritation, something stirred in her at the sight of him and her pulse rate accelerated.

No way. Not again. This is getting to be a habit.

Annie regained her voice and in a sharper tone than she'd intended said, "What are you doing here, Master Sergeant?"

"Perimeter patrol," Shay said, his tone curt. "What the hell are you doing wandering around alone at night...again?"

Annie bristled at the implied criticism, and when she spoke, her voice had risen. "It's a bit of a coincidence that we keep meeting like this, isn't it? And I don't think I need your permission to take a walk by myself."

"Lower your voice. Sound carries at night," Shay said. "It's not a good idea for women to walk around the base alone. As much as I hate to say it, there're some unsavory assholes here."

Annie folded her arms. "Is that an order?" she asked, and winced when she heard the petulant tone in her voice.

Why can't I act normally around this man? He always seems to be able to push my buttons – in the wrong order.

Shay was silent for a moment then said at last, "Whatever. It's up to you whether you listen to me or not," and to Annie he sounded bored and disinterested.

He kept turning up when she least expected him, usually scaring the shit out of her, and it always seemed to be the case that each time, they ended up irritating each other and bickering like children.

He'd kissed her without her say-so, even if she had enjoyed it – which she would never divulge to him – and he was irritating as hell with the way he always managed to whittle down her resistance each time they spoke.

She didn't want to keep arguing with him because it made her feel uncomfortable and pulled her in two directions – annoyance because he wound her up and her own undeniable feelings of attraction for him, which seemed to be getting stronger whenever she was near him.

"Look," she said. "I'm sorry. The last few hours have been lousy. It seems that we're destined to keep bumping into each other, whether we want to or not, so can we get past the juvenile conversations and act like adults?"

Annie could have sworn she saw a smile twitch Shay's mouth, then he frowned. "You're so full of yourself, McKendrick," he said. "Are you always so damn charming to the people you meet?"

Annie's temper began to flare. *Goddamn it. This guy makes my blood boil. Why can't he be civil for just one second?*

"I don't give a damn what you think of me," she said. "I take my walks because I want to be alone, so if you'll excuse me, I'll say goodnight, Master Sergeant."

He can stuff that where the sun doesn't shine and make of it what he wants. She moved to walk by him.

Her arm brushed his and thoughts and wonderings about him filled her mind. She was in no doubt he was all alpha male, confident as hell and not afraid to show it—physically, vocally or through his actions.

If he made a mistake—after all, he was only human—he would likely get over it fast and move on, because he would eventually succeed if he kept trying. Shay O'Rourke would not give up just because he'd failed once.

She also thought he didn't like to lose. He would always want to win, and if he did, he would probably beat the hell out of a person to make them remember it.

She could picture him walking into a room and his sheer presence with how he stood, walked, his voice and how he carried himself would make people turn and look, especially the women.

She'd noticed that he swaggered—not in a bad way—but that he had pep and meaning in his step, was in control and knew where he was going. He didn't need approval from others and didn't suffer from a herd mentality. He wasn't afraid to rock the boat when it was needed.

He was dominant, direct and without doubt a risk taker. He would never stay within his comfort zone and would always step up and get the girl. If he didn't manage it the first time, he would try again.

With those thoughts in mind, Annie knew that if he wanted her, she would have no defenses against him.

As if confirming her thoughts, she had taken only a single step when Shay reached for her and grasped her arm, bringing her to an abrupt halt. She was a little taken aback, and for a moment, she wanted to wrench free.

A split second later, in a complete about-face and in line with her confused feelings for him, she felt the warmth of his hand on her skin and her senses sizzled.

Despite their confrontational words, his touch was doing all manner of things to her and she wanted him to grab her like he had when he'd kissed her the first time and pull her into his arms.

"I need to talk to you," he said.

"Can't it wait?" she asked, her voice uneven.

She was positive her tone showed what effect he was having on her and she was glad the darkness hid the blush that surely stained her cheeks.

"No, it can't."

"Okay. So talk…and please let go of my arm."

Shay ignored her request. "Not here. Our profiles can be seen by the security teams."

With his final comment, he tugged her toward the shadows lurking behind the shower trailer and drew her beneath a window from which a dim radiance shone on them both.

Annie's heartbeat became erratic when he pushed her against the cold metal side of the container and moved toward her until he had her hemmed in. She could have sworn his gaze roamed her face, then her body, and heat coiled like a dead weight in her lower stomach.

He slid his rifle strap off his shoulder, leaned the weapon against the trailer then took off his helmet and dropped it to the ground. When he removed his tactical vest and let it fall to join his Kevlar, Annie's pulse fluttered wildly and her heart beat so hard she thought it might leap from her chest.

What's he doing?

The question formed in her mind, but when she opened her mouth to vocalize the words, the only thing she could do was gasp for air.

For a moment, Shay stared at her then skimmed her body once more, first downward then upward, and at last he raised his gaze to hers.

His eyes gleamed and held a frightening intensity, as if he wanted to devour her, and tension crackled between them and heat swarmed about her neck and into her cheeks.

He leaned forward, rested his hands on either side of her head and bent close to her. "I've got you now," he said, his voice deep and husky.

Annie couldn't unlock her gaze from his and she swallowed and tried to regain control of a situation that seemed to be gaining frightening momentum.

"You don't *have* me," she said, but there was very little conviction in her voice and she cleared her throat. "You...wanted to talk to me."

Shay moved his face a little closer. "I did?"

Annie nodded like a marionette doll. "You did."

"Later."

Annie almost collapsed in a boneless heap on the ground.

Later? What's going to happen between now and later? Have I missed something?

"You're so goddamn gorgeous," Shay said.

Annie couldn't process his words, and like an epiphany, she knew what was going to happen and it meant she had a choice to make. She could either run away from him as if all the hounds of hell were chasing her or she could stay and take whatever consequences resulted from being with him.

She knew at once there was no decision to make — or not one that made any sense to her anyway, and she didn't move. Instead, she said, "I am?" and wondered if she'd lost her mind, because the two-word sentences were all she could think of to say.

"Yeah, you are," Shay said and moved one hand from where it was resting on the trailer and traced a finger down her cheek and along her lips.

The digit left a tingling sensation in its wake. Annie swayed and almost melted against him but stopped herself from doing so just in time.

Anticipation built inside her. She was far from naïve with regards to men, but Shay O'Rourke was not made in the same mold as those she had known in the past, including her ex-husband.

His sex appeal was off the charts. Her body responded to him without conscious thought. Going by their first kiss and remembering the way *she* had reacted, if he tried anything, she wouldn't resist him.

He was not the badass marine she'd believed — now revealing his true self and, while doing so, unknowingly demolishing the barriers she had built around her emotions.

Once she crossed the boundaries and entered some form of relationship with this man, who was doing an expert job of turning her into a mindless wanton, it would open a door she wouldn't be able to close.

Before she could say or do anything, Shay touched his mouth to hers and her thoughts splintered and scattered. The horrible images of the last few days were wiped away. She closed her eyes and savored the warmth of his lips, and her traitorous body welcomed his touch.

Annie wondered—in a small part of her mind that wasn't sparking with desire—how she could have ever tried to deny that she was interested in this man, and she returned the kiss with eagerness and was lost.

Shay broke away from her mouth and began to kiss her neck, finding and lingering at the place where a small pulse beat fast and delicately beneath her skin. He licked a swirling trail along and around it, eliciting a moan from her and sending a series of wild tremors rippling through her body.

As he continued to leave liquid-hot kisses against her skin, a tight and almost painful knot of sensation formed in the deepest regions of her belly and she arched her spine, soft sighs and whimpers encouraging him to continue and increase what were surely the most intense feelings she had ever experienced.

As if the sound of her passion was a trigger but still not touching her with his hands, Shay suddenly slammed his mouth into hers again, his lips hot and eager, and sexual awareness traveled through Annie straight to her core. Her legs almost buckled.

She slid her hands up his muscular arms and along the slope of his powerful shoulders to the back of his neck and lingered against his warm skin before she trailed her fingers through his short hair.

He withdrew his mouth from hers once more and stared at her. She saw his heated gaze and the expression in his eyes and knew instinctively what he wanted from her.

He knows that I sense what he wants and that I want it too.

Still looking into her eyes, Shay moved in close to her until his pelvis was touching hers. He put his arms around her waist and tightened them about her. He pulled her into him and the feel of his body made her hot with pure *need*.

God, I want him so much.

The words played in Annie's mind, but she had no time to savor the kick of lust in her belly, because he moved his hands to her hips, grasped them, hauled her onto her toes and pushed her backward so she was pinned to the hard surface behind her.

Shay kissed her face and neck before returning to her mouth, where he ravaged her with his tongue.

Moisture dampened the insides of her thighs and she had the urge to rub herself against him, or anything, to relieve the tingling pressure that was making her gasp for air. It was almost unbearable and she swayed a little under the gust of heat that enveloped her.

To steady herself, she clutched his shoulders and aligned her body to his. She pulled his head toward her so that his lips pressed harder to hers.

He glided his hands up her spine, kneading the sensitive nerves there with his strong fingers, and his touch burned through her T-shirt to her skin. She drank in the feel of him.

His grip on her tightened until she felt both pain and pleasure, then he withdrew his arms from around her and ran his hands down each side of her body, ending at her hips before coming to rest on her stomach.

Her muscles quivered and she shivered when, using the palms of his hands and his fingers, Shay began to knead her lower abdomen, moving downward lower and lower.

Annie sagged, feeling hypnotized at the slow and exquisite circling motion of his thumbs, which moved tantalizingly, millimeter by millimeter, to the place where she was crying out to be satisfied.

She thrust herself close to his body, sandwiching his hands between them, the touch of their bodies increasing the pressure of his thumbs against her.

Shay kissed her harder and with escalating passion, and she moaned, grinding her hips against his, felt the hardness of his erection and relished its restrained power and the way it pushed against her.

She was aware of the electrically charged atmosphere building between them and pressed herself against him, gliding her palms from the back of his neck, along his shoulders and down his arms.

Annie noted the play of the muscles in his biceps as he moved and wished she could feel the warmth of his skin against hers.

She was desperate to get past the barrier of his uniform and she drifted her fingers to the waistband of his fatigue pants. She hesitated then pulled his combat shirt free, thrust her hands beneath it and flattened her palms against his stomach.

His skin was warm and his belly flinched at her touch. She moved the palms of her hands in a massaging motion around to his back and traced the outline of his muscles. They rippled and flexed with his movements. She admired their definition, and once more, lust and need knotted her stomach.

He tightened his arms around her until she could barely breathe, but she didn't care. She wanted to prolong his response and glided her fingers from each side of his belly to meet in the middle before once more trailing them out to his hips.

Shay's muscles contracted and she repeated the action, hearing a deep growl come from him before she dragged her nails across his skin, not hard enough to hurt him but with enough pressure to cause him to shiver.

His obvious arousal thrilled her, and when he crushed his mouth to hers, lips fierce and eager, she sank against him.

He moved his hands from her back to her waist then pulled her T-shirt from the waistband of her fatigues. He ran his fingers across her skin and she mewled without restraint.

She reveled in the warmth and roughness of his palms as he trailed them from her abdomen, up her ribcage and unerringly found her breasts.

He cupped one and glided his palm over its curve before he pulled, squeezed then flicked her erect nipple through the thin material of her bra and teased it with his thumb.

When he moved to her other breast, lavishing it with the same attention that he had given the first, Annie arched against him and she wanted to beg and plead for him to take her.

As if he sensed what she wanted and needed, Shay withdrew his hand from beneath her top, left her mouth and cupped her face in his hands.

He didn't speak for a moment, his breathing harsh and ragged, then he said, "I want you so damn bad, but it ain't gonna happen," and he let her go and stepped away.

Annie stared at him, her body trembling from the onslaught of passion that had her in its grip. Her voice was uneven when she asked, "Why?"

"Not here," he said. "I've never taken a woman in this sort of situation before and I ain't gonna start now. You're worth more than that."

Annie tried to dismiss the ache of unfulfillment that had taken up residence inside her, and bitter disappointment welled at his withdrawal, but she understood the reason why and nodded. "What now?" she asked.

Shay bent to pick up his tactical vest and put it on. "Now? I'm gonna take you back to the hospital. Then, I'm going to go back to my tent and take a cold shower. On second thoughts, I might make that two."

At his inference that he was as turned on as she, her face flushed. He put on his helmet, picked up his rifle and slung the strap over his shoulder.

Annie remembered how the whole thing had started, and in attempt to lower her pulse rate, she said, "You said you wanted to talk to me."

Shay stopped what he was doing and the expression on his face went from warm to grim in the space of a few seconds. "Shit. I did, didn't I?" He half-turned to look out at the parked helicopters and said, "Not sure you're gonna like what I've got to say."

He was silent again and Annie grew impatient. "Tell me," she insisted. "It can't be that bad."

"You think?" Shay said, then seemed to come to a decision. "Okay. Well. We've met before, Annie. We've never actually spoken. Well, we have, sort of…but, I went to Langley High School in McLean."

Annie stared at him. When memories tumbled into her mind of a tall and handsome boy with long, dark hair and green eyes, she stiffened.

Before she could say anything, Shay continued, "I was a senior and you were a sophomore. Remember your graduation night? My sister, Megan, and your date? That was me, Shay O'Rourke."

"You?"

Annie studied his features and she could have kicked herself when she saw a slight resemblance to the boy who she'd had an unrequited crush on in high school and the girl's brother who had turned up when she'd caught Cory Anderson with a young woman at the graduation ball.

She was speechless and felt all kinds of a fool that he'd slipped her memory, and she also understood why he had triggered such sensual and erotic emotions in her. Her body and subconscious had known who he was and what he meant to her all along, even if those feelings had been those of a young girl.

"So, we have a history. I had a feeling we'd met and I thought I recognized your name. I'm a goddamn asshole and I feel ashamed."

Shay shook his head. "Don't beat yourself up about it. But, yes, we've got a bit of a past."

Annie nibbled her bottom lip. "I should apologize for being a fool, for forgetting about you."

Shay stepped toward her and cupped her chin with his hand. "No apologies necessary," he said. "At least you're not skinning me alive with those goddamn beautiful eyes of yours."

"No, I'm —"

Annie's words were interrupted as he bent his head toward her and teased her lips with his tongue before he kissed her, once, twice, lightly, then pulled her almost roughly to him and kissed her hard.

It was brief but powerful and the sensations inside Annie skyrocketed again, but it was over too soon and he backed off, and she was left feeling disappointed for the second time.

"We need to go," he said.

Annie pulled herself together and, hoping she could move with some semblance of normality, followed him out from behind the trailer. They walked alongside the hospital in silence and her mind was a hive of thoughts and emotions that she wondered if she would ever be able to resolve.

She mentally hugged herself when she thought about what had just happened between them, but there was a slight element of doubt and concern about their future underlying the erotic desire she'd discovered in his arms.

A few yards from the emergency entrance, Shay put a hand on her arm and brought her to a stop. "I'm gonna leave you here."

Annie turned to him and studied his face. There was a small grin playing about his mouth, and he stared at her and caressed her arm with his thumb. "I'll catch you later and we'll continue this."

"Absolutely," Annie said, her stomach muscles fluttering at the thought.

Shay took two paces back from her and tipped his chin. "Be careful," he said, then he about turned and strode away from her, his outline fading into the darkness.

Annie watched him go and wished she could've gone with him.

What have I gone and gotten myself into?

Her mind on Shay, Annie remained where she was for a few moments, then she brought herself back to the here and now and decided that it might be prudent to get back on duty, because she'd been gone long enough.

She had a feeling she wouldn't be able to perform her job with any degree of accuracy or concentrate with her mind so full of him.

Chapter Twenty-Three

Shay was gear-prepping for an early patrol the next day but he couldn't concentrate, which was a first. His movements were methodical because he'd carried out the task so many times that he could do it with his eyes closed, but his mind was elsewhere and he wondered what the hell was wrong with him.

Like I don't know the answer to that.

Annie had been on his mind. He'd always had feelings for her, ever since high school, but it was only recently that he'd realized how deep they were.

The sexual chemistry between them was unmistakable and undeniable, and he thought she felt the same about him, but — and it was a reluctant admission — his emotions went way beyond mere attraction.

He was irritated with himself that she occupied his thoughts so much, taking his focus and concentration away from his job, which was dangerous enough without him being distracted by a woman.

Regardless of how many times he gave himself a mental kicking, he couldn't get her out of his head, and he'd asked himself the same question over and over. *What am I going to do about it?*

Shay finished checking his equipment and placed his pack on the floor by his cot. He glanced around him at his men and cocked an eyebrow when he realized how quiet they were.

Some were cleaning weapons while others were checking their gear and the rest were lying on their beds reading or dozing.

Their usual monkeying around was absent and he guessed it was because of the shit that had gone down over the past few days.

Seasoned marines they might be, but they were still human, and if they hadn't reacted to the incident with Stork and the deaths of the recon squad, he would have been concerned.

"Hey, you."

Shay half-glanced over his shoulder. "Who the fuck —?" he said under his breath.

He didn't say anything else when he recognized the man striding toward him. It was the new guy who'd joined them to replace Stork. Shay hadn't had an opportunity to get to know much about him. In fact, he'd forgotten his name, but from what he could sense from some of the team, they weren't enamored of him.

He saw the expression on the man's face and wondered what fuckup had happened to make him look so pissed off.

Before the man had even reached Shay, he said, "You, fucker. I saw you with my wife."

Stunned, Shay could only stare at him. *What the hell?*

The man went on, "You've crossed the wrong guy, pal. No one fucks with me or my wife."

Shay felt the first stirrings of anger and clenched his hands into fists at his side. From the corner of his eye, he saw Webber, who was lying on his cot, lower the pornographic magazine he was reading, and the expression on his face was the same that would be on all his men's faces.

Tension ramped up in the tent and Shay sensed Delta stir at the implied threat to their team leader.

"What *have* you been up to, Sarge?" Sergeant Miller said out loud. It wasn't a question that needed answering.

His tone was full of forced camaraderie, but Shay knew the man was sounding out the situation and would be ready to act if the implied confrontation became a reality.

Shay tried to keep his voice calm and neutral when he said to the newcomer, "Sorry, buddy. Can you run that past me again, 'cause you lost me after you called me a 'fucker'?"

The man stopped a couple of paces from Shay and pointed a finger at him, the digit only a few inches from his face.

The hostile invasion of his personal space set off an alarm in Shay that warned he might be kicking seven shades of shit out of the guy if the dude didn't back off.

From the corner of his eye, he saw Hammond and Sergeant Jackson stop what they were doing and turn to face them. Both folded their arms. To an onlooker, they might have appeared curious and relaxed, but Shay recognized that the stiffness of their postures portrayed something else entirely.

"Are you a fucking dick?" the man said, his voice furious. "Do you have a hearing problem? I saw you with my wife the other night behind the shithouse."

"Yeah, that's what I thought you said," Shay said, his temper beginning to boil. "You wanna take your finger out of my face, buddy, before I break it off and ram it down your fucking throat?"

The soldier hesitated, but he must have seen something in Shay's face that told him the master sergeant would carry out his threat, because he drew his hand back.

There was a short silence then the man continued, "Annie McKendrick is my wife and we have a kid. So, *buddy*, if you don't wanna spend the rest of your life walking around looking over your shoulder, keep your fucking hands off her."

At the mention of Annie's name, Shay's insides froze and his hand twitched with a momentary urge to punch the guy in the face.

She's married? She would've told me.

"You want me to take this dickhead outside and fuck-start his face for you?" Harris said, his voice breaking the heavy silence that had fallen. "Just say the word, Sarge."

"Nope," Shay answered and moved a pace toward the other man. "Listen up, fuckwit. I'm only going to say this once because you ain't worth telling twice. You don't come swanning in here mouthing off and acting like a fucking shithead unless you know what you're talking about and you've got the facts to back up your runaway mouth.

"I'm also your team leader, and if you don't wanna find yourself fragged one day out on patrol, I'd think *very* carefully about what you're saying. Do I make myself clear…Corporal McKendrick?"

Josh McKendrick stepped backward and glanced around him. "Oh, yeah, I get it. You dick my wife and now you ain't got the guts to own up."

Before Shay could stop himself, he'd grabbed the marine by the throat. "Cut that shit out," he said his tone low and menacing. "*Now*. I don't dick someone else's wife. I don't have to. Unlike you, I can get my own women without poaching someone else's. I could eat a bowl of alphabet soup and come out with a smarter statement than the one you've just made.

"Secondly. You fuck with me again and you'll need to start keeping *your* head on a swivel, looking for stray bullets that might come your way. So, take it up with my ass, because that's the only thing that gives a crap. Now get the fuck outta my face before I do something I'll regret, and go prep your gear."

Shay was tensed with fury, one emotion he'd thought he had under control, and he worked to stop himself from beating the man to a bloody pulp.

The corporal's face was growing puce in color and Shay released the man from his vise-like grip.

He was supposed to be a team leader and a marine, not an adolescent schoolboy who'd just found out his girl was going with someone else.

Josh McKendrick glared at him, his face twisted with what looked to Shay like hatred, and he knew he would have to keep an eye on him and thwart any threat he felt might come from the man.

"Just keep your fucking hands off her," the corporal said and, without thinking, Shay lunged at him.

Brax grasped his arm and said in a joking manner, "Now, now, Sarge. Let's not kill the fucktard. You might find yourself in heap big trouble and the little shit ain't worth it."

Shay allowed himself to be pulled away but he didn't take his eyes off McKendrick.

"He heard you, *pal*," Brax said to Josh. "Bug out, unless you want to find yourself in the hospital."

Josh McKendrick opened his mouth to say something more, rubbed his throat and decided against it. He about-turned and strode to his cot with the pile of gear lying on its mattress.

Shay pulled his arm away from Brax. "I'm okay," he said, although he was still furious and struggling to control it. It must have shown, because Brax backed off and raised his hand in a pacifying motion.

Shay clenched his hands into fists and tried to forget about what he'd just heard. The words 'wife' and 'married' kept pounding in his head, and the more he thought about what the man had said, the more the fury seethed in his mind.

"What was that all about?" Brax asked.

Shay stared at him and remained silent.

They had known each other for two tours of Iraq and were good friends, but Shay had no intention of disclosing what the confrontation had been about.

Brax wasn't stupid and that was confirmed when the sergeant said, "The medic who came on patrol with us?"

Shay was wrong-footed. "I don't know what it's about, but I aim to find out."

"Listen, buddy. A broad ain't worth all the heartache," Brax said.

Shay glared at his friend. "This one is," and he turned and hurried from the tent.

Outside, Shay strode across the graveled area in front of the accommodation. His breathing was ragged with anger and it felt like every single muscle in his body was coiled as tight as a snake that was ready to strike.

He was barely aware of his surroundings until he reached the marine Raptor sign at the edge of the road, where he came to an abrupt stop. He breathed easily for a few moments and tried to calm down.

What the hell am I doing?

For him to go storming over to see Annie and demand to know the truth was not who he was. He had never let his emotions take control of him, and he wasn't about to let it happen now. He wasn't an adolescent and should never have reacted the way he had when told she belonged to someone else.

Feelings for a woman had no place in his immediate plans, and regardless of how he felt about Annie, this was not the time nor the place. If she was married, then so be it. He'd been a fool and should have known better than to get involved with her.

He needed to turn his back on her and forget what had happened between them.

Shay sighed and about-turned to make his way back to the tent. As he did, despite the strong words to himself, he couldn't help but feel his spirits sink at his decision and a sense of loss when he realized he would never see Annie McKendrick again—if he could help it.

Chapter Twenty-Four

Annie relaxed against the support that held up one of the hospital shelters and reveled at the warm night breeze caressing her bare arms. She sighed with enjoyment.

She was still tired — nothing new there — but some of the tension caused by the fatigue had eased from her body and she felt a little more alert and less full of nervous energy.

The field hospital had received no casualties over the past twenty-four hours but, prior to that, they'd been busier than usual. During the lull — probably the prelude to chaos — the team had taken the opportunity to get some rack time, eat, shower, clean and sanitize the field hospital and inventory supplies and drugs. Once they'd completed those tasks, they'd been ordered to check and recheck everything again until they could have done it blindfolded.

Annie had tried to get some sleep, but with her state of mind as it was, she'd found it impossible to relax for even a few minutes. So, while everyone else either slept or occupied themselves with other things, she'd ventured outside to get some fresh air in the hope it would help her relax enough to sleep.

While the usual bitter odors tormented her sense of smell, the temperature was invigorating and, for the first time in quite a while, she felt revitalized, full of energy and ready for whatever life had to throw at her.

She noticed that the base was no longer as quiet as it once had been. More personnel had been arriving by aircraft almost daily and two rows of accommodation tents were now occupied.

Soft amber glows came from their interiors and she could hear muted voices, doors slamming from close by and faint music that must have come from a radio. The new sound went some way toward making Sykes a less lonely place to be.

Annie's thoughts turned to Shay and she wondered where he was. She hadn't seen him for almost two days, and while she understood he had other more important things to do, she had vague doubts that perhaps things had gone too fast between them and she'd frightened him off by her eager response.

She also realized that she had trust issues because of Josh and that she needed to resolve them. Breaking the promises to herself that she wouldn't ever get involved with anyone again had confused her and sent her emotions into a tailspin. Based on those issues alone, a new relationship, particularly in their present situation, shouldn't have been in the cards.

Annie felt a little down at her thoughts and she straightened and turned to make her way toward the hospital entrance. She needed to get some sleep while she could, because staying awake was not an intelligent option.

Energy and strength to do her job was a necessity and being depleted of both was a recipe for disaster. Being concerned about whether a man had decided not to have anything more to do with her needed to be at the bottom of her bucket list.

She was about to enter the hospital when she heard someone call her name. She was taken off guard and the first thought that entered her mind was she hoped it wasn't Josh paying her another visit because she didn't have the time or the patience to deal with him right then.

Annie stopped, turned from the direction she was going in and looked toward where she thought the voice had come from. She saw Shay standing on the path ahead of her and her heart lurched with excitement. Her next response was a smile of delight that he'd come to see her. She forgot all about her decision to get some rack time and she hurried toward him.

His face was in shadow but as she got close to him, she saw him more clearly and noticed his rigid posture and inscrutable expression with no smile of welcome for her. She knew something was wrong and her step faltered.

Upon reaching him, she stopped a foot or so away and when he didn't speak, her smile disappeared.

"What's wrong?" she asked, her voice quiet.

Shay looked at his boots then returned his gaze to hers and she winced from mental discomfort when she saw the icy look in his eyes.

At last he spoke, but his tone was emotionless. "Strange thing happened to me a coupla days ago. I got a visit from this dude. He's the new guy that's been transferred to Delta to replace Stork. He was crazy pissed and gave me a load of bullshit about how he saw me with his *wife*.

"By the way. No offense, but he's an utter dick. The fucker then had the balls to roast my ass about how I needed to keep my hands off you because you and he were *married*. He also said you had a kid and that if I didn't stay away from you, I'd need to start looking over my shoulder."

Shay paused, glanced off toward the helicopters then faced her again. "The guy was a real lucky bastard. I wanted to kill him. I don't take to being accused of something I haven't done *and* called a liar. What do you make of that, Annie?"

Annie's heart sank at his words. *Josh. He must have seen me and Shay behind the restrooms and he's still suffering from the delusion that we're still together.*

She could sense Shay's anger — whether from jealousy or at the thought of being duped by her — and she placed her hand on his forearm to try and reassure him. His muscles were tense and he didn't respond or move at her touch except to clench his jaw, which caused a small muscle to flicker in his cheek.

Even though she was innocent and couldn't control what Josh said or did, Annie wanted to repair any damage her ex had caused before it got out of hand.

"Josh and I aren't married," she said. "We were, but we divorced about a year ago. The reason? He bugged out of our marriage two weeks before my son, Aiden, was born. So, yes, I do have a child and I *was* married, but that's as far as the truth goes. My *ex*-husband has decided he wants us to try again and I told him that'll happen when hell freezes over. I can't help what he thinks or wants."

Her words trailed off when Shay failed to respond to her explanation and she wondered if he believed her. She moved her hand from his arm and stared at him, not knowing what to say next to convince him.

She was surprised when he reached for her hand and took it in his.

"C'mon," he said. "We need to find some place to talk. I'm fucking sick of being on display in this goddamn place."

He about-turned and tugged her to follow him. Her boots were unlaced and she stumbled but she went anyway, wondering where he could take her where they would be unobserved.

Shay led her between the first and second rows of shelters until they were some distance from the hospital. He stopped at one of the tents in the first row, let go of her hand and bent to unzip the door flap. Once it was open, he pulled the canvas to one side to widen the gap, stepped to the left and gestured for her to go in ahead of him.

Annie tried to read the expression in his eyes. They were still empty of emotion, and her heart began to beat erratically with the onset of nerves. But she complied with his request and went into the dim interior.

Once inside, she surveyed the long, narrow space and noted the rows of metal cots and the stack of folded blankets to her right before she turned and watched Shay as he followed her inside and resealed the door.

Annie had no idea what was going on or what he had in mind. She felt like a gauche schoolgirl alone with a boy on their first date, and even though it wasn't true of her and Shay, she still felt shy and uneasy.

He came toward her, and when he was a pace or two away, he stopped and folded his arms. It was now light enough outside for her to see him and she noted he appeared to be more relaxed.

While she couldn't blame him for believing Josh — her ex-husband was a wishful thinker and could be very persuasive in that respect — she was irritated that Shay had jumped to the conclusion she had been keeping him in the dark about her personal life.

Annie was growing annoyed and it showed in her voice when she asked, "Nothing to say?"

"Oh, yeah. I've got plenty to say," Shay replied but didn't elaborate.

Annie huffed in exasperation and gestured at their surroundings. "Why are we here?" she asked. "I thought you wanted to talk, so why don't you?"

Shay shrugged. "We need to talk all right, but I'm not one for fancy words or playing mind games and hearing or giving bullshit."

Annie raised her chin in defiance at his statement. "You don't mince your words, do you? Are you insinuating that's what I'm doing?"

"Nope."

Annie nibbled her bottom lip. "Look. I told you the truth about my marriage. Josh is an asshole and I never lied to you. The opportunity never arose for me to tell you my life history. That's all I have to say."

Shay unfolded his arms and nodded. "I believe you," he said.

Annie almost sighed out loud with relief, then flinched with surprise when he reached out his hand and took hers. He turned it palm upward and began to circle the center of it with his thumb.

His simple touch ignited heat trails in its wake, sent tingles up her arm and set her pulse racing. She tried to ignore how his touch made her feel, but failed.

"I'm an asshole," Shay said.

Annie glanced at their entwined fingers, her complete attention captured by what he was doing.

I can forgive you for being an asshole if you keep doing that.

Shay brought her hand to his mouth and kissed each knuckle in turn, and she jumped as if she'd been burned. He grinned at her as though he knew full well what he was making her feel and continued languidly stroking her.

Annie was mesmerized by the sensual movement creating a simmering heat in her body. She tried to make light of the situation and said, "You're a marine. That's to be expected."

He grinned again and the feeling of her nerves sparking like tiny electric shocks moved from her arm to travel down her spine. It felt as though all the strength had drained from her legs, leaving her without the ability to stand.

"I'm crap at this romantic shit," Shay said, keeping up the gentle circling of her palm. "So, I'll just come out with it. If it sounds juvenile, well, it'll be the best I can do." He hesitated then went on, "I've been crazy about you since high school. I wanted to ask you out on a date then but I didn't have the guts and I let you go."

Annie's heart lurched with shock at his words, and for a moment, she was speechless. She knew he was waiting for her response by the expectant look on his face, and there was no way she could let him think she wasn't going to answer.

Her voice was husky when she said, "Why didn't you just ask me?"

Shay laughed out loud but there was no amusement in the sound. "You're kidding me, right? Annie, I'm sure you heard I was no angel. The whole school *thought* they knew who I was and all about my family." He paused and his tone was bitter when he continued. "They judged me and them on how we lived, and they made assumptions about things my dad did, without the true facts.

"You were way out of my league. Right or wrong, I thought you were too good for me. Other guys talked about how...hot and rich you were and how money in McLean talks. There was no way I was even going to go near you."

Heat flushed Annie's cheeks and a wave of excitement surged through her. A flood of emotions—desire for him, a feeling of loss because of the years they'd missed together and a depth of feeling she'd never experienced for a man before—left her dizzy.

"You *are* an asshole," she said, but her tone was low and gentle. "You didn't know me and yet you made a judgment based on what you thought I was like."

"Your parents would have kicked my ass if we'd started dating," Shay responded. "As I said, you were out of reach of *my* sorry ass."

Annie shook her head. "I'm no angel either, Shay. I also have a badass temper, I'm impulsive and I'm stubborn. But my dad was a career marine then an engineer. My mom was a nurse. They've worked hard all their lives and they've never flinched at doing it. They aren't the type of people who look down on others who are...more disadvantaged than them.

"They taught me their values. They let me make my own mistakes—and there've been plenty of those—but they brought me up to learn by them. They've always trusted me and supported my decisions. I know they would never have judged you for being who you are or for what happened to your family."

Shay released her hand. "That's all I needed to hear," he said and stepped close to her, clasped her hips and tugged her toward him until their bodies were almost touching.

"So, how do you feel about me?" he asked, a slight grin touching his mouth.

Breathless at how close he was and trying to be nonchalant about her answer, Annie said, "You're so full of yourself, Master Sergeant. You can't spring those lines on a girl and expect her to have an immediate answer. But...as I'm not your normal everyday type of girl, I suppose you could say I feel the same way. I hope that answers your question."

Shay's gaze roamed her face, then he cupped it in his rough palms, causing her to utter a squeak of surprise.

"Copy that," he said and bent his head toward hers.

He brushed her lips with his—light and tender. His hands were warm on her skin and she wanted to melt into him.

Annie lifted her hand and touched the side of his face. Stubble rasped under her fingertips and she trailed them along his jawline and felt a faint flicker of a muscle beneath his skin—an emotional response.

With urgent need, Shay kissed her and his breathing quickened. Her whole world narrowed until it was just the two of them. She was cocooned in a desire that was building to a slow burn.

In a part of her where the erotic side of her nature stirred, unfulfilled, she wanted Shay O'Rourke and she had to use all her control to restrain herself and not kiss him harder.

Shay moved his hand around to her back and rested it there, his touch burning through her T-shirt to her skin like a brand. Then he trailed his fingers up her spine until he reached the base of her skull, where he clenched his fingers in her tousled hair, then relaxed them to cradle her head.

With a demanding increase in pressure, he pulled her head forward until his mouth was harder on hers. Their kiss deepened and desire burned like fire at the juncture of Annie's thighs. She tightened the muscles to increase the pressure and prolong the pleasurable tingle.

Annie glided her fingers from his neck and meshed them in his short hair. He shivered at her touch, and at his response, she wanted much more than a mere kiss from him.

He pressed almost tentatively into her and tightened his arm about her until she could barely draw enough oxygen into her lungs to breathe.

She had to have more from him and she tilted her head back and arched her neck to present it to his mouth, and as if he knew what she wanted, he burned a trail down her smooth skin with his lips to the pulse beating rapidly in her throat and he nipped the area.

Needles of exquisite sensation shot through her and she moaned and pushed her hips against him. The blood sizzled in her veins, and she grasped the waistband of his combat pants and tugged him closer.

She could feel his erection — *How hard he is!* — and she moved her hips in small circles, rubbing her pelvis against his. He groaned and trailed his fingers upward until they came to rest on one of her breasts. There he paused, as though he thought he may have gone too far, but Annie pressed her hand on top of his to urge him to continue.

Shay drew back and, for a few seconds, he and Annie stared at each other, searching each other's face.

"Don't stop," Annie whispered, reaffirming what she wanted, and after uttering a low growl, he kissed her again—this time deep and rough, tasting as if he were hungry for her.

Annie placed her palms flat on his chest then slowly slid them down to where his T-shirt was tucked into his fatigue bottoms, and she tugged it free. She thrust her hands inside, traced the sculptured landscape of his well-defined pecs and ran her fingertips downward from his chest to his abdomen.

Shay groaned and Annie withdrew from their kiss and looked at him from beneath her eyelashes. His jaw was tense and his eyes had darkened.

Annie pushed the T-shirt farther upward and bent her head to lick the area between his nipples and place featherlight kisses on his skin. A faint voice inside her protested that she was making all the moves and was acting like a hooker out to make a quick buck but she didn't care. She knew exactly in what direction the situation was going and was helpless to stop.

"Take off your top," she ordered and without hesitation, Shay obeyed. She placed the palms of her hands back on his chest, marveling at the ripple of muscles, then, sensuously, she ran her hands down his sides and curved her fingers along his stomach, eliciting a strong contraction of his muscles.

Annie stood on tiptoe and rotated her hips against his cock. He clutched her to him and jerked his hips, and more wetness dampened her panties as her sexual desire for him rose higher until the unsatisfied pleasure was unbearable.

Her nipples had hardened and chaffed at the cups of her bra, and the friction created a heady sensation of fullness and sensitivity, and while she loved Shay's demanding kisses, she wished he would turn his attention to her breasts.

Shay grasped the bottom of Annie's T-shirt, tugged it upward and over her head then dropped it to join his on the floor. He paused, his breathing ragged and stared at her.

"You're so beautiful," he exclaimed huskily. "Take that thing off." He gestured to her bra.

Annie reached up behind her back and unfastened the catches. Then, as though she were performing a striptease, she held the bra to her breasts to prevent it falling before she was ready and she lowered her shoulder to allow the strap to slide halfway along her upper arm.

She performed the same action with the other arm, paused a moment, staring into Shay's eyes, then she lowered her hands from her chest to allow the bra to fall away from her bare breasts.

As it did so, she wondered, with a mild sense of worry, what would happen if someone came into the tent and caught them. She would be mortified and they would both be in deep shit, but her concerns drifted away and she gasped when Shay cupped one of her breasts and gently circled her erect nipple with his thumb. He bent his head and kissed each in turn, finally settling on one, and he licked it in in a slow, circular motion before he moved to the other, leaving a glistening trail. She moaned and thrust her hands into his hair.

He took one of the nubs into his mouth and teased the hard bud before lashing the highly sensitive area with his tongue. She tossed her head back, and when he nibbled the delicate skin there and grazed it with his teeth, a wild shiver raced through her body and she clutched his shoulders.

Shay straightened to his full height and stared at her. His look scorched her as it raked her body and the sensation sent her pulse rate rocketing.

"Do you know how much I want you?" he asked, and bent his head and kissed her ear. "I've wanted you ever since I laid eyes on you."

His breath was hot on her skin and sent scintillating prickles of want from her breasts down to her stomach and from there to the place where she wanted him desperately.

A fierce tremor traveled to Annie's center, and when he clasped her bottom and pulled her even closer so her hips were crushed to his, she squirmed at the exquisite pressure.

With a low growl, Shay picked her up and she hooked her legs around his hips, her unlaced boots falling from her feet in the process. She strained to press herself against the outline of his cock and she ground her hips against it to create a hot and delicious friction between them.

He bucked his pelvis against hers in response and Annie moaned, trying to muffle the sounds against his bare shoulder.

For a few moments he moved his legs as though he were kicking something, then he dropped to his knees and lowered her onto a bed of scattered blankets.

Annie fell backward and Shay bent over her, kneeling between her open legs, arms either side of her head, supporting him.

Her heart was pounding so hard that she thought the whole of the forward operating base would be able to hear it.

"Are you sure this is what you want, Annie?" he asked, his voice hoarse.

Annie kissed his mouth and licked his bottom lip. She clenched his biceps with shaking hands and her voice was low and seductive when she answered him, "Shay? Shut up."

"Yes, ma'am," he answered and his kiss was brief but hard, his tongue darting possessively into her mouth, after which he traced her lips then left sensual, liquid-hot kisses first on her face, then her jawline and her neck, where a pulse raced beneath her highly sensitized skin.

Annie tilted her head into the rough bedding to give him the room he needed and she was lost.

Chapter Twenty-Five

Shay lowered himself between Annie's legs. He rested on his elbows, one on either side of her, and she clasped each of his hands, threading her fingers through his. He pressed them down, his grip tight enough to almost crush her fragile bones.

The intense burn of sexual excitement between her thighs increased and the firestorm encompassing her body grew white-hot. She didn't know how long it would be before she demanded he make love to her.

Shay let go of one of her hands and entwined his fingers in Annie's hair. He pressed his mouth to hers, the kiss hard and hungry, and she experienced the helplessness, the sinking yielding to him and the surging warmth that left her limp each time he touched her.

He left her mouth and, with reverence, he kissed each of her breasts in turn then took a nub into his mouth. His teeth grazed the sensitive skin and she cried out and gasped at the assault of his mouth, and he licked a nipple teasingly.

Annie squeezed his fingers in response, urging him on. He circled a rigid bud slowly with his tongue then he took it into his mouth and sucked it so she writhed in pleasurable torment.

Shay rocked his groin against hers in a steady rhythm, and at last he released her hand and slid his palm down her body until he reached her hip. He gripped her bottom and lifted her until his burgeoning, covered shaft was crushed between them.

She pushed her hand between their hips and moved her fingers downward until she reached the waistband of his combats.

She pressed against the outline of Shay's stiff cock then traced its hardness with her thumb and forefinger. He uttered a low moan and his body tensed.

Annie rubbed him slowly and firmly with her palm, creating a fiery frisson, and he thrust his hips in time with her own actions.

She reached for the button of his pants and, taking her time, undid it and grasped the zip to slide it down. She inserted her finger inside his shorts and moved it in a teasing motion back and forth, the digit caressing the tip of his dick.

She circled the bulging glans with the fleshy pad of her thumb and trailed a finger along the smooth, engorged vein on the underside, and his rock-hard member glided through her grip, pre-cum easing her way.

Annie plunged her entire hand inside and buried her fingers in the thick hair that nestled his cock. She stroked the area for a few moments then grasped the hot length of him and began to move her hand up and down.

Shay groaned gutturally, clamped his hand on top of hers and stayed her movements. "Stop, Annie. Be careful, because I want you so damn bad."

When she looked at his face, his eyes were closed and his jaw was clenched. She released him because she sensed he was on the verge of losing control.

A silken wetness coated her inner thighs and she ached to have him inside her. She wanted Shay with a rough and bittersweet passion that only he could satisfy and it took an enormous effort to stop herself from guiding him into her and losing herself. She had never experienced anyone like him in her life.

Annie half-turned on her side and pushed him until he rolled away from her onto his back.

Shay raised his head and looked at her with heavy-lidded eyes. "What's wrong?" he asked.

Annie didn't answer. Instead, she raised herself and leaned over him. She kissed his chest, feeling his muscles twitch at her touch.

A primeval excitement coursed through her when she recognized the power she possessed to turn him on.

Shay's gaze was molten and she licked her bottom lip, lowered her head and trailed it along to his nipple, where she nipped at his skin.

When she stared at him once more, the expression on his face was one she understood well, because it showed the want and need she shared with him.

She slid her fingertips to his chest then his stomach, trailing them lower and slower until she reached his waist.

Annie stopped, prolonging the moment and making him wait before she grasped the material at each side of his combats, and when he raised his hips for her, she pushed them down to his thighs.

She scanned his tan torso, dark against the brilliant white of his shorts, and admired the contours. Then her eyes rested on the outline of his cock that tented his underwear before she tugged them downward and released him from confinement.

His dick reared outward from its nest of hair and, almost nonchalantly, she trailed her fingers along it and circled the crown then raised herself to her knees and kissed his stomach.

She traced her tongue and lips along his body, in a slow and seductive crawl, teasing the skin of his stomach and his lower belly, and he pushed his hips at her and uttered a growl deep in his throat, as if in anticipation of what she was going to do next.

She bit his stomach, kissed one hip bone then the other and raised her head. "Are you trying to tell me you want me to stop?" she asked.

Shay's voice was a hoarse whisper and he sounded distracted when he said, "Do I want you to — ? Nope. No way."

She nibbled her bottom lip and rested her hand on the hot, silken skin of his cock, then grasped him firmly. He throbbed in her palm and she squeezed him. He gave a deeper growl, like an angry wolf, which sent warmth pooling between her legs.

"I'm so glad," she said and left a moist trail with her tongue across his stomach, from one side to the other. "Otherwise" — she kissed the glans of his cock — "we'd have to take a rain check."

Shay's breathing was ragged and he gasped, arched and his dick brushed her face. "You've got no chance of that, lady," he said and his voice sounded harsh and uneven.

Annie traced his length with a finger. Her whole body was hungry for him, and she rubbed her cheek on the satin-smooth crown and squeezed his straining shaft. "I guess—"

She bent over him once more and paused, teasing him deliberately, then slowly licked him and created intricate circles along his skin until she took the glans in her mouth, sucked once and released him.

She was panting when she glanced at Shay again, loving and wanting to see his reaction to her ministrations. He looked at her and their gazes locked, the sexual tension between them heightening, both knowing what the other wanted and anticipating and savoring the outcome.

Annie gave him a last wanton look and licked along his length. He was rock hard and bucked his hips to meet her.

Without pausing, she gripped him and began to squeeze and release him intermittently. At the same time, she took him into her mouth.

Shay's moans and grunts excited her and she sucked hard and pumped him. With each pull of her mouth, she extended her reach and he rested his hand on the back of her head and guided her. Annie obliged by taking him even deeper.

She tasted the faint salty tang of him and loved how he filled her mouth. She stroked his balls, cupped them and marveled at how tight they'd become.

Shay's breathing sped up and his groans increased. "Holy. Fucking. Shit," he said and his hips moved hard, signaling he was on the verge of his climax.

Annie's own desire was a burning need and she moved her mouth on him faster, alternately lapping at him with her tongue and moving her hand until she heard him exclaim in warning, "Annie—"

Shay grasped her arm and she stopped, releasing him. He drew her roughly up beside him and forced her to lie on her back.

He rose to his knees and moved between her legs. His hands were shaking when he reached for the button on her combat pants and he fumbled with it.

He finally managed to unzip them and she lifted her hips so he could pull them down her legs. Once he'd removed them, he threw them over his shoulder. His gaze roamed her body and she felt scorched by the hot look he gave her.

At last, his eyes met hers and he winked, which was totally at odds with the intensity of the passion they shared, before he grasped her panties and tried to yank them off.

He was rough. There was a sudden ripping sound and the delicate material came away in his hands. He tossed them aside to join her discarded trousers.

Shay grasped her hips and tugged her toward him. He skimmed his hands from her hips downward to the front of her thighs, then trailed his fingers inward before he pushed her legs farther apart.

He massaged the hyper-sensitive skin there before he touched her entrance. A sensation like an electric shock torched her and settled as a sizzling blaze in her stomach.

She was gloriously wet and her nipples were swollen and aching. She moaned and thrust her hips against his roaming fingers, desperate for him to enter her.

Continuing his assault on her body, Shay inserted one finger, then a second, before he thrust them both deep into her.

He rubbed her in a circular pattern and Annie yelped.

"Shay," she murmured, "please."

Tension built in her muscles and her climax coiled inside her. The sensation peaked and she fell over the edge into her orgasm with a shattering pleasure that made her cry out.

Shay gave Annie no chance to recover. He shuffled his way forward on his knees then lowered himself on top of her.

His erection prodded her and, when he moved, his dick throbbed against her thigh. She was desperate for him and wanted him to make love to her — hard — and she tried to settle on his cock so he could enter her.

Annie circled his hips with her legs and pulled his pelvis downward so he nudged her entrance. He moved over her clit with a slow and delicious rhythm.

She tried to meet his straining cock and whimpered when he avoided entering her. Instead, he took hold of himself and rubbed her folds. She closed her eyes and ground against him, the delicious friction building into an excruciating pleasure.

Annie slid her hands from his ass up to his back.

He lowered himself onto her once more and she kissed his shoulders in different places, sucking and nipping the skin

Fire coiled in her belly and spread outward until she felt that if Shay didn't make love to her right then, she would catch fire.

Shay left her mouth and kissed her neck and shoulder, leaving a scalding trail across her skin, and volcanic shivers rippled through her.

"You smell so good," he murmured.

Annie could only moan in response, because the desire was becoming uncontrollable and had rendered her speechless.

Shay seemed to lose patience and, rising once more to his knees, he clasped her hips and raised her. Annie understood, and as she stared into his eyes and aligned herself with his cock, he thrust into her in a single smooth move.

Annie gasped. "Oh—" she said.

For a few moments, they were both still, then she bent forward and kissed his shoulder and neck. She clenched her legs around his hips and her whole being became focused on that one point where their bodies joined.

Shay pushed himself farther into her and rotated his hips, his dick touching the walls at her center. Annie shut her eyes, clawed at his sweating chest and bucked her hips, frantic for release.

"Open your eyes, Annie," Shay ordered in a low but compelling voice. "I want you to watch me when I come and I'm gonna do the same."

Annie obeyed him without question, and he thrust back inside her, his stiff shaft plundering her. The friction created an intense wave of pleasure and she cried out, encouraging and urging him to take her over the edge.

Shay quickened his pace, and with deep and powerful strokes, he rocked against her clit and an incredible need ignited and consumed her.

As their passion rose, Annie began to utter little encouraging moans and Shay's thrusts grew more forceful. He hammered her with savage, relentless strokes.

As her onrushing orgasm began to spiral out of control, she forgot where she was and who might hear and her whimpers grew louder as she clawed at Shay's shoulders. Their gazes locked and he moved his cock in tiny plunges, as if he only had a tenuous self-control remaining. She sensed he was as close to coming as she was.

Annie's orgasm rolled over her and her climax exploded. She tensed, every nerve on fire and her body quivering.

The pleasure was so overwhelming that she wanted to scream. As her muscles clenched tight around his cock, Shay jerked his head back, gave a guttural moan and rammed into her one final time before he came hard.

As he emptied himself into her, Annie's heart thundered in her chest and she gasped for air. She felt the dampness of sweat on his back and she lightly ran her fingers through the moisture then caressed him.

Panting, Shay licked the shadowed hollow between her neck and shoulder, kissed her moist skin then pulled out of her. He rolled off her and tugged a folded blanket under his head. He stretched out, pulled her to him and hugged her, and she kissed a tiny pulse that raced in his neck.

Annie nestled into him, murmuring endearments. She nuzzled his sweating chest and neck then rested her forehead at the base of his throat. She wanted to stay in his arms for always.

Shay brushed wispy tendrils of hair from where they clung to her damp forehead and he stared into her eyes. "Holy shit," he said.

Annie's lips were bruised and swollen from his forceful kisses. "Is that a good 'holy shit' or a bad 'holy shit'?" she murmured, her voice hesitant.

Shay traced a thumb along her mouth and she kissed it before licking the tip. He jerked his hand away and his grin turned into a lazy, satisfied one. It was sexy as hell, like the man himself, and it captivated her.

"It's neither," he replied. "It's a *wow* holy shit."

Annie's laugh was seductive. "Marks out of ten?" She lowered her gaze and stared at him from beneath her eyelashes.

Shay was silent for a moment, as if thinking. "Off the charts."

A meaningful silence flowed between them, then he twisted his lips in a grimace. "Sorry to destroy the moment, but I think we need to get outta here. We don't wanna push our luck."

Annie sighed and shook her head. "Do we have to? I mean, I know we do, but I want to stay here all night," she replied, contentment flowing through her body.

Shay stroked her arm with his finger making her skin prickle and a corkscrew of desire coiled in her stomach.

"Yeah, it definitely sucks, but it's gotta be done," Shay replied.

Annie pouted but untangled herself from him and got to her feet. She turned in a circle, hunting for her uniform, and happened to glance at Shay.

He was staring at her body with an expression of lust on his face.

She struck an exaggerated sexy pose and placed one hand on her hip. "Like what you see, Master Sergeant?" she asked in a seductive voice. "Changed your mind about staying?"

Shay grinned. "I'm getting there," he replied and looked down at his semi-erect cock. "But nope – and that's against my better judgment."

Annie laughed and turned back to looking for her clothes. After discovering various items which appeared to have been scattered all over, she collected them and began to dress.

Once she and Shay were ready, they folded the blankets and restacked them then checked the shelter to ensure they had left nothing behind. She found her shredded panties and, with a smoldering look at Shay, she pushed them into the pocket of her trousers.

At last, Shay moved to the door flap and bent to unfasten it. Before he did, he stopped and glanced at her. He looked sheepish and he cleared his throat before he said, "You know, Annie. You're some kinda woman. Just remember, you're mine and no ex-husband is gonna go near you."

Annie's stomach muscles quivered and warmth heated her face. "That's a bit arrogant," she said and smiled to take the edge off her words. "But I can deal with it."

Shay nodded and raised the zipper. He pushed it open a little before putting his head out and he glanced around before beckoning her to come to him. She stood by his shoulder, he took her hand in his and they stepped outside.

It was daylight. Annie wasn't sure how long she and Shay had been together, but it must have been some time, because the sky was blue, the sun was up and the temperature had risen.

There was nobody in their immediate vicinity, although Annie could hear voices coming from the occupied accommodations, and she was relieved, because a man and a woman exiting an empty shelter would have looked very suspect.

Shay resealed the tent then drew her to stand between it and the next one, where they were partially concealed.

He dropped her hand, turned to face her and pulled her to him. They stared at each other.

Shay ran his finger down her cheek then said, "I gotta go. I've been gone too long. My guys will be coming up with crazy ideas of what I've been doing, none of them polite. I'm going outside the wire tomorrow for a few days. Not sure of the mission duration but I'll come and see you when I get back. Okay?"

Annie's anxiety surged. The dynamics of their relationship had changed. If she guessed right, then Shay felt the same way she did and that meant caring and worrying more about each other's safety.

The emotion wasn't necessarily a bad thing, but it wasn't good either. It shifted the focus from alertness and concentration to something that could result in combat ineffectiveness. It was a callous way of looking at their relationship, but where they were, their lives were full of danger. The slightest lapse could literally mean death.

Annie swallowed the words of concern she wanted to say and nodded. "Everything's good," she said with bravado. "I won't be going anywhere."

Shay kissed her hard then let her go. He tipped his chin and said, "Go. Get outta here."

Annie stepped away from him and smiled. She drank him in so she could keep the images in the forefront of her mind when things got tough and she needed him.

He backed away from her, offered her a lazy grin then about-turned and walked away.

Annie watched him as his pace quickened and she wondered if she would see him again, but she dismissed the thought as soon as it popped into her mind.

Of course she would. Now she had things to do and people to see and she needed to be gone. She walked away from what she now called *their* place and took a winding route through the surrounding accommodations until she reached the rough path that ran parallel to the tents.

Her pace slowed and she thought about the past few hours she'd spent with Shay. She blushed when she remembered their lovemaking and how she'd been so uninhibited and eager for him.

Annie touched her lips and found them tender, and as she moved, there was a pleasurable soreness between her thighs, evidence that Shay had left behind elements of his forceful sexual appetite.

She couldn't help but smile at her recollections and she hugged herself with hot delight when she thought of seeing him again.

She was approaching the hospital, tucking in her T-shirt and hoping it didn't look as though she'd spent her time with a very sexy and rough marine, although she was sure it was written all over her face.

Annie stopped when she heard a man's and a woman's voice coming from near the hospital. She wouldn't be able to slip inside unnoticed.

Okay. I'll just have to wing it.

She went on and looked to see if she could tell who the people were, and she discovered a couple in each other's arms, standing to the rear of the shelters.

She was shocked to see the distinct figure of Captain Euan Lloyd but nearly gasped out loud when she recognized the slim woman with the long and curly red hair as Freya.

Oh, whoa. I wasn't expecting that. I am not *seeing this. Most definitely not.*

She tried to lighten her footsteps, but that was no mean feat in heavy combat boots, so, keeping her eyes on the figures and getting ready to run if she was spotted, she started to walk as though she were out on patrol— heel to toe, heel to toe, hoping her footfalls were muffled.

She thought she'd gotten away with it when Freya turned her head toward Annie. If her friend had been

Superwoman, she would have been pierced with laser eyes and struck down in her tracks.

Caught in the sergeant's line of fire, Annie snapped her head forward and almost ran the rest of the way to the entrance. She darted inside and headed at a fast walk to the laundry tent, where she could not only hide from what was going to be a very irate friend but where she could make a coffee while in the process of being a coward.

Annie heard heavy footfalls from somewhere behind her and knew her sergeant was tracking her with deadly intent. She reached the shelter with what felt like minutes to spare and set about filling the kettle and turning it on to boil.

She was setting out two mugs on the table when she heard the boots reach her location and come to a stop.

Annie half-glanced over her shoulder, saw Freya, who had a wary expression on her face, and smiled. "Hey, you. I'm making coffee. Want one?"

Freya didn't answer, but she entered the tent and walked past Annie to lean against the table and folded her arms.

"Yeah, I will. Thanks," she said at last.

Annie went back to spooning coffee into the cups then folded her own arms to wait for the water to boil.

The silence was heavy between the two women, with unspoken questions from Annie remaining unanswered.

"You didn't see that," Freya said in a low voice.

"What?" Annie said, turning to her friend.

"Out there. You didn't see what you saw."

Annie frowned. "That sounds a bit...convoluted," she said. "I absolutely didn't see what I thought I saw, though."

Freya sighed. "Good. I'm glad."

Annie stared at the kettle and the steam starting to come from its spout, and couldn't resist saying, "My lips are sealed."

Freya snorted with exasperation. "Annie—"

"Well, they are. Tightly zipped shut. I promise."

"What part of 'you didn't see anything' don't you get?"

"I'm so offended," Annie said.

"Huh." Freya fell silent until she continued, "Okay. I 'fess up. I suppose you've figured it out."

Annie looked at her friend once more. "Jeez, Freya. It was right under my nose. How long's it being going on?"

Freya sighed again. "Since the first week of deployment."

Annie was startled. "Yikes. That long? You dark horse. How did I not know?"

"I hope nobody knows and it needs to stay that way," Freya answered. "Regulations and all that fraternization with the lower ranks shit."

"That must be tough."

"Yep, it sure is. But we do get our moments of alone time."

Annie went to her friend and hugged her. "I'm seriously glad for you," she said. "You deserve somebody good."

Freya cuddled her back. "Thanks, honey. Now, are you gonna tell me where you've been for the past coupla hours? And don't tell me you went nightclubbing."

Annie turned her back on Freya, went to the kettle and watched its machinations with exaggerated concentration.

"Let me guess…Master Sergeant O'Rourke."

Annie swung around to confront her friend and saw the self-satisfied grin on her face. "Okay. You saw us?"

Freya shook her head. "Nope. Your body language has been crazy ever since you met him. You go into defensive mode when questioned about him and your evasiveness was off the charts. Classic romance or lust symptoms."

Annie's cheeks heated and Freya laughed out loud. "Gotcha," she said. "Is it serious?"

Annie nodded. "I think so," she answered.

"Lotsa luck, babe. You deserve him. He's a catch."

Annie smiled as she remembered the time they had spent together. "Luck back atcha," she said. "Now, are you gonna let me make this coffee or are we gonna let the kettle boil itself to death?"

Freya joined Annie in laughter, and for a few moments, things seemed almost normal. Annie reveled in it, because there was no way to tell if it would last for much longer.

Chapter Twenty-Six

"This is CNN News bringing to you breaking news that the Operation Iraqi Freedom invasion has begun. We will stay on the air with special bulletins giving you, the people of the United States, as much information as we know concerning this momentous occasion in our history.

"We now bring to you reports of the events that preceded the opening salvoes of this Middle Eastern war."

Annie sat huddled on top of the clothes washer, clasping her blood-spattered arms around her knees and pulling them to her chest as if they could ground her, her forehead resting on them, eyes closed.

She didn't want to be reminded of the past few hours. All she wanted was to have some peace to gather her strength, but her mind kept flipping back and raking up images she wanted to forget but couldn't dismiss.

For two days, there'd been no respite. Sleep was a vague memory and washing or taking a shower were a distant dream. They'd eaten on the move, but even that simple action had been infrequent, and her body had existed on grabbed crackers, candy bars and mouthfuls of water.

Supplies and drugs had been depleted at an astonishing rate, and once no longer available, improvised procedures with what was left had been carried out. Central lines had been done without sterile gloves because access needed to be gained within moments or the patients would have died.

They'd managed to give antibiotics, and the casualties had received infection-control measures once stabilized, but on many occasions, there'd not been enough time to deal with sterile techniques.

Some of the injured medevacked to the field hospital had stayed in her head and couldn't be dismissed. There had been a United States soldier who'd been within ten feet of the impact point of a large mortar round and had suffered severe extremity and soft-tissue wounds, including a traumatic amputation of the right hand, a left arm radial artery injury, a near amputation of his left leg and acute injuries to the right.

The team had operated and stabilized him and he'd been medevacked to Mosul, but his low moans of pain while he'd been with them had been pitiful.

A twenty-four-year-old British Royal Marine with multiple AK-47 gunshot wounds... He had been shot through the right side of his chest and the right and left lower extremities. He was now at the combat support hospital in Mosul for ongoing care, but while with them, he'd pleaded for his mother.

A twenty-year-old male soldier had been injured in the right side of his neck when his forty-millimeter grenade launcher had misfired and exploded as he'd attempted to clear it.

The patient had presented completely alert with normal vital signs. He'd complained of mild hoarseness, and upon examination, it had been discovered that a fragment had entered through the right side of his neck. There were no overt signs of vascular injury, the surgical team had performed damage control surgery and he'd been medevacked out. While he'd been with them, the sound of his crying had been almost soul-destroying.

Those patients had been a small part of a mass casualty event that had almost overwhelmed the forward surgical team.

Annie released her knees, raised her head and pressed the heels of her hands to her eyes, trying to crush the harsh pictures into oblivion. She wanted to run but there was nowhere to go. She needed to forget but she didn't know how.

Shadows crept in from the periphery of her mind and she felt a gnawing fear that she wasn't going to be able to handle what was to come over the next days, weeks or months.

She teetered on the edge of a depthless abyss and was one step away from tumbling into it and being sucked down into its stygian horrors.

She didn't want to die. She yearned to go home. She wanted her son—to feel the baby softness of his skin, the fine silkiness of his hair and to hear his gurgles of laughter. She needed Shay, his strength and his passion that could wipe out the churning emotions of dread and fear that were all but consuming her.

Like a child, she also wanted her parents. She craved the feelings of protection and love that she had experienced from them until she'd joined the Army and had left the haven that had been her home.

But there was no going back. Her life was here and now and she had to deal with it. No matter that she wanted to lie down and sleep or run as fast as she could — she wouldn't quit, she wasn't going to shut down and she wasn't going to stop trying.

She heard the crackle of the tent flap and turned to see who had disturbed her.

Freya approached and held out a bottle of water. The sergeant remained silent and Annie took the proffered drink, cleared her dry throat and said, "Thanks," in response.

With a hand that trembled, she fumbled with the cap, managed to unscrew it and took a mouthful of the lukewarm liquid. Her friend leaned against a table and Annie noticed that strands of the sergeant's hair had come loose from her normal harsh bun and hung untidily about her pale face.

Her eyes held a faraway expression, and for the first time since she'd known her, Annie could see that Freya was as shell-shocked as the rest of the forward surgical team.

Annie straightened her legs and swung them so she was sitting on the edge of the clothes washer. She stared at her bottle of water, as if all the answers to her problems were contained in the clear liquid, then said, "How're things out there?"

At first, she thought the sergeant hadn't heard her, then Freya turned her gaze on her. "Quiet...for the moment." She paused. "That won't last. What about you?"

Annie shrugged. "What can I say? There're no words —"

Freya interrupted her. "No, there aren't."

They were silent for a few moments, each deep in their own thoughts, unwilling or unable to talk. At last, Annie asked, "How many patients do we have?"

Freya sighed. "Seven at the last count. Three are ready to be medevacked out. Then we can move the two in the rest area into the care unit. But don't hold your breath that it'll stay that way."

Annie slid off the edge of the washer and regained her feet. "I guess I'd better go see to the clearing up." She sipped from her water and stretched.

"Yep," Freya agreed. "We need to get it done, just in case we get more incoming."

The conversation between them was mundane. Annie couldn't think of any words she could use to support her friend. It was beyond her to sort out her own feelings at that point and she was certainly in no position to allay any fears the sergeant might have.

As much as she wanted to, the only solution to her own chaotic emotions was to file them away in her mental strongbox, to seal them in until she had space and time to deal with them in her own way. Until then, she was useless to anyone else.

Freya straightened. "Okay. Let's —"

Her words were cut off when the harsh sound of the klaxon rent the air. They stared at each other and a shiver ran along Annie's spine.

"Here we go again," Freya exclaimed and flung her bottle in the sink, hurried to the door and stepped out into the tunnel.

Annie threw her bottle on the floor. There was no time to wash the blood off her hands or change her fluid-soaked scrubs. There were no more moments where she could catch her breath or find a safe place for her thoughts. Her mental box was full and all she could do was run to do what she could.

Annie followed Freya and they ran to the operating room. Once again, the essence of war and the physical evidence of death and destruction struck her as she saw the forward surgical team preparing for what was to come.

The alarm stopped abruptly and Annie grabbed a mask and tied it on. Gathering her reserves of energy, she joined three people jogging out of the hospital to wait for the incoming medevac.

Outside, it was dark. Annie looked up at the night sky and wondered why the moon still shone and the stars carried on twinkling. In other parts of the world, life was going on as normal while she and her colleagues stood in the cold in a war-torn country.

She saw the red light in the cockpit from the inbound Blackhawk and watched as it flew over the perimeter of the base on final approach. It hovered, flared then touched down and she and the others ran toward it, their actions shifting to what was needed.

The group of four ducked beneath the slowly spinning rotors and stopped at the open side door of the helicopter. The litter was slid into their waiting hands, each taking a far corner of the stretcher and automatically assessing the patient for excessive bleeding and shock.

A medic jumped from the cabin and began to explain to them the nature of the injuries and treatment given. When he had completed his report, Annie and her colleagues turned and began to jog across the gravel toward the emergency entrance.

They were approximately twenty feet from the helo when the base siren began its nightmarish rising and falling. Giant Voice—a loudspeaker system that imparted strategic information and warned of incoming enemy missiles — joined it by announcing in emotionless tones, "Incoming. All personnel take cover."

The medic to the left of her cursed out loud and Annie's heart raced. Icy fear coursed through her veins and someone shouted, "Let's get inside, people, before we're fucked." Then she heard another noise that dried up all the moisture in her mouth. She lifted her gaze and stared in the direction of one of the Patriot missile platforms.

Time seemed to slow down. There was a second, louder noise that sounded like cold water thrown onto a hot skillet, then a nineteen-foot long, four-hundred-pound Patriot warhead — one of sixteen in the launcher — roared upward into the sky.

At an approximate speed of five thousand and sixty-two miles per hour, it trailed a white and vaporous elongated cloud of rocket propellant, and moonlight glinted on its dull gray fuselage. The hush of the desert was shattered as the roar of its ignition turned into a deep crackling bellow, like that of a jet fighter with its engines on reheat.

Unable to tear her gaze away, Annie followed its path. She knew with a deep sense of foreboding that its course was programmed to intercept incoming hostile ordnance that was heading to their location, and she scanned the sky but couldn't see anything en route toward the base.

She knew it was there and coming, because the Patriot had locked on and nothing would keep it from what it was created to do.

Annie and the others were still moving toward the hospital, but she kept her eyes on the missile, and when it suddenly arced and veered left at a forty-five-degree angle like a striking snake, she gasped.

A tiny bright light was growing larger at an astonishing speed and heading on a straight trajectory toward her. She stumbled in horror.

It was getting close and there were probably only seconds before it would impact her surroundings.

Please, God, let it be shot down. I don't want to die.

The plea ran through her mind, and within a second of thinking it, there was an enormous explosion hundreds of feet in the air outside the perimeter.

The Patriot had successfully intercepted the enemy rocket and the resulting dazzling white light burned her eyes. She watched as the two missiles disintegrated into a shower of flaming red splinters of metal that hovered for a moment then slowly, like the incandescent sparks from exploding fireworks, began to drift downward toward the earth.

The medic ducked and swore again and the nurse in front of Annie said, "Shit," in a high breathless voice.

Nobody spoke until they'd reached the entrance to the hospital, where they were met by other members of the surgical team and the casualty was handed over for assessment.

Freya approached Annie and put a hand on her shoulder. "What the fuck was that?" she asked.

Annie clasped her hands together to stop the shaking that had seized them, then leaned forward to catch her breath. "Incoming hostile missile," she answered at last. "A SCUD. We were lucky. A Patriot intercepted it."

Freya nodded. "Okay. Let's get back to work and hope that's the last we see of those things."

* * * *

Some hours later, Annie had cause to reflect on Freya's words. Casualty-wise it was quiet. All the patients had been medevacked out, except for the recent admission, who remained under observation.

There had been the distant sounds of explosions and gunfire and the constant activation of the base siren had started to fray everyone's nerves, including her own.

Each time the silence was ripped apart by the warning sound, Annie's heart rate increased and the tension in the hospital rose until it was almost palpable.

She would find herself holding her breath and waiting to see if whatever had been launched at them had been intercepted. Each time she heard the explosion confirming a hit, she sagged with relief.

The major had ordered all personnel to wear tactical vests and place individual weapons in areas where they could be to hand and used, if necessary. The body armor restricted movement and was uncomfortable but Annie was convinced that a few hours of discomfort more than made up for being shot or hit by flying shrapnel from high explosives.

The sirens had at last ceased their unearthly howl and Annie found herself cleaning and setting the triage area to rights, mainly to keep her mind occupied and her nerves calm. The rest of the staff had taken the opportunity to go to the rest area to eat, and she had found herself alone.

Even though she was occupied, Annie's thoughts turned to Shay and their last meeting. She remembered their lovemaking — how her body had responded to him without inhibition and restraint and how he had made her feel. Heat suffused her face and she was relieved there was nobody with her, because she was sure she was blushing.

She thought she was in love with him. People said a person would know if they were in love, but loving someone so soon after meeting them went against everything she believed about relationships.

If she was, then all the promises she'd made to herself meant absolutely nothing. She could be honest and say with certainty that she'd fallen for him in a big way, but love? She shied away from the truth of that, but her pulse fluttered when she wondered if he felt the same way about her.

Her thoughts turned to his mission and her anxiety stirred. She was sure that if anything happened to him, her life would never be the same again. Something would be ripped from her that could never be replaced and she prayed to whoever might be listening that he would be safe.

The turmoil of conflicting emotions made her uneasy. She was an adult, but right at that moment, she felt as though she was a teenager again, experiencing the adolescent chaos of the crush she'd once had on Shay. She had to get her head on straight and put her personal issues aside.

Annie sighed and glanced around her to confirm the area was as clean as it could be and ready for any casualties that might arrive.

She went back into the operating tent, checked to make sure the section was also ready and decided to join the others in the rest area. She was hungry and thirsty and needed a moment or two to relax.

She was about to make her way there when the sirens sounded again and she hurried toward the tunnel that went into the next shelter. She was near it when her whole world exploded.

Time seemed to stand still and the lights went out. She was hit by a wave of hot air and a concussive force pummeled her body. The blast lifted her and she was hurled some distance across the tent to collide with a solid metal object. She hit the floor hard and something heavy toppled onto her chest, pinning her to the surface beneath her.

The pain was instantaneous. Her sternum felt crushed, her breath left her lungs and she screamed inside as she tried to draw in a breath. She couldn't expand her chest fully and, with terror gripping her in its talons, she tried to push the weight off her, but she was weak and the item wouldn't budge.

Dust was heavy in the air, adding to her inability to breathe, and her chest tightened. Unbidden thoughts flashed through her mind.

I can't breathe. I'm going to die. Aiden! Shay!

She would never see her son again. The relationship between her and Shay would cease to exist, as would she, and the thought was as painful as the injuries to her body.

I won't die like this.

Someone screamed and glass shattered. The smell of burning stung her nose and she heard the crackle of fire. There was distant shouting, then something hit her head and the side of her face. There was another explosion — this time of agony — then…blackness.

Chapter Twenty-Seven

Annie regained consciousness, trembling. Her heart raced and her muscles convulsed. Pain lanced through her chest and she moaned, the sound like that of a wounded animal. A relentless pounding resonated inside her skull and the constant tremors seizing her limbs turned to violent shivers that racked her slim frame.

The unrelenting torment became secondary when she realized with mind-numbing shock that she couldn't see.

She fought to open her eyes and her fear became white-hot needles of terror when her eyelids refused to obey her brain's commands. She refused to accept that she was blind and, determined not to let panic overwhelm her, she forced herself to take a deep, calming breath to try to quell the dread that threatened to choke her.

Her muscles became rigid with tension and she lay still and tried to slow the frantic beating of her heart. After a few moments, she attempted to open her eyes once more, but it was as though they had been gummed shut with a very effective sealant.

At her persistence, a sharp stinging sensation assaulted the delicate tissue and Annie gasped. The discomfort increased in severity, but despite that, she was unwilling to give up. Her perseverance won out when in small increments, her lashes tore away from the fragile skin beneath her eyes and she managed to open them, even though it was only to the merest of slits.

Electric light almost blinded her and she blinked and winced at her eyes' tenderness. They burned and smarted, as if a handful of sand had been flung in them. But, little by little, her vision cleared and she felt an enormous sense of relief.

Her small moment of triumph was crushed when the throbbing in her head ratcheted up until she thought her skull was going to break open. Nausea coiled in her stomach and all she could hear was the sound of her wavering breaths, loud and guttural in her ears.

Spasms snatched at her limbs again, causing them to twitch and tremble. Sharp stabs of pain of varying degrees of intensity flayed at her body and panic surged through her once more. She wondered what was wrong with her.

Annie drew in another deep breath and let it out. *Get a hold of yourself, girl. You need your wits about you, not to go into panic mode.*

The pounding in her head faded to a level she could deal with and the tension eased from her muscles. She sighed and stared at the ceiling. She immediately recognized where she was and some calmness flooded through her.

I'm in a hospital. So, I've been in an accident but I'm safe!

It was at that point that the veil of amnesia lifted from her mind, and with the physical force of a hammer blow, memories surged back of the field hospital being hit.

A single blast followed by a concussive force that lifted her off her feet and threw her across the operating room, where she came up hard against some form of metal equipment.

She heard a piercing scream and the sound still resonated in her head. It was the last noise she heard before something heavy impacted her chest – almost crushing her – and another object landed on her head and face. There was an intense moment of agony then...nothing.

Annie licked her dry and cracked lips and winced as pain streaked down the left side of her face. It felt as though somebody was attacking her cheek and jaw with needles and it brought tears to her eyes. She froze, as though by doing so, she could banish her discomfort to the recesses of her brain.

She wanted to scream but was able to suppress the sound, because she knew if she allowed the noise its freedom, she wouldn't be able to stop.

By degrees, the pain faded to a tolerable level and she released her pent-up breath. Aside from her other injuries, which appeared to be minor, she now knew her face was hurt and it must be quite bad. Whether it was a bone fracture or a significant wound, there had been some damage done.

She had to know the extent of her injuries. Once she had that knowledge, she could begin to deal with the fact that she was hurt. She would know what it was and could start on the emotional road of accepting whatever disfigurement she had sustained.

With that aim uppermost in her thoughts, she forced the memory of what had happened at the hospital to the back of her mind, and with the utmost care, she flexed her jaw then opened her mouth.

At the movement, it felt as though someone was cutting her face with a knife. The skin on her cheek and jaw was tight and inflexible, and it was such a sickening sensation that she dry-heaved and thought for a moment that she was going to be ill.

Annie was stubborn and determined not to let the discomfort divert her from gauging the level of damage she'd sustained, but, as she persisted, the pain increased and became almost unbearable. She relaxed her features and lay still, willing the torment to pass. Her heart raced with anxiety when she realized her facial injuries were far more serious than she had initially feared.

When there was nothing but a dull ache remaining, and although she was reluctant to cause herself any further suffering, she was compelled to investigate further. Without wasting any more time, she tried to raise her hand so she could touch the wound.

Something tugged at the crook of her elbow, restricting movement and causing a brief twinge then tenderness. She gritted her teeth, lifted her head from the pillow and moved her arm so she could see what was causing it.

An eighteen-gauge catheter had been inserted into a vein with double tubes running from its hub up to two clear bags of fluid. They hung from a stand and she tried to read the small labels, then studied them and at last identified fluid resuscitation for circulatory shock in one and what appeared to be antibiotics in the other.

An ambulatory heart monitor sat on top of a tall aluminum trolley to her right and a quiet blipping impinged on her hearing. The sensor placed on the finger of her right hand sent signals to the machine, and she saw a white strip of paper with green tracing dangling from it. She tilted her head to see if she could work out if everything was normal, but couldn't decipher the results.

She stared at the screen with its ever-changing readouts and saw that her blood pressure, pulse and respiration were within normal parameters, so she was still very much alive. Once she had that confirmation, she turned her attention from the machine and gazed at her other hand.

Annie swallowed and wished someone would bring her some water to drink. Her throat had already been dry, but now her mouth was completely devoid of all moisture and her tongue felt as rough as sandpaper.

Dismissing the images of a glass of cold water full of ice, she raised her free hand so she could look at it. Her fingers quivered with faint tremors — whether from anxiety or weakness she couldn't tell — and she curled them into a fist before straightening them once more. She shut her eyes and rested her fingertips on her left jaw.

She felt swelling and hissed through her teeth. It encompassed the whole side of her face and the tenderness almost made her cringe, but she carried on tracing the distention along her cheekbone.

She'd barely moved them an inch or so before she discovered what was wrong. It wasn't until she'd reached the outer corner of her eye that she knew what injury she had sustained and its extent.

Her eyes filled with tears but she blinked them back and tentatively touched along the length of the wound. She noted its curved scimitar-like shape that started approximately one-half inch above her cheekbone before it swept down almost to the corner of her mouth.

Annie noted the raised rigidity of it, the puckering of the skin and the soreness, and her heart sank. She had no idea how many stitches there were, and while she knew the repair would have been done with the utmost care to lessen scarring, she was in no doubt she would be marred for life and probably would require cosmetic surgery, if she were vain enough to want to put herself through that procedure.

Right at that moment, however, she couldn't even begin to think about what she would do until she saw and came to terms with what she would look like when the wound had healed.

A smothering wave of tiredness, both mental and physical, washed over her and she rested her hand back on the blanket. She wanted nothing more than to relinquish control, wallow in self-pity and cry her eyes out or, at the very least, go back to sleep and hope that when she woke up, everything would have been nothing but a nightmare.

Annie didn't have the luxury of any of that. She chastised herself for her weakness and told herself she should be grateful because she was still in one piece *and* alive, which was something she couldn't say for others.

She needed to get back on her feet and return to the surgical team, because they would need every available pair of hands. With that in mind, it was going to be impossible for her to sit around and do nothing while others were fighting, hurting and in some cases, dying.

Okay, Annie McKendrick. What's done is done. Start as you mean to go on.

She thought about Shay and emotion tugged at her heart.

Is he still out there?

Will he come and see me when he finds out what's happened?

Will he still want me when he sees my face?

What if he decides I'm not the woman I was?

Doubts about whether he cared enough for her to be able to look at her warred with a shameless yearning to see him. Just his presence alone would be enough to strengthen her resolve and boost her confidence to get through what she had to.

Annie felt alone with no answers to the questions that churned through her mind, and she pushed all thoughts and feelings with respect to Shay toward the virtual bottomless black box with its reinforced lid where she banished all memories and images that had the power to hurt her.

There was no time for a pity party, and at last she was able to concentrate on her present situation without distractions. Mindful of her injuries and the needle in her arm, she started to push herself from her reclining position to a point where she was almost sitting and she rested against the pillows at her back.

Her body protested the prolonged activity, and sharp discomfort corkscrewed in her sternum and powered through other areas of her body before fading to dull aches. When she realized she wasn't about to fall apart, she relaxed and looked around.

She was in a ward, and she could only think that she'd been medevacked to the combat support hospital in Mosul, which would have been the closest to Sykes.

All the beds were occupied by patients who appeared to be either sleeping or unconscious. Some had green curtains pulled around them for privacy and she could hear a murmur of voices from behind one and a low moan from another.

Heart monitors, including her own, blipped quietly, air conditioning hummed in the background and, in a distant part of the hospital, she could hear hurrying footsteps then a loud metallic crash as something dropped to the floor.

Her gaze settled on two nurses in green scrubs who appeared from behind separate curtains. They began to move from patient to patient, lifting clipboards from the ends of the beds and studying them, their footwear squeaking annoyingly on the green linoleum floor.

On hearing the noise outside the ward, one of the nurses turned to look in the direction of the double swing doors, as if she expected them to be flung open at any moment. She must have noticed that Annie was conscious, because she put the chart she was holding back in its place, about-turned and walked toward her.

"Welcome back," she said when she reached Annie's bedside and smiled. "How're you feeling?"

Without waiting for an answer, she placed two fingers on the pulse site on Annie's right wrist and glanced at a small watch pinned to the breast pocket of her top.

Annie licked her dry lips. "Like I've been trampled then dragged by a herd of elephants. Can I have a drink, please?"

The nurse remained silent for a moment longer then moved to a battered green bedside locker on Annie's left.

Annie turned her head gingerly and watched as the nurse poured half a glass of water from a full jug.

She reached out and gave the plastic container to Annie. "Here you go. Sip it. Don't gulp."

Annie did as she was told, almost moaning out loud when she took her first mouthful, relishing the liquid lubrication that soothed her parched mouth and throat.

Once she'd drunk her fill, she settled back against her pillows once more and studied the nurse.

"Will I live?" she asked, her voice hoarse.

The nurse moved to the foot of Annie's bed and unhooked her chart. She made a notation on it then put it back. "The name's Charlene," she said. "And yes, you'll live. You were lucky."

"What injuries do I have?" Annie asked, then pointed to her face. "Apart from this, of course."

Charlene gave Annie her full attention. "It's doctor's rounds soon. He'll chat with you, explain things and go over the next steps."

The nurse smiled at her once more and walked away to another patient's bed.

Annie felt frustrated at the less-than-satisfying response but was all too aware she was not the only patient that needed attending to. Regardless, she wanted answers, and as time passed – slowly – she grew impatient. By the time she finally heard voices in the corridor outside the doors and a small group of medical personnel entered the ward, she could have thrown something in frustration at the delay.

Her gaze rested on a harassed-looking Army captain leading three members of his staff. The group approached her bed and the officer unhooked the clipboard from its foot.

She grew uncomfortable when he remained silent while he studied her notes. She itched to say something but quashed her impatience. She wouldn't interrupt a doctor when he was concentrating.

Annie watched the captain for what seemed like minutes when it was probably only seconds and noticed he had stubble along his jawline, as if he hadn't shaved for a while, and there were dark circles beneath his eyes.

She was almost sure he hadn't slept for a few days, possibly since Operation Iraqi Freedom had begun. They would have been busy with casualties, and she felt a sense of guilt at her almost surely minor injuries compared to what they'd had to deal with.

At last, the officer replaced the clipboard and folded his arms. He directed his gaze toward her and a small smile broke the hardened planes of his face. "Glad to see you awake. How do you feel?"

"I'm good, sir," Annie answered, determined to convince him she was well enough to be discharged.

The captain continued to stare at her with an intense look in his blue eyes, as if he didn't believe her. "Uh-huh. Any headache?" he asked.

"It was pretty bad when I woke up, sir, but it's okay now."

"Do you remember what happened?"

Annie hesitated for a moment then nodded. "The hospital was hit by a SCUD," she replied. "Was anyone else hurt?"

"A few bumps and bruises," the officer said. "Everyone was very lucky. You suffered the worst of it."

A chill swept through her and she pleated the crisp white sheet that covered her. "Am I okay?" she asked at last.

The captain nodded. "You will be. You sustained a nasty hit to your head, resulting in a contusion, a swelling on your brain and a slight bleed. We had to put you into a drug-induced coma so the hematoma could reduce and to enable us to monitor the bleed. The last scan we gave you showed the trauma has decreased and there should be no further problems."

Annie nodded, inhaled a deep breath and let it out slowly. "How long was I out for and what happened to my face?" she asked.

"You've been here for a week. The object that hit your head also cut your face and caused a laceration. It was quite long and deep but it was clean and needed no debridement. We had to give you quite a few stitches. I know it might feel bad now, but it will heal and eventually will only leave a faint scar.

"You also suffered severe bruising to your sternum and various cuts and bruises. You're on the mend now, so you're a pretty lucky young lady."

Annie didn't feel lucky, because she'd lost a week of her life. Her parents would be freaking out and she wondered if Shay knew, but she managed a slight smile anyway. "When can I get back to Sykes?" she asked.

"Not for a couple of days, I'm afraid," the officer answered. "We need to give you another scan, check your cognitive functions and get those stitches removed. Once I think you're fully recovered, you'll be discharged."

"Thank you, sir," Annie said and wondered what she was going to do with herself for the next few days.

"Okay. Well, I'll check you over and see how things are going."

Annie felt like a robot when she said again, "Thank you, sir," but there was nothing much left to say.

The captain carried out a thorough examination, checking the pupil reaction of Annie's eyes, her blood pressure and pulse. He also had one of the nurses extract the catheter from her arm.

He probed the wound on her face, seemed satisfied then prodded her sternum. Annie guessed he was happy that everything was as it should be and he finally smiled at her and said, "You appear to be on the mend, McKendrick. You can get up and walk around for short periods of time.

"Take it easy, though. No rushing around, wild dancing or anything like that. I want you to keep taking the painkillers, because no doubt you still have a headache, no matter what you tell me." The captain raised an eyebrow knowingly. "If you start to get any dizziness, double vision or vomiting, you're to inform one of the nurses. Is that understood?"

"Yes, sir," Annie replied meekly, almost rolling her eyeballs.

I'm a medic, for God's sake. Like I don't know the symptoms of a brain injury.

"Okay. I'll leave you to rest or whatever."

The captain nodded at Annie and moved away from her bed to walk behind the closed curtains of the patient opposite her.

Annie huffed and folded her arms. She knew the saying that medical professionals always made the worst patients and she would have to hold her impatience in check, but she wanted to get back to the base so she could put this behind her.

She was jerked from her thoughts when Charlene approached her.

"Good news?" she asked.

"Sort of," Annie replied. "Do you have a mirror?"

Charlene pursed her lips. "We do," she said. "Are you sure you want it?"

Annie shrugged. "Not really, but I need to see what I've got to deal with."

"Okay. I'll be back in a minute."

The nurse walked away and left the ward, leaving Annie alone and wondering if she was doing the right thing.

Am I ready for this? Do I really want to see how messed up I am?

Nerves knotted her stomach and she felt sick. She closed her eyes and bit her bottom lip. She had to see her face to be able to move forward.

"Are you okay?"

Charlene's question startled her and Annie jumped and her eyes flew open.

"I'm good," she replied and took the small hand mirror that the nurse held out to her.

For a moment she almost changed her mind. It was no big deal to see herself right at that moment. She could wait until the stitches were out and the wound might look better. If it was as bad as she thought it was, it might set her back.

Her usual stubbornness took over and she lifted the mirror so it was positioned in front of her. Her heart jerked when she saw her face.

She already knew there was swelling and she'd guessed at the length of the wound, but she swallowed when she saw how bloodshot her left eye was and the livid yellow, green and purple of the surrounding socket, the colors spreading outward onto her forehead and vanishing into her hair and down to her ear. She had one hell of a black eye.

The laceration itself had been repaired with minute stitches, but the skin of her cheek was raised in a ridge and puckered, distorting her features on that side of her face. It was a deep, angry red, although there was no sign of infection, which was some consolation.

Annie's heart sank. She'd never been vain about her looks, so it wasn't a case of being devastated that she would be scarred. The thought uppermost in her mind was how she would look to Shay and how it could affect his feelings for her. If she saw a look of revulsion on his face when they next met, it would break her heart.

Tears filled her eyes again and she despised how emotionally weak she'd become. She lowered the mirror and turned to Charlene, who had stayed by her bedside.

"I don't want any visitors," she said, and her words sounded like a death knell over her relationship with Shay.

Charlene was quiet for a moment. "Can I ask why?" she asked at last.

"I need to deal with this on my own...for now. Come to terms with it. Get myself well. I need to take a step at a time."

"Okay, if that's what you want. I'll inform the ward staff."

Annie felt desperate. "*Nobody*," she emphasized and heard the quiver in her voice.

Charlene stared at her then nodded. "I understand. Get some rest."

The nurse turned and walked away, and Annie lay back against her pillows and closed her eyes.

She was so tired. Her body hurt and so did her face, but none of her physical injuries could hurt her as much as the pain in her heart.

Chapter Twenty-Eight

It was mid-afternoon and two days after Annie had awoken from her coma. She sat on a rickety wooden bench in a small courtyard situated in the center of the hospital, waiting for a ride back to base on a Blackhawk helicopter that was coming in from Sykes to pick up supplies.

She'd been discharged that morning with a reasonably clean bill of health and she was now adhering to the Army's oft-quoted phrase 'hurry up and wait'.

Her bed had been needed by another patient and, as she'd had no gear to take with her apart from her ripped and stained uniform, which she was wearing, she'd decided to find somewhere peaceful in the medical facility where she could wait alone.

The quadrangle was just such a place. It wasn't much to look at, being a barren and sandy area enclosed on all sides by white-washed brickwork with square glassless windows and open to the sky.

Someone had placed a couple of benches in the meager shadows thrown by the overhanging roof of the hospital's internal walls, and perhaps the same person had planted two Tamarisk trees in wooden tubs, their leaves now covered in dust and wilting in the heat. Both actions might have been an attempt to make the environment appear pleasing to the eye, but the well-meaning thought hadn't worked.

While Annie was sequestered from the noise and organized chaos of her ward, the sunlight bounced off the walls and made her squint. It was hot and the heavy air was stifling. She was growing uncomfortable.

She was also thirsty, so she undid the cap of her bottle of water, sipped at the warm contents and thought back over the past forty-eight hours.

Annie had undergone another scan, the results of which had shown that the swelling in her brain where she had been struck had disappeared. She'd also sat through a series of tests — which she had passed with no problem — and was relieved that the blow had left no lasting disturbance to her cognitive functioning.

She still had a large, vivid bruise over her sternum and lower ribs, but apart from some pain when she coughed, she had no permanent effects from the injury.

The worst part had been when the stitches in her face had been removed. The wound had still been very sore, and while she knew what to expect from the snipping and tugging of having them extracted, the resultant pain had brought tears to her eyes.

After looking in the mirror the first time, she'd refused to do so again. She'd decided there was no point making herself feel worse about the disfigurement and she would need to bide her time until she had healed.

Once she'd seen her reflection for the second time, she had still sported a black eye, the colorful bruise marring her forehead and eye socket and extending downward to her jawline. The only good thing about the whole situation was that the inflammation had decreased, although the scar remained livid and pronounced.

The physical evidence of her injury would fade with time but the mental scars she'd received would take longer to heal. There was nothing she could do about any of it except get back to work and hope she could deal with her emotional turmoil when and if it became a problem.

When Annie had asked, nobody in the hospital seemed to have had any information on how Operation Iraqi Freedom was progressing. She knew war had been declared — she remembered the radio broadcast with clarity — but she'd lost a whole week of her life and had no idea whether any of her work colleagues had been injured in the attack on the field hospital. The nursing staff had no further details of what had happened.

She'd noticed an increase in incoming and outgoing patients on her ward and the staff were no longer as relaxed as they had once been. They rushed from one casualty to another with a sense of urgency, and as soon as the ill person had been removed from the critical care list, transferred to the recovery unit and their bed had become empty, there seemed to be only enough time to clean the bed space and change the linen before it was filled with another severely injured and usually unconscious casualty.

When Annie was mobile enough to get about on her own, she'd begun to make forays from the ward to other parts of the hospital. She had noticed a rise in noise levels in the corridors and a familiar tension in the atmosphere, like what was felt in the field hospital when the surgical team dealt with mass casualties. It had triggered a sense of urgency and frustration within her that she should be doing something to help.

She'd begun to grow bored with her enforced incarceration. While she knew she needed to heal and the feeling was unreasonable, she wanted to be back at the base and doing her job. Having nothing to do was ratcheting up her levels of impatience.

Now, she sat alone, waiting for her transport to take her to the airfield, and she tried not to think about Shay. He'd been on her mind a lot, even though she'd tried hard to focus on her recovery and not allow thoughts of her own personal situation get in the way of what was important.

Annie wondered if he knew what had happened to her and whether he'd tried to see her. If he was back at Sykes, then he did, but this wasn't a normal situation. Relationships could flourish in a combat zone, more intense and passionate than usual, but for the past few hours, she'd heard distant gunfire and explosions from within Mosul itself.

The noises had sounded like a firefight, which could mean war had come to the city. If that was the case, she doubted Shay would have had the time to even attempt to visit her. If by some miracle he *had* shown up at the hospital and been turned away at her order, then she only had herself to blame.

Annie's request not to receive visitors had been a knee-jerk reaction to memories of her disastrous marriage to Josh. The callous way he'd left her because she was pregnant shortly before Aidan's birth was an event that she didn't want to repeat.

She'd fallen hard for Shay, after promising herself she wouldn't be so gullible again, and after seeing her injury, she had presupposed, in a childish way, that he would be turned off by it and cut off their relationship. She'd judged him to be just as shallow as her ex-husband, which meant she might have destroyed any chance she had with him.

She'd had an idea that if Shay thought she wasn't interested and had stopped their newly formed relationship, he wouldn't come back and she would never see him again. *That* thought hurt more then she thought possible.

Annie sighed and glanced at her watch. There was still another hour before she needed to leave and she didn't want to sit around in the heat any longer, so she decided she would go hunt down a cup of coffee, which would waste a little more time.

She was about to stand when she sensed somebody watching her. The hair on the nape of her neck prickled and unease crept down her spine.

She scanned the courtyard, and when her gaze reached the open wooden door — the entrance to the area — her heart missed a beat then raced on at breakneck speed. For a moment she couldn't breathe and her stomach churned with nausea.

Shay was leaning against the doorframe watching her. His arms were folded and his legs were crossed at the ankles, but despite his casual stance, he looked far from relaxed. Even over the distance between them, she could see his face was emotionless and the tension he was feeling was evidenced by his rigid posture.

Annie froze. She was unable to move and she couldn't speak. Seeing him there was a shock, but then warmth flooded through her at the sight of him.

Her feelings were subdued and replaced with agitation when Shay uncrossed his arms and straightened. When he started to walk toward her, she wondered in a fleeting moment of desperation if she could run — and if she did, would he come after her.

On getting out of bed that morning, she had arranged her hair in a messy bun and now she quickly pulled out the borrowed hair grips and shook her head so a curtain of unruly hair fell to hide the left side of her face.

She didn't want to be at a disadvantage, so, clutching the water bottle as though it had the ability to keep her grounded, she rose and waited for Shay to reach her.

When he was a foot or so away, she dipped her head so he couldn't see her face, stayed mute and waited for him to speak.

When he also stayed silent, she said in a low voice, "What're you doing here?"

There was a moment's pause, then Shay said in a calm and cold voice, "What? Are you serious, Annie? What the hell do you *think* I'm doing here?"

Annie shook her head. All thought of how to extricate herself from the meeting and the ensuing conversation had disappeared.

"How did you find out where I was?" she asked and realized at once that it was a stupid question.

There was anger in Shay's voice when he answered, "Try this. Twenty-four hours ago, I get back from a mission and dump my gear. I attend a debrief and I get informed that the base was attacked with a SCUD and the field hospital blown up…with one casualty.

"Like the nut job I am, I leg it over to the hospital and speak to a certain Sergeant Marshall. It was a day of revelations, because she told me that it was my…*you* that'd been injured and medevacked to Mosul.

"In one helluva coincidence, my platoon and I have been given new orders and we've been transferred to Mosul because of all the shit that's kicking up here, so we move out. As soon as we land and, despite the fact that I could get shit-canned for doing it, I head over here, only to be told that you wanted no visitors—which, I guess, included me. That was a kick in the balls, to be blunt. Why, Annie?"

Annie licked her lips and swallowed. Then, against her better judgment, she said, "I don't want to get into this now, Shay. My transport is picking me up soon to take me to the airfield so I can get back to Sykes."

Shay didn't respond for a moment. When he spoke again, his voice was devoid of emotion. "Oh, okay. *You* don't want to get into it now. What the *fuck*? What's all this about?"

Annie knew he wouldn't leave her alone until she gave him an explanation, and she did owe him one, but she couldn't find any words to justify why she'd acted as she had.

He took a pace toward her and she stiffened. His closeness to her was a distraction and she felt the sensual pull of him and wanted to sink into his arms. She needed to move away from him before she changed her mind but there was no room to move. The edge of the bench was against the back of her knees and she was trapped.

Shay cupped her chin with his left hand and raised Annie's face so she was looking at him. With his right, he pushed the curls of hair away from her other cheek and stared at the scar. She saw a flicker of emotion in his eyes but his expression didn't change to one of revulsion or disgust.

"Is that the reason?" he asked at last.

Annie suppressed the feelings his touch had triggered and her voice was emotionless when she said, "Josh dumped me just for being pregnant. I wasn't about to let it happen again."

Shay traced her lips with his thumb and she shuddered. The barrier she'd erected began to crumble under his caress.

"I care that you've been hurt," Shay said and his tone had gentle undertones, his anger absent. "I've told you before that I ain't good with fancy words, so I don't give a flying fuck what you look like. Don't put me in the same class as your asshole of an ex."

He let go of her chin, moved his hand and cupped the side of her face.

Annie felt the warm roughness of his palm against her skin and she wanted to close her eyes and incline her head so she could nuzzle into it and savor his touch.

Shay moved even closer to her. "You need to listen to me, Annie. I've let you go three times and I'm not gonna let it happen again. Do you really think my feelings for you would change because you've been injured and you look a bit different? If you think that, then I'm gone."

Annie scanned his face and eventually settled on his eyes. After all, the old saying was that they were a window to the soul. She saw the truth of what he was saying in them and her own filled with tears and a small sob escaped her.

"No," she said at last. "I did think that—but not now. I was wrong. I'm sorry."

Shay stared at her, his green eyes as cold as a mountain lake. He was obviously calculating if she was telling the truth. At last, he moved toward her until there was no more distance between them.

Annie was of the same mind and met him. When they came together, his arms went around her in the intimate and demanding way she had come to love and need.

He held her tightly, as if he never wanted to let her go. Even though her bruises thrummed with discomfort at his grip, she thrilled at the feel of him, clasped her hands behind his head and pressed herself to him.

Shay and Annie stared at each other, their mouths so close that she could feel his warm breath on her lips. She wanted him to kiss her hard so their passion could wipe out the physical hurt of her injuries and the nightmare of the past few days and his need for her would help her begin to heal.

Shay touched her lips with his and his tongue teased their softness before he drew back. Annie stood on tiptoe and kissed him in answer, first on his mouth, then his nose and finally his jaw, and he grinned in alpha-male triumph.

He met her mouth in a searing kiss, the force of it causing the laceration on her face to twinge in protest. She ignored the pain and focused on his touch. She teased his hair with her fingers and delight coursed through her when he shuddered.

As with their previous kisses, their passion flared quick and hot and Shay drew away from her lips. "We need to stop," he murmured and tightened his arms about her waist. "Wrong place — and definitely not now."

Annie teasingly nibbled at his bottom lip before she said in a husky voice, "You love it."

"You got that right," Shay replied and proceeded to show her how much he did by kissing her forcefully and skimming his hands along her spine to caress her ass before he glided his palms around to her stomach.

Annie gasped and a fire ignited in her lower belly. She whimpered with a building need.

At last, Shay released her and stepped away. "The patients will have a field day if they see us," he said, his breathing harsh and uneven.

Annie smiled at him. "We'll make their day," she said then frowned. "Did you say you've been transferred to Mosul?"

"Yeah. The natives have been fighting. It's not a good sign in the current hostilities. It could end up being a shit fest, so we've been ordered to peace-keep. In other words, don't shoot until they shoot first or we see the whites of their eyes."

"Will you...be safe?" she asked and tried to keep the anxiety from her voice.

"Nobody is ever safe in a war, Annie," Shay answered. "I'll do my best, but I can't make any promises."

Annie slid her hands from the back of his head and rested the palms against his chest. "I'll see you when I see you, then," she said with as much bravado as she could muster.

Shay rested his forehead on hers. "You can count on it," he replied and his tone was soft. "As I said. There's no way I'm gonna let you go. I'll get back to you...somehow. Just be there."

Annie nodded, the depth of feeling that she had for him welling up and lodging in her throat, almost choking her.

Chapter Twenty-Nine

May second, zero-seven-thirty hours

It's been thirty-two days since I've heard from Shay.

The forlorn words popped into Annie's mind. She stopped wiping down the triage table and, for a moment, she wanted to leave what she was doing and hide. Fear that something might have happened to him — that he'd been killed — knotted her insides.

She knew it was a baseless anxiety. She'd gone into the relationship with her eyes wide open, aware that Shay might not come back to her. He had a job to do and he was good at it. But she couldn't get rid of the dark thought that fate sometimes had a habit of stepping in and destroying lives. A person's destiny couldn't be predicted, most particularly when they were on the frontline.

An icy trickle ran up Annie's spine. She didn't want to think about him, so, as had come to be the norm when suppressing her emotions where he was concerned, she pushed the thoughts to the back of her mind and continued with what she was doing.

Her mind drifted back to memories of the unrelenting stream of casualties — military, civilian, the enemy and, most pathetic of all, children caught in the crossfire — all maimed and suffering from disfiguring injuries.

After treatment, some had survived and had been transferred out to a hospital that hadn't yet been destroyed by weapons of war. Others had died and the mortuary dome had filled up, emptied then been refilled on an almost-daily basis.

She'd become almost desensitized to the horror and trauma, erecting a mental barrier to protect her from the emotions that came hand-in-hand with working in a frontline field hospital. She'd had to, otherwise she would never have been able to function.

Every day she carried out her duties as she'd been trained to do but had drawn back mentally from feeling sadness and guilt at what she witnessed. To allow herself to form a bond or care about the patients she looked after — even if it was only for a short time — would have been her undoing.

Annie remembered the names of some of the places she'd heard on the radio where prolonged and bloody fighting had taken place — the battles of Nasiriyah, Najaf, Basra and Karbala — and she wondered when it would end, if it ever did.

She was exhausted, as was everyone in the forward surgical team. On more occasions than she could count, they'd had to use the rest shelter as a makeshift recovery area for those coming around after surgeries when the care unit was full. This meant that she and her colleagues were limited to catching, at most, an hour of sleep anywhere and whenever they could. Even sixty minutes was a rare treat and only occurred when there was a brief lull in incoming patients.

Annie sighed. She tucked a loose skein of hair behind her ear and grimaced at the feel of the unwashed strands between her fingers. She would give anything for a hot shower and at least six hours of uninterrupted sleep. It wasn't going to happen in the foreseeable future, though, so she would just have to put up *and* shut up.

"Well, that's the best we can do," Freya said and moved to stand beside her.

Annie turned to her friend and, with an effort, smiled. "How're we doing for supplies?" she asked.

Freya leaned against the table and shook her head. "Not good. We're low on almost everything, including blood products and drugs. The hospital in Mosul being blown up really screwed us over." She sighed and massaged her forehead with her fingertips. "I've got no idea what'll happen if we get a mass casualty event."

Annie was at a loss for words, a state of mind that had been frequent with her of late. Conversations about everyday trivia and thinking normal thoughts were things of the past. She seemed to have lost the art of living, along with all the emotional traits that made her a human being. Sometimes she felt that she was just existing without a soul.

She cleared he throat. "It's quiet for a change," she said.

"Yeah, too quiet," Freya replied but didn't elaborate.

Annie studied her friend. There were dark circles beneath the sergeant's eyes and her dull and lifeless hair was coiled into a messy bun. What struck a chord with Annie was the thousand-yard stare that had dimmed the sparkle in Freya's green eyes. She had a feeling that what she was seeing almost certainly mirrored was in her own.

"Any news from —?" Freya began.

Annie interrupted her before she could complete the question, "No." Her tone was sharp and she tried to soften it when she continued. "Nothing."

"I'm sure he's fine."

Annie shrugged. "Don't say anything more, Freya, please. If I think about him, I'll fall apart and I've got a job to do."

Freya squeezed Annie's arm. "This whole shitfest is falling apart. Now, let's get out of here and grab a coffee before our luck runs out."

Annie nodded. She turned to leave when someone behind her said, "Annie."

For a moment, Annie's mind went blank and she stopped. She recognized the voice. All sound faded away until she existed in a vacuum of silence. Her heart began to race, her stomach churned with nausea and she closed her eyes.

She wanted to turn around but she couldn't. The voice was Shay's but she was afraid that her mind might be playing a cruel trick. If she looked behind her and he wasn't there, she would break.

Freya moved alongside her and Annie felt her friend's warm breath against her ear. "Annie, don't just stand there. Get your ass moving. Go to him."

Cocooned as she was in her mind's quiet, Annie heard the sergeant's boots move passed her and she watched as Freya left the triage area.

Annie wanted to call out to her to stay with her, in case it was just her imagination that she'd heard his voice, instead, without any further hesitation, she about-turned in the direction of the emergency entrance.

A small sound — a whimper encompassing all the sudden emotions that surged through her — escaped her when she saw Shay watching her from across the width of the shelter.

She stared at him speechless then, not wanting to be away from him for another second, she ran to meet him.

Annie almost cannoned into him but he caught her too him and tugged her in roughly against him. She threw her arms around his neck and rested her forehead in the hollow between his shoulder and neck.

He smelled of dirt and sweat. Dust and sand from his tactical vest stuck to her cheek but she didn't care. All that mattered was that he was here with her and she was in his arms.

Shay ran his hands — flat against the cotton-clad skin of her back — upward, stopping when he reached the area between her shoulder blades. He massaged the muscles there, warmth from his palms penetrating the thin material of her T-shirt.

Annie was unable to stop herself from pressing her body into his, and at that point, he skimmed the palms of his hands downward over the lower part of her spine to clasp her bottom, pulling her even closer.

Annie lifted her head to stare at him and Shay grazed her cheek with his lips, before moving on to kiss the soft area of her neck just below the curve of her ear.

"You smell so good," he whispered, his breath warm on her skin.

Annie nuzzled his neck, tasting him with the tip of her tongue. She inhaled, the smell of him tantalizing her senses.

She leaned back in his arms and studied his face. He hadn't shaved in some time, an action that probably hadn't been high on his bucket list. His tan face was smeared with dirt and there was a small bloody gash on his right cheek, the wound now crusted over.

But it was Shay's eyes that caused Annie concern. They were empty of emotion, like a green lake barren of life. The planes of his face were hard and a small muscle flickered in his jaw.

Annie touched the cut with her fingertips and broke the silence between them, "Was it bad out there?"

In response to her question, his arms tightened around her waist.

"Yeah," he replied and didn't say anything else.

Annie wanted to push him with further questions but she sensed that what he'd seen and done were subjects he didn't want to discuss. Instead, she tightened her arms around his neck and gently caressed the back of his head.

Her voice was low when she said, "You're back. I have you now."

At that precise moment, he filled her world with the sheer impact of his presence and she needed to dwell in the moment instead of what was going to happen in their future.

Shay tightened his arms about her, lowered his head and kissed her mouth. It was tender, one that was made even more sensuous and provocative because of its gentleness. Annie returned it with all the feeling she had for him.

The stubble on his jaws scratched the tender skin of her cheek and chin but the prospect of discomfort from stubble burn the next day was negated by the firm touch of his lips on hers.

Without conscious thought, Annie opened her mouth, and at her silent urging, Shay kissed her with more force. Her breathing quickened and his uneven breaths grew in synchronization with her own.

He moved one of his hands from her bottom, skimming his palm up the length of her spine to the base of her skull. His kiss grew rough with urgent need and Annie winced as he bruised her lips, but she stayed silent.

Shay released her abruptly and Annie almost staggered backward.

"I'm sorry," he said, and his voice was hoarse.

Annie shook her head and cupped the side of his face with her hand. "There's no need to apologize. We can get through this."

She knew that whatever had happened to him during the previous month had profoundly changed him. Something was eating away at him but she couldn't delve too deep without causing him to withdraw from her. If he wanted to tell her, he would — but in his own time.

If he went back out to fight again — and she knew he would have to — and if he wasn't killed and they both survived, she was sure they would be together at the end of it all. How long that would be, she had no idea. They still had much to go through. Their future couldn't be planned or predicted. To do so would almost be a curse on their survival and happiness. For now, they had these few moments alone...together. She would wait and she would be there — willing to surrender to him whenever he wanted and needed her.

My Shay, my forever love.

Want to see more from this author?
Here's a taster for you to enjoy!

Ambush of Love
Sharon Kimbra Walsh

Excerpt

Scorched by the searing sun, the arid, parched land stretched for miles in all directions. Stunted, prickly thorn bushes grew randomly, eking out a poor existence, roots buried deep beneath the seared landscape, always searching for moisture to sustain life.

Twisted, spindly trees struggled pathetically to survive on the desolate, barren land, their branches stripped of all but the hardiest of leaves, even those curled into withering parodies of life in an attempt to hide away from the unsympathetic sunlight.

Approximately two kilometers away, a range of tall mountains—cleaved asunder here and there with deep crevices and fissures—thrust serrated summits toward a sky of washed-out blue, a vast canopy of emptiness without even the smallest wisp of moisture-bearing cloud in evidence. Jagged profiles wreathed in thin vaporous mists, the craggy, rocky slopes were dotted with threadlike waterfalls, the tumbling flows sparkling in the rays from the glaring, bloated sun.

Clouds of dust—disturbed by the patrol—hung motionless in the still, hot air, minute particles finding their way through the fine seals of ballistic combat helmets into eyes and mouths and inside combats, chafing skin raw. The air was hot and dry, so much so that if inhaled, it leached all moisture from lips and dried up saliva in mouths.

The tall British army officer paced slowly along what passed for a road – a poorly maintained track full of deep ruts and potholes – his stride relaxed and methodical, primarily to remain focused on his immediate surroundings but also to conserve energy.

He rolled his shoulders in an attempt to ease the weight of his bergen. Alert for signs of snipers or IEDs, his keen eyes ceaselessly roamed about him, his modified SA80A2 with its underslung grenade launcher, SUSAT sight and common weapon sight tracking every movement.

Lieutenant Nick Ryan – aka LT or 'the Old Man', thirty-two years of age – was starting to feel tired and thirsty and his feet hurt. His body armor with its hard and soft plates – configured for additional freedom of movement for this specific mission – felt as though it had doubled in weight, his pack as if it were filled with blocks of cement. His combat shirt and T-shirt beneath were soaked with sweat.

He was eager – as he assumed the rest of his men were also – to get back to the FOB, the forward operating base – for a mission debrief, shower and scran. At this stage of the mission, however, his sole aim was to get Bravo Recon Section through the next few clicks alive and in one piece.

He had learned the hard way – through the lack of focus and mistakes of others – that one moment's loss of concentration could result in someone being hurt or even killed. He therefore pushed all thoughts of future comforts to the back of his mind – a feat that had served him well on past deployments — and stepped away from his position as point man at the head of the patrol.

Turning to face the line of men behind him, he noticed that while they still maintained a ragged formation, their movements were lethargic, with shoulders slumped and feet stumbling through the fine dust and sand. He realized that concentration within the section was beginning to flag, a dangerous situation while in an area teeming with insurgents.

Nick spoke a password into the confines of his helmet then waited for the voice-activated heads up display, commonly called HUD, to stream onto the inside of his tinted full-face shield. After a few moments, flickering green lines resolved themselves into schematics of route maps and combat situation reports — sitreps. He uttered a different password and the displays faded, leaving behind their PSMs data that kept him updated on their physiological status.

He studied the readouts sent directly to his personal central information system from the medical sensors embedded in the thin lining of his men's desert, multi-terrain pattern combats. They showed the body temperatures, heart rates, hydration and stress levels of each man and he found himself smiling with amusement.

Individual biomedical data showed the slightly decreased heart rates and respiration of almost every member of Bravo Recon. It appeared that his men were dozing on their feet, as if they were out for an afternoon stroll through a park at home instead of the inhospitable climes of Afghanistan.

Deactivating the PSMs, he said, "Comms," which triggered his communications system and abruptly said, "Come on, lads. We're nearly home."

His voice entered the communications network of his section and from there into each individual helmet. His mouth twitched again with amusement as at least half of his men's heads jerked up, their bodies reacting with surprise at the sound of his voice.

"Two more clicks and you can have your downtime. I know this heat is a bastard. You're all knackered and probably thirsty, and you want to get back to the FOB. This is the time when your concentration will start to lapse and you could lose focus. If that happens, make no mistake, you will get your backsides kicked.

"The mujis will have us bagged and tagged by now and they will have intel on us. More than that, they'll know how long we've been out and that we're tired and, therefore, easy pickings. You all need to stay alert and concentrate. You are at your most vulnerable right now because being nearly back at base. You're only focusing on that. Right now, you need to keep eyes on at all times, no matter how crap you're all feeling."

Nick's intention had been to shake Bravo Recon from their heat-induced torpors, and he hoped that his words had made the appropriate impact. He was satisfied when they straightened their shoulders, their pace quickened and they lifted their SA80A2s a little higher, the action offered as a warning to any hostiles who might be observing them.

He returned to his position as point man and checked the immediate area. He quickly noticed two Afghan men approximately twenty meters away, puttering slowly along on dilapidated motorcycles. They were keeping pace with the section, watching them through binoculars, their worn-out engines sounding muted in the still air.

Nick felt a rush of adrenaline and quickly lifted his right arm out to the side in the direction of the intruders, raising two fingers. Activating his comms, he ordered, "Eyes right, Bravo Recon. Two dickers at twenty meters."

Lifting his weapon, he aimed it at the Afghan men. Keeping his keen gaze on them, he heard the faint noise of rifles lifted in unison behind him and he raised a hand in an attempt to stop someone's twitchy finger from increasing its pressure on a trigger, thereby causing an international incident.

"Wait out," he ordered calmly.

The Afghanistan men, seeming to realize that they were now objects of interest, immediately turned their motorcycles about and sped off in the opposite direction.

Nick waited until the bikes were some distance away before lowering his hand, then his weapon. He kept his gaze on the fleeing men, quickly disappearing into a shimmering heat-haze. His irritation quickly turned to anger as he supposed that intel regarding the number of men in his patrol, amount of firepower and weapon type was probably speeding on its way to enemy commanders.

Christ! Bloody bastards!

"Move out." Raising his right hand, he gestured for the patrol to move on, aware that Bravo Recon Section might be on the receiving end of an ambush before reaching the safety of the FOB.

* * * *

Corporal Jessie McAllister—twenty-four years of age—stared out of the open side door of the army Wildcat Mk2 helicopter. Squinting in the harsh sunlight, she watched the shadow of the helo flashing across the parched landscape beneath her, and her spirits sank even further.

"Holy shit!" she exclaimed and heaved a sigh of resignation. She glanced quickly over her shoulder at the other passenger to see if he had heard her unladylike expletive, but as he had done the whole trip, the soldier continued to ignore her. Feeling as though she wanted to poke her tongue out at him for his ignorance, Jessie turned back to her study of the countryside spread out below her.

Oh, perfect. My home for the next six months is going to be Hell.

Prior to her deployment, her parents — military veterans in their own right — had given her the benefit of their vast knowledge, regaling her with stories of their experiences in country — both good and bad. The reality, however, was beyond her wildest nightmares. Her impression of her new country — Kunar Province in the Korengal Valley — had deteriorated from resigned acceptance to dislike, the further she had traveled from Base Kandahar.

From what she had seen so far, most of Afghanistan consisted of flat beige and ochre-crackled earth, dotted with sparse, stunted vegetation, broken up by irrigation ditches and dry, shallow wabis. No sign of human habitation broke the empty monotony of the landscape, not even the mud and brick ruins of a compound or a single animal racing to find shelter from the inhospitable conditions. The tableland looked unforgiving, lonely and abandoned.

Since her arrival in country, Jessie's spirits had plummeted lower at every turn, until at last she'd begun to question the choices she had made over the last year, decisions that she now considered she'd made rather hastily.

Since she'd been a child, she had wanted to emulate her parents and join the military. She'd opted for the Marine Corps and had passed the tough basic and advanced medical training with ease. Now that she was here on her first overseas deployment, she found herself wondering why she had done it, constantly asking herself what she was doing on the front line instead of being safe at home with a nice boring nine-to-five job.

If the men and women with whom she had spoken had told the truth, it was a man's world in Afghanistan, and women should have no part in it. That particular label hadn't changed much over the years. With major advances in technology and a reorganization of the US armed forces, there still appeared to be a lingering ingrained sexist attitude toward females.

The US military seemed to want to keep women in desk jobs, forgotten about and therefore out of trouble. Much to Jessie's annoyance, it appeared that according to general opinion, women—even though they had proven themselves on par with men—appeared to remain the weaker and lesser-skilled sex.

In relation to herself, a tiny cog in the US military machinery—for some unknown and completely illogical reason—had decided to attach her to a British unit. Why the British army needed a US Marine medic she had no idea, but she had accepted the new orders with resignation and equanimity.

Her one failing grace was that she had inherited her father's stubbornness, a fact that her mother had brought up to her on a number of occasions. So with this ammunition, she was determined to prove to herself, to the men of her new world and to the authorities, that they were wrong and that she—as a woman and an individual—was perfectly capable of fulfilling a combat role.

As much as she tried to convince herself that acceptance meant nothing to her, Jessie was conscious of a feeling of apprehension about her imminent arrival at her new home. The thought of what her new section's reaction to her presence might be had created a nauseating coil of dread in the pit of her stomach. Her nerves swooped and jived like a plague of agitated butterflies, and she felt a little sick.

She swiped at a droplet of sweat that had trickled from beneath her helmet. Even with the side door of the Wildcat pushed all the way open and a wind howling around the interior, the heat was almost unbearable. Dressed in full battle gear, including the new lightweight PPE, her personal protective equipment, it felt as though the blood in her veins was quickly heating to the boiling point.

Her helmet with its nine-millimeter thick mandible guard and HUD face shield — configured and contoured to fit the shape of her skull and the sides of her face — constricted her head like a metal band. Perspiration coated her face and long strands of wayward hair, having managed to creep from beneath the confines of the helmet, flew about her face, clinging to her cheeks and finding their way into her eyes and mouth.

Clamping her weapon between her knees to prevent it from slipping from her grasp and flying out into the slipstream, Jessie straightened in her seat and ran gloved hands across her face, attempting to free the latticework of hair entwined across her nose and mouth.

God, I'm so tired.

With twenty hours of flying time behind her, combined with the energy-sapping heat, she felt as though she could sleep for a week. Top of her list, however, when she finally arrived at the FOB, was a shower. She had her doubts, though, that she would find anything remotely like one in existence. She had a sinking feeling that she would inevitably end up having to share ablutions with the men, causing embarrassment for all concerned.

Jessie sighed and gave up trying to tuck her wayward hair out of the way. She turned to stare out of the door once more, this time raising her head to look up at the blue sky. She wondered if some form of epiphany would suddenly strike her from the heavens, enlightening her as to how she could extricate herself from the mess in which she now found herself.

Instead, the harsh brightness almost blinded her. Her eyes watered and burned, and she cursed herself for not having the foresight to lower her face shield, just another mistake to add to her steadily lengthening list.

Lowering her gaze, she waited for her vision to clear, then stared in the direction they were flying. Through a rippling heat-haze, she made out the first signs of civilization in the shape of a compound located at the base of the mountains. The helicopter had started to make a smooth descent in that direction and, as they neared it, Jessie supposed this was to be her final destination.

She could make out a large, rectangular base surrounded by what she estimated to be four-meter high walls of cream-colored Hesco. Anyone trying to scale the heights would find it impossible to negotiate the smooth angle and achieve a breach. High steel gates broke up the straight lines of one wall, while security towers covered in khaki-colored camouflage netting loomed strategically at the base's four corners.

It had to be FOB Elabat in all its glory.

She heard the rotor blades slow as the Wildcat continued its rapid descent. With the sound of the moaning wind diminishing inside the fuselage, she slung the strap of her SA80A2 over her shoulder, reached for her pack and kit bag to prepare for the landing and braced her booted feet against the ridged metal floor.

They appeared to be approaching an area of flat land some meters distant from the FOB, and Jessie edged closer to the open door, dragging her bulky kit with her. Poking her head out, she kept an eye on their approach for any sign of insurgents popping their heads up to observe the actions of the helicopter.

She was also able to gauge the security of her new home. Bordering the FOB on three sides were piles of spindly, half-dead thorn bushes, felled trees and large piles of boulders with a ten-meter deep no-man's land between the vegetative barrier and the base walls. It meant that an insurgent attempting to get close to the base would have to cross it in full view of two of the security towers, and she felt a modicum of reassurance in that.

The helicopter landed smoothly and delicately with barely a bump. After getting to her feet, Jessie crouched slightly then jumped down to the hard, dusty ground. Clouds of dust—stirred up by the rotor blades—immediately engulfed her head and body, and she coughed and spluttered.

Waving a hand in front of her face, she tried to protect her eyes from the stinging particles. Belatedly, she lowered her face shield, grabbed her pack and bag and took a few stumbling steps backward, ducking beneath the slowly spinning blades. The soldier passenger—still acting as though she did not exist—leaped down to take up a security position alongside the helicopter, keeping a watchful eye on their surroundings.

Undecided as to what to do next, Jessie looked around. The co-pilot joined her and, as she glanced at him, she saw that he was staring at her with a wide grin on his face. Reaching around her into the Wildcat's interior, he grabbed for a large khaki sack just inside the door and, as he did so, his body—intentionally or otherwise — brushed against hers. He winked and jerked his head sideways.

"Well, come on then, darlin'. You hang around out here and you'll get your pretty backside shot," he shouted.

Jessie heard the note of contempt in his voice — as if she had broken some important cardinal rule. Hot and tired, she glared at him, biting back words of retort. As if dismissing her as being of no consequence, the co-pilot turned his back and jogged away, holding the heavy sack as though it weighed nothing, his weapon held casually at his side.

Feeling slightly defeated, Jessie started to follow him. As she came out from beneath the shadow thrown by the helicopter, the searing heat instantly beat down onto her head and body, enveloping her in what felt like a stifling blanket. Her heavy pack swung violently from one shoulder, the kit bag seemed maliciously intent on tripping her up and the SA80A2 pounded her back like a wild thing. Her breath hissed harshly through gritted teeth, sweat trickled down her face and her lungs felt tight and burned from the hot air.

She guessed the distance to the base to be no more than one hundred meters or so from the landing zone, however, after only accomplishing half the distance, it felt as though she had completed a ten-kilometer exercise run, carrying full equipment. A sudden anxious thought that she might well pass out from heat exhaustion before reaching the heavy gates crossed her mind. She quickly quashed the notion, noticing that one of the gates was already open in anticipation of their arrival. Two soldiers stood on either side of it with weapons raised.

Reaching the base, the co-pilot entered and, with relief, Jessie prepared to follow. It was at this point that her legs — weak with fatigue and the excess weight she carried — suddenly buckled and she tripped, stumbled and almost fell flat on her face.

Struggling to regain her footing and what little composure she had left, she heard a derisory chuckle from one of the soldiers on security duty, felt a hard hand on her back and a shove almost aided her in completing her tumble to the ground.

Home of Erotic Romance

Sign up for our newsletter and find out about all our romance book releases, eBook sales and promotions, sneak peeks and FREE romance books!

About the Author

Sharon spent eight and a half years in the Women's Royal Air Force. Originally based in London, after she met her husband, Sharon relocated to Scotland to settle in Edinburgh. Already loving the country after having been stationed there during her time in the military, Sharon has never looked back. She lives with her husband and rescue West Highland Terrier, Snowie, (who thinks that she is a Rottweiler in disguise).

In 2014 Sharon started to have visions of writing a contemporary military romance. The ideas started to pile up and there was nothing for it but to get them down on her laptop, regardless of time and place.

Sharon loves to hear from readers. You can find her contact information, website details and author profile page at https://www.totallybound.com